"What do we know, really know about this woman?" Lynn asked

"Not much," Cal said. "Daddy met her at a party. She went to Smith, lives in Boston and is an investment banker." He grinned. "Sounds like a barrel of fun."

"Sounds t'me like she's gonna be as useless around a ranch as teats on a wild boar," Hank grumbled.

Tyler walked to the front windows and saw his father's Cadillac drive through the gate. "Well, in a minute we'll know more about her. Put on your party manner. They're here."

The front door opened and closed. A minute later a willowy, young blond woman in a striking green coatdress preceded J.T. into the room. The brothers and sister exchanged quick, stunned glances. Hank's jaw dropped. *God A'mighty, what in the hell's gotten into the boy?* he wondered. *He oughta adopt her, not marry her.*

Special thanks and acknowledgment to Barbara Kaye
for her contribution to the Crystal Creek series.

Special thanks and acknowledgment to Sutton Press Inc.
for its contribution to the concept for the Crystal Creek series.

Published March 1993

ISBN 0-373-82513-7

DEEP IN THE HEART

Dear Reader,

Welcome to Crystal Creek! In the heart of Texas Hill Country, the McKinneys have been ranching, living and loving for generations, but the future promises changes none of these good folks could ever imagine!

Crystal Creek itself is the product of many imaginations, but the stories began to take shape when some of your favorite authors—Barbara Kaye, Margot Dalton, Bethany Campbell, Cara West, Kathy Clark and Sharon Brondos—all got together with me just outside of Austin to explore the Hill Country, and to dream up the kinds of romances such a setting would provide. For several days, we roamed the countryside, where generous Texans opened their historic homes to us, and gave us insights into their lives. We ate barbecue, we visited an ostrich farm and we mapped out our plans to give you the linked stories you love, with a true Texas flavor and all the elements you've come to expect in your romance reading: compelling, contemporary characters caught in conflicts that reflect today's dilemmas.

So one of the McKinney boys wants to break away from cattle ranching to start a winery on his daddy's beloved ranch, to increase the profit potential. A sharp Austin lawyer upsets the neighborhood by opening a dude ranch that will attract city slickers to a working ranch community. A career-minded country-and-western singer falls for the local sheriff, and an insurance scam involving some prize horses lands one of the locals in jail.

These are just a few of the story lines that will draw you back month after month to Crystal Creek, where power and influence live in the land and in the hands of one family determined to nourish old Texas fortunes and forge new Texas futures.

C'mon down to Crystal Creek—home of sultry Texas drawls, smooth Texas charm and tall, sexy Texans!

Marsha Zinberg
Coordinator, Crystal Creek

A Note from the Author

Having grown up in cattle and oil country, I've met plenty of J.T.s in my day. J.T. is a widower and owner of the grand Double C Ranch near the town of Crystal Creek, Texas. Stubborn and opinionated, he's a man accustomed to doing things his own way. But when he falls for Boston socialite, Cynthia Page, he sends shock waves through his family. His grandfather, his grown children, even his servants are horrified that J.T. plans to marry a woman twenty years his junior, and an outsider to boot.

I loved doing this book. The mere thought of a woman like Cynthia locking horns with a man like J.T. intrigued me from the beginning. I hope you will find it equally fascinating.

Barbara Kaye

Cast of Characters

AT THE DOUBLE C RANCH

J. T. McKinney — Rancher, owner of the Double C, his family's ranch. A man who knows his mind.

Cynthia Page — Bostonian bank executive, who sets the Double C on its ear.

Tyler McKinney — J.T.'s eldest son, a graduate of Rice University. Now he wants to grow grapes in his daddy's pasture.

Cal McKinney — J.T.'s second son, a rodeo cowboy who loves 'em and leaves 'em.

Lynn McKinney — J.T.'s only daughter. She bucks the trend by raising Thoroughbreds in Quarterhorse country.

Hank Travis — J.T.'s ancient grandfather. Old Hank has seen and done it all.

Lettie Mae Reese — Cook. } Together they know all
Virginia Parks — Housekeeper. } the household secrets.

Ken Slattery — Foreman at the Double C.

AT THE CIRCLE T RANCH

Carolyn Randolph Townsend — J.T.'s sister-in-law and neighbor.

Beverly Townsend — Carolyn's daughter and a former Miss Texas.

Lori Porter — Carolyn's cousin. Lori lives at the Circle T and keeps the ranch accounts.

AT THE LONGHORN

Dottie Jones — Owner of the Longhorn Motel and Coffee Shop.

Nora Jones — Dottie's son's ex-wife.

Martin Avery — Mayor of Crystal Creek.

Bubba and Mary Gibson — Old friends of J.T.'s.

Nate Purdy — Crystal Creek's family physician.

Vernon Trent — Real-estate agent.

Wayne Jackson — Sheriff.

CHAPTER ONE

"IF THIS GAL'S really a Boston blueblood and so god-damned rich and successful, what makes her think she wants to come down here and live on a Texas ranch?"

The questioner was a gnarled, wizened nonagenarian named Hank Travis. The person he asked the question of was his grandson, John Travis McKinney. J.T., seated at the desk in his study, glanced up from the market reports he had been reading. "Tell you what, Grandpa—when the lady herself gets here, ask her that question."

"Humph." Hank ran a hand over his hair, a mop he was careless about getting cut. Surprisingly, it was more salt-and-pepper than white, and he had lost very little of it. His face was deeply tanned and had the texture of a relief map. It usually sported a faint stubble at the chin because Hank hated to shave.

"You forgot to shave this morning," J.T. noted.

"Didn't forget. Didn't want to."

"Reckon you could get around to it before this afternoon?"

"Maybe, maybe not," Hank said. He had developed the permanent squint of a man who had spent most of a long, long life in the outdoors. The squint was magnified by wire-rimmed, thick-lensed eye-glasses, but the eyes behind them were alert and incisive. They seemed to telegraph a message: I've got all my marbles and a few of yours as well. "Boston, of all places! You couldn't find a homegrown gal?"

J.T. grinned. "Now, how can I answer that? I happened to meet Cynthia, that's all. We clicked."

"Humph. Cynthia. Even her name sounds highfalutin. Tryin' to remember if I ever knew a Cynthia. Don't reckon I ever did. I 'spect this one'll stay maybe a week. Bet she's never even had her hands dirty."

"Wouldn't know, Grandpa. They've sure been nice and clean every time I've been with her."

Hank dragged on the hand-rolled cigarette that smelled to J.T. like a pile of burning manure. One of the old man's greatest worries was that the day would come when he could no longer buy the "makin's." As it was, a drugstore in town ordered the papers and tobacco especially for him. The one and only time J.T. had admonished him about his smoking, Hank had fixed a withering look on his grandson and said, "If they're gonna kill me, they'd better hurry 'fore something else beats 'em to it."

"Sit down, Grandpa," J.T. said. "Take the load off your feet."

"Naw, I'm gonna go sit on the porch a spell. The women are in such a stew they're plumb drivin' me nuts."

Hank turned to leave the room. He walked with the aid of a cane, necessitated by a hip injury suffered in an oil well blowout during the sixtieth year of his life, long after he should have quit the oil patch. He actually needed to use a walker, but he'd told J.T. he'd go off in the brush and shoot himself before he'd use that confounded contraption. The cane was bad enough. How he hated it! It was a symbol of old age and infirmity.

J.T. watched Hank leave the study. In December his maternal grandfather would be ninety-nine, and it certainly looked as if he was going to live to celebrate his hundredth birthday. There were those who said he was too mean to die. J.T. admired him as he had admired few men in his life, but even he admitted Hank was a crusty old bird who took some getting used to. He recalled something Martin Avery, his attorney, had said two years ago after a particularly trying confrontation with Hank. "No one has the right to be so goddamned feisty at ninety-six!" That, J.T. decided, summed up his grandfather far better than he could.

Hank had hardly cleared the room when Virginia Parks, the McKinneys' housekeeper, sailed into the study. She was carrying two identical flower arrangements, one in each hand. "J.T., here are the centerpieces the florist sent. We're using the blue tablecloths tonight. What do you think?"

"Nice," he said, with a marked lack of interest.

"That won't be too much blue?"

J.T. frowned and shrugged. "I don't know. That's hardly my department. They look okay to me. If you're worried about them, get Lynn's opinion." His eyes again fell to the reports on his desk.

"Lettie Mae wants to know if the all-white china is okay with you."

"Sure."

"Did you go over the seating arrangement I showed you?"

J.T. looked up. "The what?"

"The seating arrangement I worked out." Since Virginia's hands were full, she cocked her head toward the desk. "It's right there at your elbow."

J.T. looked first to the right, then to the left. He had forgotten the piece of paper she had given him the day before. Picking it up, he scanned it and saw it was a diagram of some kind. "What did you say this is?"

Virginia sighed. "The seating arrangement for dinner tonight. I gave it a lot of thought. I'm putting Mr. Avery at the right of your lady friend—"

"I wish you would stop referring to her as my 'lady friend.' Her name is Cynthia. If you don't feel comfortable with that, call her Ms. Page."

"Of course," the housekeeper said stiffly. "And I've put Tyler and Cal at her table, too. You know Mr. Hank will eat at six like he always does, so he probably won't even put in an appearance. You and Lynn can hold forth at the other table. That way, all the guests are seated near some family member. I seem to remember reading that's proper."

"For God's sake, Virginia, this isn't a state dinner at the White House! These people have known one another half their lives. They don't give a damn who sits where. Just holler, 'Come and get it,' and let them all fend for themselves."

Virginia sniffed. "I thought this had to be so perfect. After all, how many times have we had a guest of honor from Boston?"

At that moment, Lettie Mae Reese, the cook, walked into the room and came to stand beside Virginia. For perhaps the thousandth time in his life, J.T. thought what a formidable pair they were. Virginia, sixtyish, silver-haired and pleasingly plump, and Lettie Mae, fifty-three, tall, thin and with skin the color of café au lait, ran his household with a skill and precision that would have put a drill sergeant to shame. They would gladly run every facet of his life if he would allow it. Though they often exasperated him to the point of tears, he didn't know what he would do without them.

"J.T., we might want to reconsider tonight's menu," Lettie Mae said.

"Why?"

"You wanted me to barbecue briskets, right?"

"Right."

"And Mr. Avery and the Purdys are going to be here?"

"Yes, of course."

"They were here for dinner a couple of weeks ago, and that's what we served. They're going to think I don't have any imagination."

J.T. simply stared at her a minute before saying, "Lettie Mae, Nate Purdy would eat barbecued something every night of his life if he could. And Martin's a bachelor with the palate of a mountain goat. He'll eat anything. Have the briskets."

The cook shrugged. "Okay, if you say so. Are you bringing your lady friend back here for lunch?"

"Her name is Cynthia. No, we'll stop for something. You two have enough to do as it is."

"Don't you think it would be nice to serve dessert and coffee in the living room after dinner? I read somewhere that it's stylish."

"Hell, no! I hate balancing food on my knee. When I eat, I want a solid table under the food."

"How long are you going to be working in here?" Virginia asked. "We have to vacuum and dust this room."

Standing, J.T. kicked back his chair with the heel of his boot and reached for his brown felt Stetson. "Well, I can see I'm not going to get any work done this morning, so guess I'll head on in to Austin."

"Isn't it a little early?" Virginia asked. "I thought you said the plane didn't get in until after eleven."

"I want to talk to Ken before I leave, and depending on the time, I might make a pit stop in Crystal Creek." He started to leave the room, but at the threshold he stopped and turned. "Did you tell the kids I want them here this afternoon?"

Virginia and Lettie Mae nodded in unison.

"Good. See you later."

The two women stared after his retreating figure. "He's as jumpy as a long-tailed cat," was Lettie Mae's verdict.

"I guess it's important to him that we all like her," Virginia said.

"I guess. Nothing personal against the lady in question, but I don't think I'll ever be able to accept another woman in this house. This is Miss Pauline's house."

"Life's for the living. Let's try to keep that in mind, for J.T.'s sake."

Lettie Mae nodded and headed back to the kitchen. Virginia carried the flowers into the dining room. The mahogany table that normally stood in the center of the big room had been moved to one side, and a long, folding table had been set up parallel to it. Both were covered with blue linen cloths. She set an arrangement in the center of each, then stepped back to view the effect. No, there wasn't too much blue, she decided. Everything looked beautiful.

The McKinney household had been a beehive of activity for days, a refreshing change of pace. At one time, entertaining on a lavish scale had been the norm rather than the exception of the Double C Ranch, but years had passed since J.T. had wanted to throw a party. It was nice to see him excited about something, and Virginia was as curious about the woman from Boston as everyone else was...and just as apprehensive.

For five long years the housekeeper had fretted over
J.T. After his beloved Pauline's death from breast
cancer, he had withdrawn into a shell, seldom leaving
the ranch, attending few social functions, seeing only
a few close friends. The Double C became the be-all
of his existence. Virginia had found herself constantly admonishing him to buy some new clothes, get
a haircut, go out more, have people over, and J.T. was
not a man who took kindly to "mothering." Gradually, however, he had mended and decided to reenter
the world, but his old vigor seemed to be gone forever.

Then about six months ago he had changed dramatically. He'd become alive and vital again—much
more like the man who had built a middling-size ranch
into a showplace. It hadn't taken long for observers to
find out the reason for the startling metamorphosis—
a woman. Specifically, a woman he'd met at a party in
Austin, a woman named Cynthia Page, who lived in
Boston. Virginia reckoned J.T. had spent a small for-
tune on flying back and forth—at the controls of his
Baron when weather permitted, taking commercial
flights when it didn't. Suddenly, literally overnight, he
had found there was more to life than the Double C.

Now the Bostonian was coming for an extended
visit, so that meant things were serious. Virginia wasn't
quite sure how she felt about that. On one hand, she
conceded that the woman had been good for J.T.
There was a sparkle in his eye and a spring to his step
again. On the other hand, Virginia found it hard to

accept that he had found someone to take Miss Pauline's place. They all—she, Lettie Mae, Mr. Hank and J.T.'s children—were having trouble with that one. In their eyes, only Pauline could be Mrs. J. T. McKinney. As Lettie Mae had said, this was Miss Pauline's house; J.T. had built it for her. Her touch was everywhere.

Virginia shook herself out of her reverie. A world of things needed to be done before the party tonight. A bartender and a mother-and-daughter cleaning team had been hired to help out, but most of the work would be left to Virginia, Lettie Mae and the cook's young helper. J.T. had said he wanted the party to be special, so they all were committed to making it as perfect as human hands could. Virginia just hoped the woman from Boston turned out to be worth it.

J.T. PAUSED when he stepped out onto the front porch and made a lingering survey of his domain. Fall in the Hill Country of Central Texas was always a delightful time of year. This morning there had been the faintest touch of crispness in the air, meaning that the worst of the summer heat was behind them. That was probably the most welcome weather event of the entire yearly cycle. In an area of the world where summers were long and hot, fall was possibly the most welcome season of them all.

To anyone who knew the Hill Country as well as J.T. did, there was an enchantment to the place that could be matched nowhere else on earth. For one thing, it possessed a goodly amount of old-world charm in its stone fences, houses, barns and villages. The first settlers in the area were Germans who came to Texas thinking they had purchased prime coastal land. What they found when they arrived were limestone hills and Comanches. But there was also plenty of cedar and oak, secret valleys, breathtaking views and a network of waterways fed by deep cold springs. And the pretty, orderly farms, ranches and towns of today were a testament to the tenacity of those Germans who stayed and made the most of what they had.

On this October morning, the Double C seemed to be dozing in the sun, but behind the scenes plenty of work was being done. J.T.'s pride in the place was limitless. He had lived on the ranch all his life, having been born there fifty-five years ago. It had been a much smaller operation then, not much more than a mom-and-pop stock farm run by his father, Calvin, and his mother, Emily, along with two aging hired hands. But over the years, as market conditions and his own financial circumstances had allowed, Calvin had picked up a few more acres here and there, all the while patiently upgrading his herd and making sure his only child, John Travis, learned every facet of the cattle business. He had done the job well, so well that when he and Emily were tragically killed in an automobile accident during a vicious storm while on vacation in Galveston, J.T. had been able to step in and take over the ranch with scarcely a ripple in its day-to-day operation.

That had been twenty years ago. Calvin Carl Mc-Kinney, the source of the ranch's name, wouldn't have recognized the present-day Double C. Its size had more than doubled to ten thousand acres, making it the area's largest ranch, and its grounds and buildings were impressive. Its hub, often referred to as head-quarters, was the stately, white two-story house J.T. had built for his wife, Pauline Randolph McKinney, after his parents' deaths. Behind the house was the swimming pool he'd had installed when his oldest child, Tyler, had begun pestering him for one. Be-yond the pool were the outbuildings—the stable, the foreman's house, the bunkhouse and a guest house—all of them painted the same dazzling white as the main residence. Asters and chrysanthemums peeked out from beneath shrubbery. Surrounding the whole were limestone hills and pasturelands where grazed hundreds of Brangus cattle, the reason for the ranch's existence.

The swimming pool, the guest house and the flow-ers all highlighted a paradox in J.T.'s personality. Ranchers as a whole were loath to allocate so much as a square foot of their precious land for anything but the serious business of raising livestock. But the Dou-ble C was J.T.'s passion, so beautifying it received high priority.

About fifty yards from this cluster of buildings was another structure that didn't look as if it belonged there, and until thirteen years ago, it hadn't. It was the stone house Hank Travis had built near Pearsall for his

wife and daughter many years ago. That it now stood
in the Double C was a testimony to J.T.'s own stubborn and determined nature. At age eighty-five, Hank
had again broken the hip he'd injured in 1953. The
doctor had laid down the law. There was no way he
could go on living alone in that house in Pearsall. J.T.
had agreed and insisted his grandfather move to the
Double C. Hank, fighting for his independence down
to the wire, had flatly refused. So, while his grandfather was in the hospital for extensive physical ther-
apy, J.T. had hired a company to, stone by stone,
move the house to the Double C.

Of course Hank had never forgiven him. At least he
said he hadn't. But by now the alternative would have
been a nursing home, and J.T. could just imagine what
Hank would have had to say about that. Personally,
he suspected his grandfather enjoyed having family
close by. After all, they made a good audience for
those oil-patch yarns of his, but he was absolutely
certain he would never hear such an admission from
Hank Travis's lips.

Satisfied that all was well with his mini kingdom,
J.T. stepped off the porch and rounded the corner of
the house, heading for the bunkhouse. As he strode
across the grounds, he carried himself so ramrod
straight, so authoritatively, that anyone watching him
would have known instinctively he was a man of importance. He was tall, six foot one, and had deep
brown eyes and dark hair that was graying at the tem-
ples and around his ears. That was the only sign of

age, for his face was remarkably unlined and undeniably handsome, ruggedly so, and his lean, muscular physique was the envy of many much younger men. His friends knew him to be loyal; his employees thought him fair. Other men considered him a "good man and a real man," while women who had known him for years thought Pauline Randolph McKinney had been the most fortunate woman on earth.

In the office at one end of the long bunkhouse, J.T. found Ken Slattery, his foreman, but Ken's craggy face didn't break into its customary smile when he saw the boss. He was, in fact, scowling darkly.

"What's wrong?" J.T. demanded.

"You're not gonna like it," Ken said. "One of the men just came in to tell me there's four more cows missing from the herd this morning."

"Son of a bitch! You're sure there wasn't a gate left open or a break in the fence somewhere?"

"He's positive. He said he personally checked."

"Well, last time I was willing to believe the two we lost just strayed off, but not now. I'm afraid we might be up against some livestock larceny."

"That's my guess, too," Ken said.

"Tell you what I want you to do. Call the Southwest Breeders' Association and talk to a man named Larry Wendt. He's a cousin of mine and an investigator. Tell him I want to see him ASAP. And tell the men to start varying their schedules. Don't check the herd at the same time every day. The thief might have familiarized himself with our routine."

"Right."

"And let's keep this under our hats until we talk to Larry. We don't want to go crying wolf, and talk of cattle rustling gets folks around here a mite nervous."

"Gotcha."

J.T. turned to leave, then snapped his fingers and turned back. "I forgot what I came out here for. There's going to be a fellow out from the County Extension Office. He'll want to take some soil samples, so let him, okay?"

"Sure. Does this mean you're going to give Tyler's project the green light?"

"Let's just say I'm thinking about it. First he's going to have to convince me it'll make us some money."

Ken was mildly surprised. For more than a year, Tyler had been talking about planting some vineyards on the ranch and going into the winemaking business. At first J.T. had said, "No way," and Ken had assumed that would be the end of it. But as the boss learned more about the Texas wine industry, he had become less adamant, and Tyler had grown more persistent. When it came to his kids, J.T. was not predictable. He put up a stern facade, but he actually doted on his offspring. Ken thought that tendency had become even more pronounced since Pauline's death. Tyler just might get those vineyards after all.

Ken was as close to the McKinneys as it was possible for an employee to be. Everything that went on in the big house was of interest to him because he was almost one of the family. Moreover, Cal McKinney,

J.T.'s middle child, was his pal, and Cal liked to talk about his dad and his siblings. So Ken knew all about Tyler's grand ambitions.

He also knew everything the others knew about the woman from Boston, which wasn't a lot, and he knew J.T.'s children were less than thrilled over the possibility of a stepmother. Ken supposed that was only natural, but he hoped they would come around. The boss had been alone and lonely too long. "Are you on your way to the airport?" he asked.

"Yeah," J.T. said. "If I don't see you before, I'll see you at the party tonight."

"Those cattle we bought from that outfit in Oklahoma will be here this afternoon. Want me to take care of it?"

"That's right, I forgot." J.T. frowned thoughtfully. "No, I'll be here when they arrive. I want to be damned sure I get what I paid for. See you then."

"Sure. Take care."

J.T. left the office and retraced his steps to the front of the house where his midnight-blue Cadillac was parked. A minute later he drove through the front gate, turned right and headed for Crystal Creek, a town located about ten miles from the Double C, some forty miles west of Austin.

The community of almost seven thousand residents was one of the postcard-pretty towns that were scattered throughout the Hill Country, and like so many Texas towns, its original commercial district had been built around the courthouse square. The courthouse shared the square with a couple of statues, an ancient pecan tree and the Claro County Library. Across the street on the right was the Crystal Creek branch of Southwest Bank, a steel-and-glass structure that stood in marked contrast to the venerable courthouse. Two blocks beyond the square was the Longhorn Motel and Coffee Shop. J.T. checked his watch and determined that he had plenty of time for a cup of coffee.

The motel itself was a clean, well-kept, old-fashioned inn that rock hounds and other such tourists seemed to find quaint, and its coffee shop served as the community's unofficial town hall. It was where Crystal Creek's movers and shakers gathered for business talk and gossip.

J.T. was too late for the breakfast crowd and too early for the coffee-break bunch, so the place was almost deserted. He sat at one of the tables near the counter and waited. Almost immediately the door to the kitchen swung open, and Dottie Jones, the Longhorn's proprietor, appeared. Fiftyish and slightly overweight, Dottie was arguably the best-loved person in Crystal Creek. She also had an overworked shoulder—more folks than she could recall had cried on it. J.T. would have bet there wasn't a thing that transpired in the town that Dottie didn't know about. Fortunately, she was remarkably closemouthed. If one heard gossip, it didn't come from Dottie's lips.

"Mornin', J.T.," she greeted. "Coffee?"

"Yeah, Dottie, thanks. Looks like you've about got the place to yourself this morning."

"We had a real busy spell about an hour ago, but it's sure quiet now." She indicated the coffeepot. "Don't worry, it's fresh. I just made it. You want it black, right?"

"Right."

Dottie carried the coffee to his table just as the kitchen door opened again. Nora Jones, Dottie's former daughter-in-law, came out carrying a tray of clean cups and saucers. "Hi, J.T.," she said with a smile. "How're things?"

"Great in some ways, not so hot in others. How's Rory?"

Nora's face lit up at the mention of her son. "He's fine. Turning into some kind of softball player."

"So I've heard."

"I understand you're about to have some company."

J.T. grinned. "That's right. I'm on my way to the airport now."

"I can hardly wait to meet her."

J.T. honestly couldn't remember talking about Cynthia to anyone but his family, Virginia and Lettie Mae, and he hadn't told even them very much. Yet everyone in town seemed to know about her. But that was Crystal Creek; news spread faster there than jam on bread. No doubt his daughter, Lynn, had told her cousin and best friend, Beverly, who had told her mother, Carolyn, who might have told her cousin, Lori, and so on. "I'll bring her by in a day or two," he promised Nora.

"You'd better."

Just then J.T. felt a slap on his shoulder. He looked up to see Martin Avery, his attorney, longtime friend and now Crystal Creek's mayor. "Well, hello, Martin. Have a seat."

Martin pulled out a chair, sat down and smoothed at his gray-streaked blond hair. "I sure could take about six months of this weather," he commented as he indicated to Nora he wanted coffee.

"It'd be easy to get used to," J.T. agreed.

The two men's friendship went back a long way. They both were natives of Crystal Creek and had run with the same crowd in high school. Both had prospered and were solid citizens who donated generously to various local charities. Both were members of the First Baptist Church, and they belonged to the same fraternal organization. It was in their personal lives that they most differed. J.T. had literally married the girl next door, for Pauline had grown up on the Circle T, the ranch adjacent to the Double C. Martin had never married, though J.T. knew for a fact he had once been deeply in love. The woman in question had married someone else while Martin was in law school. J.T. assumed the attorney was one of those men who only love once. Until Cynthia, he had considered himself to be one, too.

Nora brought Martin's coffee, and for the next twenty minutes or so the two men fell into idle talk about their favorite subjects—Crystal Creek and its inhabitants. As they talked, the tempo in the coffee shop quickened. Regulars filed in and took seats almost reserved for them by custom. There was a great deal of calling back and forth between tables. It was generally believed more serious business was conducted in the Longhorn Coffee Shop than in any office in town.

Finally J.T. looked at his watch, then reached into his hip pocket for his wallet. Slapping a dollar bill on the table, he said, "I'd better get a move on. I'll see you tonight, won't I, Martin?"

"You bet. Wouldn't miss it for the world. I'm pretty anxious to meet this Yankee gal you've taken a shine to."

"Take care." J.T. waved goodbye to Dottie and Nora as he wound his way through the maze of tables and chairs that filled the center of the coffee shop. He had reached the door when it opened, and two more customers entered. J.T.'s gaze darkened when he saw the new arrivals.

Billie Jo Dumont swept past him. "Hi, J.T.," she said.

"Mornin', Billie Jo."

Quick on her heels, which was where he seemed to stay most of the time these days, was Al "Bubba" Gibson. "Hi, podnuh," Bubba said, punching J.T.'s arm playfully.

"Hi, Bubba. How's the world treating you?"

"No complaints," he said and followed Billie Jo to a secluded booth at the back of the coffee shop.

J.T. was still scowling when he got into the Cadillac and drove off. He had known Bubba from way back; they'd gone to school together and both were now ranchers. But friend or not, J.T. would have liked to shake his pal until his teeth rattled. The relationship with Billie Jo was being flaunted openly, and that was, to J.T.'s notion, unforgivable. Bubba's wife, Mary, was a classy lady who didn't deserve that kind of treatment, and she had to know about Billie Jo. Even if the affair had been conducted discreetly, it couldn't have been kept a secret long, not in Crystal Creek. J.T. could imagine how Mary must feel, knowing her husband for thirty-five years was involved with a woman younger than their daughter.

He didn't think he was a prude, but he did have some deeply held principles, and one of them concerned marital fidelity. He had been lapdog-faithful to Pauline during their long marriage, not only because he had loved her but because he wouldn't have wanted her subjected to humiliation. And until this thing with Billie Jo had started, he would have sworn that Bubba and Mary had the same kind of marriage.

Maybe Bubba was going through a midlife crisis. He had been a compulsive womanizer in his younger days. J.T. recalled some of the locker room wisecracks. "Bubba lays everything but his breakfast eggs." Maybe being seen with a twenty-year-old woman made him feel like he'd had a hormone transplant. Frankly, J.T. didn't understand why Mary didn't pack her bags and take a nice long vacation until Bubba came to his senses.

He also didn't understand Billie Jo. She was young and very pretty with those pouty lips and all that strawberry-blond hair. Plus, she had a knock-'em dead figure. Half of Crystal Creek's young studs panted after her. Why would she want to become involved with a middle-aged married man? It was highly unlikely that Bubba would ever actually leave Mary, so what was in it for Billie Jo?

J.T. didn't know, but he did know there wasn't a damned thing he could do about it. Anyway, he had far more delightful things to think about. First of all, there was a plane to meet.

CHAPTER TWO

THE CAPTAIN had just announced they would begin their approach to Austin's Mueller Airport in fifteen minutes. The flight attendants moved up and down the aisle, gathering magazines and paper cups. Cynthia Anita Page leaned forward and looked out the window. The sky was so clear and blue it didn't look real. Her stomach churned with anticipation, and she wasn't the kind of woman whose stomach often churned, from anticipation or anything else.

But then, in all the thirty-five years of her orderly existence, she had never found herself in a situation like this. If things worked out as she hoped, she was coming to Crystal Creek to join her future husband, to meet his family and friends and to get acquainted with her future home.

During the past six months, while she was being delightfully and persistently wooed, Cynthia had often been amazed at how sure she was that she wanted this drastic change in her life. She certainly hadn't received any encouragement. Her friends back in Boston were aghast and gave the marriage, if it took place, a life span of six months. Her father, Joseph, had given her a ponderous lecture on the advisability of staying with "one's own kind." Her mother, Alicia, almost had an attack of the vapors whenever she thought about it. "Honestly, Cynthia...a woman with your advantages!" she had exclaimed only the day before while watching her daughter pack. "How could you even consider such a thing? You have some notion that living on a ranch will be romantic and adventurous, but I imagine very little of it really is."

Cynthia couldn't blame her parents for having doubts and misgivings. When one considered how they had raised their only child—Dana Hall prep school, Smith College, knowing all the right people, doing all the right things—it wasn't surprising they would feel that Cynthia was moving down in the world.

But Cynthia herself saw it differently. From the cradle she had been raised to be a lady, and she was one in every way. Everything about her spoke of status and affluence. Her blond beauty was sleek and polished. Her clothes were classic and expensive, and she wore them with the ease of a woman accustomed to the finest of everything. Her years of studying banking and finance at Smith, then her long tenure with Winwood Federal, one of the largest investment banks in the country, had made her always-keen mind razor sharp. No one questioned her competence. She was the embodiment of the ideal woman of the 1980s—upwardly mobile, bright, ambitious, well educated and with scads of disposable income.

But the 1980s were over, and she had grown restless. The high-powered life-style she had so carefully forged for herself was no longer satisfying, but she would never be content to be what her mother was—a wealthy woman of leisure who spent her days doing good works and her nights either entertaining or being entertained. Cynthia wanted more. A home and a family as well as a fulfilling career. She was aware her childbearing years were rapidly coming to an end. In J. T. McKinney she thought she had finally found the man of her dreams—tough, strong, affectionate and intelligent. When he told her his late wife had been a full partner in the Double C's operation, she had found it too good to be true. A tough, strong man who wanted more in a wife than an apron-clad helpmate was exactly what she had been looking for. Cynthia leaned her head on the back of the seat, closed her eyes and smiled, recalling the party six months ago where it all had begun....

SALLY HONECKER had promised the party would be a dazzling affair, and Cynthia wasn't disappointed. She was glad she had gone to the trouble of making the trip from Boston to attend. Trust Sally to throw an elegant party to celebrate the blooming of the first bluebonnets! Sally's and Ted's gracious Austin home was ablaze with lights, festive with flowers, and their well-heeled socialite friends were dressed to the nines.

"As far as I'm concerned," one of the guests had told Cynthia earlier, "spring officially arrives when the Honeckers give their party. It's sort of a tradition. And this year's is especially nice, don't you think?''

Cynthia thought it was a splendid party, and the weather had cooperated beautifully. The day had been sunny and mild, and the night air was pleasant enough for many of the guests to enjoy their drinks on the patio. It was a far cry from the dismal drizzle she had left behind in Boston the day before.

She strolled by the sumptuously laden buffet table, picked up a tortilla chip and dipped it into a chafing dish full of cheese dip, loaded with chiles, of course. She was, after all, in Texas. Just as she popped the tidbit into her mouth, Sally threaded her way through the crush of guests toward her. Cynthia marveled at how well her former college roommate looked. *Perky* had been the word most often used to describe Sally back in their Smith College days, and the adjective still fit.

Cynthia and Sally had been inseparable at Smith, and Cynthia still smiled when she recalled what a contrast the duo must have presented on campus. She was as blond as Sally was brunette. At five foot seven, she stood a full four inches taller than her petite friend. And their dispositions were totally dissimilar. Cynthia, much to her own regret, had to constantly guard against coming across as too prim and reserved. Sally, on the other hand, seemed never to have met a stranger. Even their backgrounds were as different as winter and summer. Sally's father was a lusty oil wildcatter who made and lost fortunes at the turn of a drill bit. Cynthia's family had been prominent in Boston banking circles for well over a century, and her mother could trace her ancestors back to colonial times. They were Beacon Hill Brahmin through and through. And yet, the two women had hit it off from the first, and thanks to telephones and airplanes, were still close friends fourteen years after graduation.

"Having a good time?" Sally asked, spearing a shrimp and plunging it into a bowl of sauce.

"Marvelous," Cynthia answered truthfully. "You have a nice group of friends. They've made me feel very welcome."

"I'm so glad you came, Cyn, but I do wish you could stay longer."

"Big old banks like Winwood Federal aren't exactly generous when it comes to time off."

"But you're such a big shot now. A vice president! It sounds so impressive."

Cynthia smiled. "Didn't anyone ever tell you that bank vice presidents are a dime a dozen," she said, though she actually was proud of what she had achieved, particularly since she liked to think she had done it without calling on her family's clout. However, even she knew that growing up in the industry had given her an edge. She'd known the ropes and had received invaluable advice from her father, uncles and cousins.

"I'll bet bank vice presidents who look like you do aren't a dime a dozen." Sally uttered an exaggerated sigh. "I don't know why I have a thing to do with you.

I'm insanely jealous of your height and your figure and just about everything else. I'm so...angular. Hardly a curve.''

"So why do you have a handsome husband and two beautiful kids, while I have a two-bedroom apartment and one largely unsociable cat?''

"It must be your own fault. I can't believe all Boston men are blind to your charms.''

Cynthia's smile faded. "Sally, you can't begin to imagine the kind of men I meet. They're focused solely on their careers and themselves, not necessarily in that order. Sometimes I think I'll scream if I meet one more man who spends the entire evening telling me the story of his life. I never seem to be invited to places where everyone just relaxes and has a good time, the way these people are.'' Her eyes roamed over the sea of smiling faces, then abruptly stopped. "Mmm,'' she murmured.

"Mmm, what?'' Sally asked.

"Now there's someone whose life story I wouldn't mind hearing.''

"Really? Which one?''

"The tall man in the blue suit by the fireplace. The one talking to your dad.''

Sally rose on her toes and craned her neck. Then she settled on her heels and smiled. "You still have good taste in men.''

"Who is he?''

"John Travis McKinney—J.T. to those who know him well, and, judging from the look on your face, I'd say you'd like to get to know him well."

"I suppose he's married and has five kids."

"Three kids, all grown. And his wife died five years ago. J.T.'s a big man in these parts. He owns the Double C Ranch over in Crystal Creek. You ought to see it. It's just about the biggest spread in the area, a real showplace. Come on, I'll introduce you."

Cynthia hung back. "That would be rather pointless, wouldn't it, Sally? Tomorrow I'll be long gone."

"Oh, come on. You'll be back for other visits, and J.T.'s a great guy to know. If the two of you get acquainted and hit it off...well, who knows? I might get you down here to Austin more often. Come on."

Cynthia hesitated, but only for a second. The man by the fireplace was simply too intriguing, and she couldn't remember the last time she'd seen a man who truly intrigued her. She and Sally wound their way through the crowd and crossed the room.

"J.T., I have someone I want you to meet," Sally said.

J.T. straightened and turned. His mouth curved into a slightly crooked, completely charming smile that showed a row of even white teeth. Cynthia felt a curious inner stirring. All of her life she had dreamed of meeting a man and experiencing an instant reaction to him. She had begun to think such a thing couldn't happen, not in real life, but now she knew differently.

What she didn't know was why this particular man had that effect on her. True, he was handsome, ruggedly so, but she'd met many handsome men. He was tall, more than six feet, she guessed, and he had the warmest brown eyes she had ever seen. She couldn't begin to guess his age, but if he had three grown children, he probably was older than he looked. He was even better-looking than he had appeared to be from across the room.

Yet none of that explained her odd reaction to him. Feeling decidedly off balance, she sensed something in the air, much as an animal senses water long before reaching it. The very atmosphere vibrated. Even as she experienced it, she couldn't believe it.

"I'd like you to meet my friend, Cynthia Page," Sally said. "We roomed together at Smith. Cynthia, this is J. T. McKinney."

Two pairs of brown eyes locked together, and for a split second J.T. and Cynthia might have been the only two people in the room. "Cynthia," J.T. said as he offered his hand. "It's a pleasure to meet you."

She took his hand, and as ridiculous as it was, she would have sworn she felt something click between them. Amazingly, from the look on J.T.'s face, she could tell he had felt it, too. Perhaps she was reading too much into his expression, but at the very least, it conveyed much more than ordinary interest.

"How do you do, J.T.?" she said in her best party voice.

"So you and Sally were roommates. Tell me the truth—how did this Texas girl really fare up there? To hear her tell it, she fairly took the northeast by storm."

"Oh, she was a charmer, all right. Take her word for it."

Sally touched Cynthia's arm. "I'll leave you two to chat. I must mix and mingle."

Out of the corner of her eye, Cynthia saw Sally's father move away and join another group. That left her free to concentrate solely on J. T. McKinney. She favored him with her warmest smile.

"Where's home, Cynthia?" he asked.

"Boston."

"Boston," he repeated, as though she had said Ankara or Calcutta. "What do you in Boston?"

"I'm a banker. Have you heard of Winwood Federal?"

One dark brow lifted slightly. "I imagine everyone in business has heard of Winwood Federal."

"Business? I thought Sally said you're a rancher."

"Ranching is business. The official name of my operation is the Double C Land and Cattle Company. Livestock raising is big business in this part of the world."

"Yes, I suppose it is a business," Cynthia said, "but one forgets that. When I think of ranching—something I confess I almost never do—I think of a lot of Hollywood nonsense about a free and easy life, roaming the wide-open spaces."

"The land I ranch doesn't have wide-open spaces," J.T. said with a grin. "My land is the up-and-down kind, full of rocks, trees and scrubs, and it happens to be the most beautiful place on earth." He took her by the arm. "Nice night, isn't it? Let me get us both a drink, and we'll enjoy them on the patio."

Even if she had wanted to say no, which she didn't, she wouldn't have. Instinct told her that people rarely said no to J.T. "Thanks. I'd like that."

He guided her to the bar, asked for a vodka and tonic at her request, a Scotch on the rocks with a splash for himself, then propelled her toward the French doors at the far end of the room. Guests parted to make a path for them. Most spoke to J.T., and he answered with, "Hi, there. Good to see you again," but he didn't slow down. Cynthia guessed he didn't care to be caught up in conversation.

The night air had cooled some, and the patio was beginning to empty. J.T. found two chairs away from the few groups that stood about in clusters. Pulling out one for her, he waited until she was seated. Then he sat down after carefully hitching his trousers at both knees. Cynthia thought what an incredibly masculine gesture that was.

"How long will you be visiting Sally?"

"I'll be going home tomorrow morning. My flight leaves at ten."

"What a shame."

Did he really think it was a shame, she wondered, or was he just making polite conversation? "I have to be at work Monday morning, you know."

"How did you get interested in banking in the first place?"

"It was almost preordained, I think. My family has been in banking for generations. It seemed natural to study banking and finance."

"Do you enjoy your work?"

Cynthia pursed her lips. "I always have," she said with a tiny frown.

"But? Why do I sense there's a 'but' in there?"

"Oh, I suppose I've reached the point of asking myself if it's what I want to do the rest of my life."

"And have you come up with an answer?" J.T. asked.

Smiling, she shook her head. "No, I'm afraid not. What about you? Do you like your work?"

"I wouldn't trade places with anyone on earth."

"How fortunate you are."

J.T. looked at her for the briefest of seconds—admiringly, she thought. Then he asked, "Are you married, divorced, thinking of getting married?"

"None of the above." Then it was her turn to quiz him. She asked the kind of questions new acquaintances ask, but this time she was genuinely interested in the answers. Gradually he opened up, though she got the impression he didn't feel easy when talking about himself. He spoke lovingly and proudly of his late wife, his children, his ranch. Normally she avoided this kind of conversation like the plague, but somehow this one was different.

The night air eventually drove them indoors, but instead of rejoining the crush of guests and drifting off, J.T. led her to a relatively secluded corner where their conversation could continue uninterrupted. The evening flew by. When the party broke up and he was forced to leave, Cynthia could honestly say she had never in her life regretted so much having to say goodbye. She couldn't even put her finger on what there was about him that made him so special. He just was.

When Sally and Ted closed the door behind the last of their guests, Ted bade the women good-night and went straight upstairs, but Sally was bursting with curiosity. "Let's have one final, tiny sip of wine, and you can tell me what you and J.T. talked about for hours."

"Was it hours? It seemed like minutes. We didn't talk about anything in particular. Mostly he told me about himself and his family."

"Really? That doesn't sound much like J.T. I think of him as the strong, silent type."

"Well, I must admit I asked dozens of questions. Now you tell me about him."

Sally turned thoughtful. "How to describe J.T.? It's not easy. Most of my information is secondhand stuff, things I've heard from Ted and others who've had direct dealings with him. I know he was a devoted husband, and he's crazy about his kids. I've heard more than one person say you couldn't have a better friend, and he really does work that ranch of his. He doesn't leave it in the hands of a manager or anything like that. Apparently that means something in ranching circles. I just know he's highly thought of.''

Everything Sally said jibed with what Cynthia hoped to hear about the man, and she thought of him for a long time after crawling in bed that night. Why, oh, why did the most interesting man she had met in years have to live half a continent away from Boston? Of course, she could come to Austin anytime she could get away. Sally had issued an open invitation years ago, and Cynthia knew it was a genuine one. She just might take advantage of it. J.T. was interested in her, too; she was sure of it. That was a comforting thought and one that enabled her to get a very good night's sleep.

CYNTHIA WOKE feeling refreshed and recharged the following morning. After a leisurely breakfast with Sally and Ted, she showered and packed. Her bags were standing at the front door when the call came.

"It's for you," Sally said with a knowing smile, handing her the phone. Cynthia's heart did a little dance as she lifted the receiver to her ear.

"Hello."

"Cynthia? J. T. McKinney. You remember, from last night."

"Of course, I remember. Good morning."

"Good morning. Ah...listen, I have some business to attend to near Boston this week, and it occurred to me that we might get together for dinner Friday night. If you don't have other plans, of course."

"Friday night? I don't believe I have a thing on tap. I'd love to have dinner. Thanks."

"Say, seven o'clock? I'll be running around in a taxi, so just give me your address."

Her first impulse was to offer to pick him up at the airport, but she thought better of it. She gave him the address, they exchanged a few more pleasantries then Cynthia hung up. Turning to Sally, she smiled triumphantly. "That was J.T."

"I figured."

"He has business near Boston this week."

Sally giggled. "I'll just bet he does. You haven't lost your touch, Cyn."

"We're having dinner Friday night. Now I guess the trick is to give him an evening he won't forget."

CYNTHIA'S SPIRITS SOARED throughout the following week. For the first time in ages she had a reason to look forward to an evening. She gave a lot of thought to where she would take him. Suspecting that a rancher would not go for dishes like scallops in ginger-cilantro cream, she eschewed the trendier restaurants in favor of one that served what might have been the best Yankee pot roast in all New England. J.T. ate heartily and raved about the food. Afterward, they lingered over after-dinner drinks and coffee in the piano bar. He deposited her at her door before midnight, made a date to see her the following day, then took a cab back to his hotel.

Saturday she gave him a tourist's-eye view of the city she knew so well. Later, when discussing dinner plans, he said, "I'm not much of a fish man, but, hell, I'm in Boston. Shouldn't I have clam chowder or something?" Laughing, she took him to the best no-frills seafood place she knew of, and again he seemed to enjoy the food. Also again, he had her home before midnight, only this time he kissed her affectionately before taking a cab to his hotel.

Cynthia was still asleep when he called Sunday morning to say goodbye. "Good morning," he greeted her brightly as she tried to shake off the vestiges of sleep. "I'm on my way home, but it looks like I'll have to come back. May I see you again next Friday?"

"Well...yes, of course." Elation swept through her. She had been sure some time would pass before she got to see him again. Squinting at the bedside clock, she was surprised at the early hour. "Good heavens, are you already at the airport? What time does your flight leave?"

"Whenever I turn the key in the ignition. I flew my plane up."

"Are you telling me you flew all the way from Texas in a little plane?"

"Hey, it's not little. It's a twin-engine six-seater."

"Those things just look so flimsy to me."

"Well, they're not, and I'm a good pilot. Friday at seven, then?"

"Yes."

"Take care, Cynthia. I really had a nice time."

"So did I, J.T. I . . . I'd like to ask you to do a favor for me, if you will."

"Of course, if I can."

"Call me when you arrive safely home."

There was a pause. She wondered if he thought her silly or was pleased by her concern. "All right," he said quietly. "I'll be glad to. Goodbye, Cynthia."

"Goodbye."

And she was restless and edgy, unable to concentrate on anything until his call came that afternoon.

THE FOLLOWING WEEKEND was a replay of the first, though they went to different restaurants and they saw different sights, off-the-beaten-track things that Cynthia enjoyed most. J.T.'s good-night kisses were a bit more lingering and insistent, though no one could have described them as passionate.

Things began to change during the third weekend. That was when she took him to meet her parents. Joseph and Alicia were gracious and welcoming; their breeding would have allowed nothing less. That very breeding, however, made them so correct and formal that they could never exude real warmth to outsiders. J.T. handled the visit with aplomb, remarking only that her parents seemed to be very nice people.

That weekend he kissed her with an intensity that left Cynthia weak and wanting more. She could feel the heat passing between them. It seemed only reasonable to expect him to ask to stay the night, but she'd not dealt with a man like J.T. before. He was the product of a different time and place. She soon realized that he regarded courtship as a ritual, a rite of passage that demanded a proper sequence of events, a certain gallantry. But at least by that third weekend he had given up all pretense of coming to Boston for any reason but to see her.

During the fourth weekend, he stopped making reservations at a hotel.

ON SATURDAY AFTERNOON a pouring rain had begun, making outdoor activities unattractive. Cynthia and J.T. holed up in her apartment. He watched a golf tournament on TV, while Tiffany, her tabby cat, snoozed on his lap. That alone made him special, for Tiffany had always been a one-person cat who lurked in corners when Cynthia had company. But the fickle feline had taken to J.T. right away.

Cynthia spent most of the afternoon puttering in her well-equipped kitchen, something she liked to do when the weather was foul. She had decided to prepare a full curry feast with all the condiments for J.T., who professed astonishment.

"You don't seem to me like the kind of woman who would cook."

"I love to cook. At the risk of sounding modest, that's probably why I'm so good at it."

"Amazing."

"Amazing that I cook? Legions of women do it every day. Was your wife a good cook?" Cynthia had never found it uncomfortable to talk about Pauline, and neither had J.T.

"Pauline never went near the kitchen. She'd always had a cook."

"So had I until I left home. Then I realized I'd better learn my way around pots and pans unless I wanted to exist on canned and frozen things. Cooking makes me feel creative, and I'm not naturally a creative person."

When she set the food in front of him, along with a basket of homemade *chapati* that he mistook for tortillas, he simply stared at the unfamiliar fare a minute. Then he dug in. After a few bites he declared it one of the most delicious dishes he had ever eaten. "Almost as good as Mexican food."

Cynthia laughed. "I'm going to take that as the ultimate compliment. It's not too hot for you?"

"Too hot? You're looking at a man who can eat jalapeño peppers off the bush."

She was certain she had never spent a more enjoyable evening. It was relaxed and curiously domestic. After J.T. had helped her with the dishes, she turned out the kitchen light and led the way into the living room. Together they sat on the sofa, very close to each other. "Music or television?" she asked.

"Music, by all means. I haven't watched much TV since 'Gunsmoke' went off the air."

Chuckling, Cynthia picked up the remote control and punched a button. Soothing strains from her favorite easy-listening station filled the room. She kicked off her shoes, tucked her feet beneath her and snuggled closer to J.T. Their arms linked; her head went to his shoulder. The atmosphere was warmly companionable and oddly strained at the same time. They were like two smitten teenagers wondering what the next move should be.

"J.T., your family—have they asked about these trips?"

"There have been some questions, yes."

"What did you tell them?"

"The truth—that my only business in Boston is with a lovely woman I met at a party."

"How did they take it?"

His hesitation told Cynthia all she needed to know. They were either taken aback, disapproving or both.

"You know how kids are," he said vaguely. "My grandfather's almost as bad."

She didn't know how kids were, but it didn't matter. She certainly wasn't going to spend any of their precious time together worrying about his family. Shifting her position, she slid her arm down the length of his shoulders and leaned forward to kiss him on the ear. He turned his head, enabling her to capture his mouth with hers. An odd sound came from his throat. Embracing her, he leaned into the kiss, deepening it until their tongues intertwined. When they lifted their heads, both were breathless. Cynthia gave him a smile that was almost shy.

"You're a lovely woman," he said. "You've injected a badly needed dose of joy into my life."

"I'm glad."

"I think I could fall in love with you if I let myself."

"Be my guest."

J.T. lapsed into thoughtful silence. It seemed to Cynthia he was waging an inner war with himself. She gingerly fingered the buttons of his shirt. "J.T., literally be my guest. Stay with me tonight."

The look on his face was indescribable. Too late it occurred to her that perhaps in his world, men did not welcome such boldness from women. She stared back at him, puzzlement in her eyes as she wondered how she would graciously handle matters if he declined her invitation.

Suddenly, without a word, J.T. got to his feet and crossed the room to the telephone. He took a card out of his shirt pocket, picked up the receiver and dialed. Good Lord, Cynthia thought. Is he calling a cab?

"This is J. T. McKinney," she heard him say. "I'm in 1104. My plans have changed, and I'll be checking out within the hour. Yes . . . thank you."

Hanging up, he turned and looked at her, his face solemn, his eyes blazing. "The doorman will get me a cab. I'll be back as quickly as I can."

Cynthia stared at the back of the door after he had shut it, utterly astonished. Any other man would have swept her up in his arms and had her in the bedroom in the blink of an eye. J.T. was going to check out of his hotel first!

But then, if he were like any other man, she wouldn't want him. Collecting her wits, she scrambled off the sofa and hurried into the bathroom to draw a tub of water. She sprinkled it liberally with fragrant oil, and while the tub was filling, she rummaged through her dresser for the frilliest, sexiest nightgown she owned. When J.T. returned a little more than an hour later, both she and the bedroom were ready for a seduction. Cynthia percolated with excitement. She wanted to remember every single detail of the night. It was a long time since she'd made love, and she'd never made love with anyone who thrilled her the way J.T. did.

He stood in the center of the room, holding a garment bag over his shoulder, looking rather uncertain and a little sheepish. "I travel light," he said.

"Let me take it. I'll hang it for you."

Turning off the living room lamp, she beckoned him with a nod of her head. He followed her into the bedroom, where one lamp shone softly, casting shadows over the four-poster, whose covers had been turned down to reveal floral sheets under a puffy down coverlet. J.T. stared at it as though it was the first bed he'd ever seen.

Cynthia hung his bag in her closet, then crossed the room to stand in front of him. Letting her arms crawl up his chest, she locked her hands behind his neck. His hands slid down her body, and his lips reached for hers. They kissed as though they had all the time in the world... and they did. They had the whole, long, lovely night.

But when J.T. lifted his head, his expression was one of utmost gravity. "My goodness," Cynthia murmured, brushing the underside of his chin with her lips. "You look so serious."

"This is serious."

"I agree... and nice."

"I'm not sure it's the best thing that could happen to you."

"Well, I am."

Suddenly his hands felt as clumsy as hams. "I feel so... inept," he confessed.

"Why on earth would you feel that way?"

"Cynthia, I was married a long time, and long-married couples just know... well, there's a sort of ritual they've learned over the years that... Oh, Jesus, I'm saying this badly, but I do so want this to be special, and I'm not sure I remember...."

"Of course it will be special. It's our first time. It will be special and memorable. Now please, J.T., let's not talk."

Her deft fingers unflicked a shirt button from its hole. With his help, she undressed him, marveling at his body's strength. Time rested kindly on him. Then she shivered as he untied her robe, pushed it off her shoulders and touched her flesh with his fingertips. She experienced an unbearable longing for fulfillment, but with some difficulty she allowed him to set the pace. When he turned to guide her between the sheets, she begrudged even that brief separation of their bodies.

At first his movements were slow and sensual, but as her eagerness grew ever more evident, he became commanding. Her responses were volcanic. When at last he entered her, she knew that anything she had experienced before this night had been merely a warm-up. This was the real thing. The completeness they found in each other was draining, numbing and completely satisfying.

IN THE WEEKS and months that followed, variations on that theme were played and replayed many times. Cynthia blossomed under the glow of J.T.'s lovemaking. But she desperately needed to know that their relationship went beyond sex. She knew she was in love, and he had told her he loved her, that she made him happier than he'd been in years. Still, it wasn't enough; she wanted more.

One night as they lay in bed, she suddenly realized they'd shared five months of weekends. He'd missed only three in all that time, twice when business demands prevented his traveling, once when he'd been nursing a nasty cold. Five months of growing ever closer, five months of her wondering. "What do you see happening to us, J.T.?" she asked.

He propped himself on one elbow to look down at her. "I don't understand what you're asking, sweetheart."

"Am I your sweetheart? For how long? Five more months? A year? Two years? Will we ever spend Christmas, New Year's Eve, the Fourth of July together? Will we ever take a trip together? Will we ever spend, say, a Wednesday together or is this to remain a Friday to Saturday romance? Do you ever intend for me to meet your family? I'm not setting conditions, but I would like to know what I have to look forward to."

There was a pause, then he expelled his breath. "Now I know what you're asking." Rolling over, he threw back the covers, slipped into his pajama bottoms and walked to the window. He stood there so long that Cynthia braced herself for almost anything—utter rejection, the end of the relationship, anything.

Finally he turned. "Do you know how old I am?"

"Well, let's see...you have a son who's thirty-four, and you were twenty-one when he was born, so with my advanced degree in finance...give me a minute and I'll figure it out."

"Be serious."

"I am serious! I think of us as being the same age when I think about age at all, which isn't very often."

"We aren't the same age." He raked his fingers through his hair and returned to sit on the edge of the bed. "But let's forget age for the moment. I want nothing more than to marry you, but—"

"I accept."

"Cynthia, living at the Double C wouldn't be anything like your life here."

"Good. I'm up to here with my life."

"And Crystal Creek isn't Boston, not by a long shot. There aren't any great restaurants or shops, no theaters...."

"Oh, J.T., that's so unimportant."

"And life on the ranch is even sleepier than it is in town. Plus, I have an aging grandfather and adult children living there. You might find it difficult to adjust to them."

"And they might find it difficult to adjust to me, right? I'd think it odd if they didn't."

They argued back and forth. Every argument he came up with was met by a more forceful one from her. Finally he reached out and rumpled her hair. "I'll make a deal with you."

"Deal?"

"Come for a visit, a long one, a few months at least. Can that be arranged?"

Cynthia pursed her lips. "I think so. I've been with the bank a long time, and I have a superefficient assistant. I can ask for a leave of absence. Oh, J.T., is that really necessary? Can't you give me credit for being able to work things out?"

"It's a whole different way of life, sweetheart. I personally need to know you're sure of what you'd be getting into."

A part of her was miffed at him for having doubts, but another more sensible part knew that he was probably right. She wouldn't just be marrying him; he came encumbered. Throwing her arms around his neck, she kissed him soundly. "When is all this going to take place?"

"I suppose you have to make arrangements at work."

"I should give them two weeks' notice."

"And I'm going to be tied up at a cattlemen's convention in Houston week after next. Let's say three weeks from now. That'll get you there at the nicest time of year."

They made plans until far into the night, and the next afternoon when J.T. said goodbye was the first time Cynthia didn't experience her usual Sunday letdown. On Monday she asked for and was granted a leave of absence. She made arrangements to farm Tiffany out with friends. She called Sally in Austin, and they talked for half an hour. Then she told her parents. And despite the latter's predictions of dismal failure, Cynthia had absolutely no doubt that her future lay in Crystal Creek, Texas.

THE GENTLE JOLT as the plane touched down snapped her out of her reverie. Opening her handbag, she took out a compact and gave her makeup a final scrutiny.

She was as ridiculously nervous as a teenager on her first date, and that was strange. She had never been even slightly nervous with J.T. in Boston. However, she conceded, this was different. This was his territory, his home turf, and, for some reason, Cynthia felt that put her at a disadvantage.

In the terminal, she spotted him before he saw her, and what she saw took her breath away. Always before, at Sally's party and in Boston, he had worn conservative business suits or tailored slacks and sport shirts. Today he had on a white shirt, starched jeans, cowboy boots and a belt with a silver buckle the size of a pancake. In his hand he held a brown cowboy hat. Why were such clothes so flattering to masculine looks? He was without question the most attractive man she'd ever known.

Then he saw her, and his ruggedly handsome face broke into a grin. Quickening her step, she walked into his arms.

CHAPTER THREE

TYLER MCKINNEY PROWLED the living room like a caged tiger, glancing at his watch, walking to the hearth, then to the front windows to peer out.

"Man, I wish you'd sit down," drawled his brother, Cal, from his prone position on the sofa. "You're making me nervous."

Tyler stopped his pacing and looked down at Cal. "Yeah, I noticed. You look as nervous as a cooked noodle."

"He has to be nervous," Lynn McKinney said as she settled into one of the wing chairs that flanked the hearth. "We all are."

"What's to be nervous about?" Cal asked. "The old man's found himself a friend. He's bringing her here, so it must be serious. Big deal. Relax."

"What if we don't like her?" Lynn asked.

"Doubt it'll make any difference," Cal said. "It's what Daddy thinks about her that counts."

"It would be awful if we didn't like her," Lynn insisted. "Can you even imagine bad vibes in this house?"

"No, but then, I can't imagine a strange woman in this house, either. We'll get used to it."

"That's easy for you to say," Lynn said. "You're hardly ever home. Tyler and Grandpa Hank and I live here every day."

From his easy chair, Hank listened to the conversation swirling around him. He still hadn't shaved, mainly because his grandson had suggested he should. He made a sound of disdain. "It's all stuff and nonsense, if you ask me. A man J.T.'s age ought'a be content to wait for grandchildren to come along." He squinted at his great-grandchildren. "Course, he's not doin' too good in that department, is he?"

Tyler said nothing. He didn't for a minute think Cal was as nonchalant about this as he was letting on, but of all of them, he would be the least upset at the thought of their father's getting married again. In the first place, as Lynn had pointed out, Cal spent most of the year following the Professional Rodeo Cowboys Association circuit, so he popped in and out of their lives with the predictability of the Texas weather. And for another, even if Cal hated the woman from Boston, he'd let it bother him for maybe ten minutes. More than anyone Tyler had ever known, his brother was able to brush aside life's unpleasantries and go on his merry way. He was a freewheeling seeker of pleasure, a ladies' man who liked to be the center of attention. That was one reason, Tyler suspected, he enjoyed rodeoing so much. Cal was a celebrity out on the circuit.

Tyler shifted his attention to Lynn. It was impossible for him to know how his sister was taking the news of their father's new love interest. She wasn't one for pouring out her feelings. For all he knew, she might welcome the presence of another woman in the house. Even he had to admit it was overwhelmingly male-dominated, and he knew that since Pauline's death Lynn had often been forced to fight to make her influence felt. Tyler was almost certain that was partly the reason his sister insisted on raising Thoroughbreds in a quarter horse state. She was making an independent statement. And since the Bostonian sounded like one of those fiercely independent modern women, she and Lynn might find themselves sisters under the skin.

On the other hand, Lynn had adored their mother. With her auburn hair and petite figure, she was the McKinney offspring who most resembled Pauline, so much so that it was sometimes painful for Tyler to look at her. And she seemed to have tried to get closer to J.T. since their mother's death, as though she wanted to protect him. Lynn might very well resent the woman from Boston.

But if she did, Tyler mused, she would just hie off to the stable and lose herself in grooming and working her horses. He himself had no such outlet, not yet. Damn, the woman's visit couldn't have been more ill-timed. Just when he'd thought he had talked his father into the wine-making venture. Now J.T. would be so tied up with his woman friend that Tyler feared his own plans would have to be put on hold.

Tyler shifted his attention to his great-grandfather. One thing no one would have to spend time wondering about was what Grandpa Hank thought of the woman. He'd just blurt it out, hurt feelings be damned.

Tyler didn't have to dig very deep in search of his own feelings about a possible stepmother. He hated the idea. He was the oldest of J.T.'s children and had been the closest to Pauline. There simply had been a special bond between them that the other members of the family recognized and accepted. To Tyler, his mother had seemed almost saintly. The thought of another woman's moving into the master bedroom and directing the household was totally objectionable to him. He didn't bother to question the rationality of it. He didn't remind himself that J.T. had been incredibly lonely for five years and deserved a second chance at happiness. It was the way he felt, and there was nothing he could do about it.

"What do we know, really know about this woman?" Lynn was asking.

"Not much," Cal said. "Daddy met her at a party. She went to Smith, lives in Boston and is an investment banker." He grinned. "Sounds like a barrel of fun."

"Sounds t'me like she's gonna be as useless around here as teats on a wild boar," Hank grumbled.

Tyler walked to the front windows again, and this time he saw his father's Cadillac drive through the gate. "Well, in a minute we'll know more about her. Put on your party manners. They're here."

Cal grudgingly struggled to a sitting position and got to his feet. Lynn straightened and folded her hands in her lap, then glanced sideways at Tyler. He had gone to the fireplace and stood with his hands clasped behind his back. It occurred to Lynn that he was standing exactly as their father did while he collected his thoughts before dealing with something he found unpleasant. Was the woman from Boston really that difficult for Tyler to come to terms with?

The front door opened and closed. A minute later a willowy blond woman in a striking green coatdress preceded J.T. into the room. The brothers and sisters exchanged quick, stunned glances. Hank's jaw dropped. Each of them had formed a vague mental picture of Cynthia Page, but none of those pictures had approached reality. Lynn thought Cynthia might well be the most beautiful woman she'd ever seen. Her beauty was cool, serene and polished. Lynn guessed *patrician* was the word for it. She felt her own face flush. She supposed she had hoped Ms. Page would be rather plain. *She's prettier than Mama was,* she thought, and it hurt.

Cal's thoughts took a decidedly different turn. Ever the ladies' man, he couldn't help but admire his father for having captured the eye of such a gorgeous creature. And because his self-confidence when it came to women was unlimited, he took a minute to wish he had been the one to have seen Cynthia Page first. No wonder his dad had been acting as spry as a spring chicken lately. But under no circumstances did Cal think he would ever be able to regard this woman as a stepmother.

Tyler was thunderstruck. Whatever he had been expecting, it certainly wasn't the woman by his father's side. *Good God,* he thought, *she's about my age! What in the devil can those two possibly have in common?* And unlike Cal, he didn't particularly admire J.T. for having taken up with a woman twenty years his junior. Tyler thought it made his father look foolish. He wondered if J.T. was trying to recapture his youth through the woman from Boston.

God A'mighty, what in the hell's gotten into the boy? Hank wondered. *He ought'a adopt her, not marry her.*

J.T. gently propelled Cynthia into the living room. Tyler noticed the possessive way his father's hand rested at the small of the woman's back, and a slow burn spread through him.

"Good, good," J.T. said, "you're all here." He guided Cynthia to the chair where his grandfather sat. "Cynthia, this is my grandfather, Hank Travis."

What a wonderfully dear old gentleman, Cynthia thought. She offered him her hand and her warmest smile. "Mr. Travis, I am delighted to meet you." Her tone was the one normally reserved for the very young or very old.

Hank scowled at the toadyism he thought he detected in her voice. Eyeing her hand, he said, "I don't like shakin' hands with a woman. Women didn't shake hands in my day. It looks unladylike. Only men ought'a shake hands.''

Cynthia was so startled she didn't know what to say. She withdrew her hand as though she'd touched a hot stove and said, "It's...nice meeting you."

Hank squinted up at her. "Why, you're not hardly dry behind the ears, are you?''

Cynthia wondered if the man was teasing her. J.T. cleared his throat and urged her toward the oldest of his children. "Tyler, I'd like you to meet Cynthia Page."

They shook hands. Tyler noticed that her skin was as smooth as thick cream and her pale oval nails were perfectly manicured. Her makeup was so flawless that she seemed to be wearing none. In fact, every inch of her was groomed to a T. She looked like someone who never got mussed. She probably slid out of bed every morning with every hair in place. *And Daddy has seen her slide out of bed in the morning!* The thought shook him to his toes. He knew that most people found it difficult to imagine their parents' sex lives, but with J.T. the difficulty was more pronounced. His father had been such a commanding presence in Tyler's life that the younger man found it impossible to believe J. T. McKinney had the same drives as lesser mortals. "How do you do, Cynthia?" he said stiffly. "Welcome to the Double C."

"Thank you. It's nice to be here at last."

J.T. urged her on. "And this is Cal."

Cal favored her with the boyish grin that had charmed legions of women. "Hello, Cynthia. It's nice to meet you."

"Thank you, Cal."

"And this is Lynn," J.T. said.

As the two women shook hands, Cynthia studied J.T.'s daughter without seeming to. Lynn didn't look a thing like her father, so Cynthia assumed the woman had inherited her mother's looks. Lynn and Cal favored each other to a certain degree, but it was Tyler who looked like J.T. In fact, he was a young carbon copy of his dad, so much so that Cynthia had been forced to fight back a gasp while being introduced to him.

She stepped back and smiled. "It's nice meeting all of you. I've heard so much about you." *Now comes the tedious part,* she thought. All that inane, awkward small talk while getting acquainted.

Actually, it was easy, because Cynthia long ago had mastered the art of keeping a conversation going no matter what. She made appropriate remarks about the weather, the beauty of the countryside and her initial impressions of the ranch. The grandfather kept watching her, as if hoping she would make a wrong move, which was a bit disconcerting. After a while, he pulled a packet of papers and a pouch of tobacco out of his shirt pocket and rolled a cigarette. She had never seen anyone do that except in the movies. But when he lit the thing, the pungent aroma filled her nostrils and made her cough. He smiled maliciously. *The old goat,*

Cynthia thought, just as maliciously. *Why are we already sparring?*

However, she gave him another chance to redeem himself. When it came up in conversation that Hank's background was not in ranching but in oil prospecting, Cynthia turned to him politely. "Oh, you're in oil, Mr. Travis?"

"In oil?" Hank cackled. "I sure have been in it...ass deep a time or two."

The corners of Tyler's mouth twitched. Cal grinned openly. Lynn looked embarrassed, and J.T. again cleared his throat. Cynthia could certainly say she'd never met anyone quite like Hank Travis before...and hoped never to again.

Tyler, Cal and Lynn, on the other hand, went through the motions of courtesy, asking her the kind of questions people ask strangers. Cynthia pretended not to notice that they seemed more curious than genuinely interested, more polite than warm. At least she was able to make sure there were no awkward, silent gaps in the conversation. But the relief she felt when J.T. got to his feet was enormous.

"You'll all have plenty of time to get acquainted later. Right now I want to introduce Cynthia to Virginia and Lettie Mae, then show her to the guest house." He held out his hand to Cynthia, who took it and stood up. Then J.T. turned to Tyler. "That load of cattle from Oklahoma ought to be here soon. Meet me in Ken's office in about twenty minutes."

"Right," Tyler said.

"Come on, Cynthia." J.T. again took her arm and led her out of the room. For several long wordless minutes his children and his grandfather simply stared after them. It was Cal who finally broke the silence.

"Whew! You gotta hand it to him. Our old man has fine taste in women."

"Me personally," Hank said, "I think the boy's goin' through one of those...whatchamacallits—mid-life something or others."

Lynn's eyes flashed. "I think it's practically obscene," she snapped. "She's not any older than Tyler."

"So?"

"So, it . . . it just doesn't seem right somehow."

"Oh, come on, Lynn. How about you, big brother? What do you think of our possible stepmother-to-be?"

Tyler would have cut out his tongue before he voiced his real thoughts about Cynthia Page. It was more than having someone take Pauline's place. Somehow the fact that his father's love interest was young, beautiful, shapely, poised—the kind of woman any man would be proud to be seen with—was too much.

Tyler's emotions were entirely at odds with the sensible man he considered himself to be. He couldn't forget the way J.T. had looked at Cynthia or the way she had looked at him. Nor could he forget her limpid brown eyes, beautiful red mouth, and the movement of her hips beneath the green dress as she and his father had walked out of the room. "Like you said, Cal, what we think about her doesn't count."

LATER, CYNTHIA STRETCHED out on the big comfortable bed in the guest house and contemplated the ceiling. J.T. had apologized all over the place for leaving her alone, but she actually was grateful for the quiet interlude. It was going to be a busy day. He had promised her a minitour of the ranch once his business was finished; then there was to be a welcoming party that night.

"I hope you don't mind," J.T. had said over lunch when he told her about the party. "It occurred to me after I'd invited everyone that I probably should have asked you if a party was okay."

"It's fine," she assured him. "I'm sure I'll have a wonderful time."

"I know women usually like to have some warning so they can plan what they're going to wear and that sort of thing."

"Don't worry about me. The years at Winwood Federal have left me pretty flexible. I can be dressed to kill in very short order."

Actually, had he asked her beforehand, she probably would have vetoed a party on the first night in favor of a quiet evening in the bosom of family. She had already decided that her first priority was to get J.T.'s family to accept her, and she was too smart to expect it to be simple.

Uneasiness—a totally unfamiliar sensation—churned through Cynthia. She found herself in the odd position of having to fit in. It was a first for her. Throughout her life, as a member in good standing of the upper, upper reaches of Boston society, she'd always assumed she would be accepted anywhere she chose to be. There were plenty of rules in that exclusive society, to be sure, but she had always followed them, and life had sailed along its smooth, predictable course. Here she didn't know the rules, so she was going to have to move cautiously and keep her eyes open, her ears tuned.

She thought about what she had seen and heard so far. The countryside was picturesque, and the ranch itself was beautiful . . . at least what she had seen of it. The house was big, comfortable-looking but a bit old-fashioned and not furnished in any particular style. If everything worked out as she hoped, the house would receive her personal touch.

She recalled the two women she had met in the kitchen, Virginia and Lettie Mae. They certainly didn't act like any servants Cynthia had ever known. There was a familiarity between J.T. and the two women she had found startling. She herself had been surrounded by servants from birth, and in her parents' house a certain formality existed between the family and those who worked for them, a correctness that was never breached. Virginia and Lettie Mae even called J.T. by his first name. That was going to be difficult for her to get used to, but when in Rome . . .

Cynthia's thoughts moved on to J.T.'s family. Her future with J.T. depended upon winning their approval. She hadn't been telling the unvarnished truth when she'd said she had heard so much about them. Her time with J.T. up until now had been so limited that they'd never spent much of it talking about anything but each other. Naturally, though, he had dropped little bits of information here and there, and now she tried to recall what he had told her.

His grandfather, he'd said, was a character, fiercely independent and earthy. That, Cynthia thought, was a classic understatement. Caustic, crochety and quite unpleasant would be more accurate. Grandfathers, for heaven's sake, were supposed to be . . . grandfatherly.

Tyler was the real businessman of the trio—thoughtful and serious, sometimes too serious in his father's estimation. An egghead, in J.T.'s words. A graduate of Rice University. Since Cynthia leaned toward the intellectual and tended to be serious, too, she had expected she and Tyler would hit if off from the beginning, but it was clear that wasn't going to happen. His aloof, almost chilly manner toward her was a major disappointment. She was an astute observer of human nature, and she hadn't been in that living room five minutes before she realized that Tyler resented her. Winning his approval was going to take more tact and finesse than she was sure she possessed . . . or had the patience to employ.

Cal was entirely different. J.T. had told her he suspected Cal had never had a serious thought in his life, and now Cynthia could see why. He was full of easy charm and came across as a carefree undergraduate student, the kind who was in hot water with the authorities half the time. But Cal hadn't gone to college, something that irked J.T. no end. He'd been too restless and too much in love with the rodeo to spend time in a classroom, J.T. had told her. "The most complicated thing about that middle kid of mine is his love life," he'd said. "It must take a great deal of careful planning to keep his women from running into one another and comparing notes." And though Cynthia knew it was too soon to draw conclusions, she had Cal pegged as a free spirit and a compulsive flirt. He had even indulged in a little flirting with her.

Then there was Lynn. When J.T. talked about his daughter he grew rather wistful. Lynn, according to him, was a quiet loner who'd never been seriously interested in one man, who would far rather work with her horses than go to parties or out on dates. In all her life she'd had only one best friend, and that was her cousin, Beverly. It was clear to Cynthia that J.T. didn't think that was right but didn't know what he could do about it. And, he'd said, his daughter had a stubborn streak a mile wide. Once she made up her mind about something, it stayed made.

Watching Lynn earlier, Cynthia had thought how stunning she could be if she would spend a little more time on her appearance. She looked like the kind of woman who hopped out of bed, washed her face, ran a comb through her hair, put on a swipe of lipstick and let it go at that. But perhaps that went with her personality. Maybe she deliberately chose not to call attention to herself. Yet it was Lynn whom Cynthia most wanted to get close to, not only because she had often longed for a daughter, but because Lynn seemed to hold a special place in J.T.'s affections. But how did one go about getting close to a quiet loner . . . and a stubborn one, at that?

So there they were—some very tough nuts to crack. Cynthia had never minded a challenge, but this one was outside her expertise. She felt somewhat like Daniel entering the lion's den. As she had left the living room on J.T.'s arm earlier, she had been overcome with the sure knowledge that if she were to get on a plane and head back to Boston in the morning, not one member of his family would think it a pity.

THE VEHICLE J.T. USED to show Cynthia around the Double C that afternoon was a vintage Jeep, one of a fleet of cars and trucks used to conduct the ranch's business. There were few roads on the property because roads took up valuable grassland. J.T. simply lit out cross-country, and Cynthia held on for dear life, feeling that her teeth were rattling as badly as the Jeep's chassis.

What struck her most about the Double C, beyond the sheer size of the place, was the terrain itself. City person that she was, she'd always pictured ranching country as an endless vista of sagebrush and cactus, but here there was something new to see beyond every rise. She saw stark limestone hills against which prickly pear did indeed nestle. Then as the Jeep topped a rise, the scene changed dramatically to one of pastureland. Cattle were everywhere, as were cedar and mesquite. A river meandered through the property— the Claro River, J.T. told her. "That means 'clear' in Spanish," he said. The river was aptly named. Never had Cynthia seen water sparkle. The ranch was far lovelier than she would have guessed, and she told J.T. as much. He was enormously pleased.

"We'll even have us a show of color in a few weeks," he said. "Maybe it won't seem like much to a New Englander, but we think it's mighty pretty."

"How many cattle do you have?"

He laughed lustily. "Good Lord, Cynthia, you're not ever supposed to ask a rancher that."

"Why not?"

"Might as well ask him to let you have a peek at his bank account."

"I guess I have a lot to learn."

"But here at the Double C we hold it to...oh, roughly twenty acres per cow unit, meaning one cow and a calf. Not everyone follows that. Overgrazing is a big problem in the West, always has been. Two many ranchers try to squeeze in all the livestock they can, but here in the Hill Country our German ancestors knew better than to do that. They came from families that had kept patches of land productive for centuries. Most of the folks around here have kept a lot of the old ways." Suddenly J.T. braked. Turning off the engine, he slid his arms around Cynthia's shoulders, pulled her to him and kissed her soundly. Then he sat back and made a head-to-toe inspection of her. "You look downright fetching in jeans."

"Thanks. I'm trying to blend in with the scenery."

"That you'll never be able to do, love. You'd always stand out even in scenery this pretty. I'm glad you're here."

"So am I."

"Should I apologize for Grandpa?"

She didn't think he would want to hear the truth. "Oh, I think he works hard at being a colorful character."

"He came of age in the oil patches of Oklahoma and West Texas, and that was a rough-and-tumble world. Not many niceties were observed, that's for sure. I'm afraid Grandpa says what he thinks and doesn't care whose toes he steps on. He has a real soft spot in his heart for Lynn, but he thinks raising Thoroughbreds in a quarter horse state is stupid, and he tells her so every chance he gets."

"How did he come to live here?"

"He fell in love with a lady from Crystal Creek—my mother's mother." He gave her a capsulized account of Hank's life, ending with the story about moving the stone house to the Double C. "What did you think of the kids?"

"Well...J.T., I only talked to them about fifteen minutes," she hedged. "But they're a handsome lot. I know you're proud of them."

J.T. nodded. "I'd be a lot prouder if one of them would get married and present me with a grandchild. Insurance for the future. Tyler's the logical candidate."

"Is there a prospect for a Mrs. Tyler McKinney?"

"Not that I know of. Tyler's always dated a lot, but he just never settled on one particular woman. And these days all he has on his mind is wine making."

Cynthia looked at him to see if he was serious. "Wine making?"

"Yeah, he wants me to turn over some acreage to him so he can plant grapevines."

"That seems a rather strange thing for a rancher to want to do. How did he get interested in that?"

"I'm not sure. I have an old friend named Don Holden. Don grew up around here, but then he went off to college at Stanford and somewhere along the way got interested in wine making. Now he owns a winery in the Napa Valley, and he's offered to let Tyler come out to California, stay with him and get a feel for the business. Hardly a day goes by that the kid doesn't stick something under my nose for me to read."

"How do you feel about a venture like that?" Cynthia asked.

"I have mixed feelings. At first I said no, and that was that. I thought it was silly. But Tyler's persistent, and I've learned a little more about the wine industry in this state since then. It's...interesting."

"I'm surprised you thought about it twice. You don't want roads because they use up grassland, yet you're thinking of a vineyard."

J.T. pushed his hat farther back on his head and grinned. "Well, sweetheart, I'm reminded of the rancher out in West Texas who leased his land to a big oil company that proceeded to drill a producing well. When the rancher was told that out of every sixteen barrels produced, one would be his, he said, 'Hot damn! Now I can afford to ranch.' If wine would pay ranching's way..."

"It just doesn't seem to me they're compatible," Cynthia insisted. "Have you studied the cost effectiveness of such an operation?"

J.T. grinned. "Ah, there's the banker in you coming out. I've got a ballpark figure of what it'll cost to get started up, yes."

"But there are so many other things you have to ask yourself, J.T."

"Like what?"

"Like...you'll be giving up land that's now being used to raise cattle. What will that cost you? And what about Tyler's time? You once told me he's the only one of your three children who takes an active part in the ranch's operation. Are you willing to do without him? Will you have to hire someone to do what he does now? Are you willing to wait for the return on your investment? I don't imagine one plants grapes one year and begins turning out fine wine the next. But let's say the venture is enormously successful. Will

Tyler want to expand? Will he then want a tasting room and guided tours? I've visited a few wineries, and it seems to me they require a great deal of land. How much of the Double C are you willing to allocate for making wine?'' She paused to take a deep breath. ''I suppose the list goes on and on, but those are the things that come to me off the top of my head.''

J.T. rubbed his chin thoughtfully. ''All I've been interested in was the start-up cost and whether or not it would make us some money.''

Cynthia carefully considered what she said next. ''You might also ask yourself if you want to go into wine making because it's good business . . . or because you want to please Tyler.''

J.T. uttered a little grunt. ''You might be right. I've always been a sucker where those kids are concerned and even more so since . . .''

The words trailed off, but Cynthia was sure she knew what he had started to say—since Pauline died. If that was true, Tyler, Cal and Lynn doubtless had picked up on it. She wondered if they took advantage of it. They'd be very unusual children if they didn't.

''Guess I'd better do some more hard thinking about Tyler's grand plans,'' J.T. went on. He leaned over and kissed her again, then started the Jeep. ''I'd also better get us back to the house, or we'll never be ready for the party on time.''

Cynthia sighed. ''What a shame. I was so enjoying being alone with you.''

"Don't worry, sweetheart. I plan on finding lots of time for us before the day's over."

The Jeep bounced and jolted across open land until they reached the ranch's hub, and J.T. halted it in front of the guest house. "I'll come over and get you about a quarter to seven," he told Cynthia.

She climbed out of the vehicle. "Thanks, I'd appreciate that."

"One thing you won't have to worry about tonight is Grandpa. He eats at six and is in bed by nine without fail. He won't even put in an appearance." He winked at her, blew a kiss, then drove off.

After parking the Jeep behind the main house, J.T. hurried up the back steps and through the kitchen door. Lettie Mae was deep in conversation with her young assistant. She looked over her shoulder when J.T. entered.

"I was beginning to think you were going to be late for your own party," she said.

J.T. didn't break stride. "I'll be ready in plenty of time. Something sure smells good."

He passed through the dining room, taking note of how festive everything looked. Nobody did this sort of thing better than Virginia and Lettie Mae, he thought with satisfaction. He had reached the foot of the stairs when Tyler came out of the study.

"Have you got a minute, Daddy?"

"I really don't, son. I'm running late."

"The Extension Office agent left some literature. I was hoping you'd find time to look it over."

"Not tonight, Tyler. It's time to party, not work."

Tyler frowned. "Have you had a chance to call Don to make arrangements for me to go to California?"

J.T. slapped his son on the shoulder. "No, I haven't, and to be honest with you, there are some more questions I want to ask before this goes any further."

"Questions? What kind of questions?"

"We'll talk about it tomorrow. Now... I've really got to run."

Tyler watched as J.T. hurried up the stairs. He felt uncasy. He sensed some change in his father's entire attitude, and that bothered him. He'd thought things were steaming right along. Now his father had more questions. Why?

Pivoting, Tyler returned to the study, closed the door and went to sit behind his father's desk. As recently as early that afternoon, when he, Ken and J.T. had been taking delivery of the cattle, his father had talked about the vineyards as if they were an accomplished fact. Then he'd gone off to spend the rest of the afternoon with Cynthia.

So, Tyler decided, it must be Ms. Page who was behind J.T.'s second thoughts. The investment banker from Boston, a person whose job it was to finance other people's ideas. And if she was anything like every banker Tyler had ever known, she was cautious to the point of absurdity. *No* was probably her favorite word. She could probably conjure up problems out of thin air, ask questions that were almost impossible to answer. And, of course, she would have a world of influence with J.T. Damn! It was bad enough that Grandpa Hank seized every opportunity to tell J.T. he thought wine making was the silliest notion he'd ever heard of. Fortunately J.T. didn't pay much attention to anything his grandfather had to say about the ranch's operation. But Cynthia?

Tyler brooded on that a minute or two before something occurred to him. No matter how strong Cynthia's influence with his father was, she didn't have what he, Cal and Lynn had—blood ties. J.T. McKinney was as high on family as any man could be. Tyler knew somewhere in the back of his father's mind was a rosy picture of his three kids marrying, having kids of their own and settling on or near the Double C forever. He could become quite eloquent on the subject when he got wound up. Once, during an overly expansive moment, he'd said he wanted McKinneys on the Double C for as long as the pharaohs had ruled Egypt. Cal, who had a hard time staying in one place longer than a week, referred to it as "Daddy's dynasty speech."

Tyler smiled unpleasantly. He had all sorts of cards left to play. He might even enlist the aid of Cal and Lynn. The three of them formed a powerful coalition when it came to dealing with their father. Not for a minute did he intend to allow the lovely Bostonian to sail in and spoil his plans.

He glanced at his watch and stood up. Right now he had to go upstairs and get ready for the party that would welcome Cynthia Page to Texas.

CHAPTER FOUR

THERE WAS a full-length mirror on the back of the bathroom door in the guest house. Cynthia stood in front of it and scrutinized her appearance. In typical masculine fashion, J.T. had given her only the scantiest guidelines about appropriate dress for the evening's party. "It's pretty casual, but I guess the women get a little more gussied up than the men do," was all he'd said, which told her almost nothing.

However, simplicity had always been her byword when it came to clothes—her mother's doing. "Make people look at you, not at what you're wearing," Alicia had admonished when Cynthia was growing up. She still abided by that general rule. The long-sleeved white silk blouse, the softly draped black skirt, the single strand of perfect pearls all constituted the simplest attire, clothes that could be worn any number of places. Leaving the bathroom, she walked to the dresser, gave herself a quick spray of cologne, slipped her feet into black pumps, then sat down and waited for J.T.

She didn't think she had been so nervous since her first day at Winwood Federal, and there were plenty of people who would have been astonished to learn that Cynthia Page had ever been nervous in her life. The aura she presented was one of such cool self-confidence that her business associates wouldn't have dreamed she ever got butterflies in her stomach. But they were churning like crazy tonight.

Cynthia wondered if what she was feeling was not so much nervousness as culture shock. She had entered a whole new world. Even J.T. was different in some inexplicable way. For one thing, he sounded different. He used words and phrases she'd never heard him use in Boston. What had come across as affable charm there had turned into an "aw, shucks" kind of folksiness here. His friends would probably have the same quality—much like the people she had met at the Honeckers' house.

That thought made her relax somewhat, since she'd never had any trouble feeling at ease at Sally's house. Then she tensed again as she reminded herself of something. At Sally's she'd never had to win anyone's approval.

She heard a light knock on the door. "Come in," she called as she stood. The door opened and J.T. stepped into the room. "Mmm," he murmured appreciatively, eyeing her up and down. "You look great."

"Thanks. So do you." He was wearing dark brown trousers, cut Western style, and a long-sleeved tan shirt, open at the throat. He also wore boots, but unlike the sturdy cowhide work boots he'd had on that afternoon, these were made of some exotic leather and polished to a high shine.

Crossing the room, J.T. took both her hands in his and bent to kiss her lightly on the mouth. "How long has it been since I told you I love you?"

She pretended to give it serious thought. "At the airport."

"That's too long."

"I agree."

"I don't want you to ever forget that I do."

"I have no intention of forgetting it. Have any of the guests arrived?"

He shook his head. "We'll have time for a quiet drink with the kids. Oh, and I asked Carolyn and Beverly to come early."

"Carolyn and Beverly?"

"Carolyn's my sister-in-law. Beverly's her daughter. They live at the Circle T. That's next door."

Since Cynthia knew J.T. was an only child, Carolyn had to be Pauline's sister. Lord, tonight she was going to be surrounded by people who had known and loved Pauline, and from all she had been able to learn, she and Pauline McKinney were as different as two people could be.

Stop that, she scolded herself. *You're not here to compete with Pauline's memory.* J.T. had always been very candid about his great love for his late wife, and Cynthia had never been even slightly jealous of her. After all, Pauline was part of the past; Cynthia was only interested in the present and the future.

"Ready?" J.T. asked.

As ready as I'll ever be. "Yes," she said.

"Then let's go."

CAL WAS THE LAST of the young McKinneys to gather in the living room. Tyler watched his brother amble across the room and almost drop in a chair. Cal never did anything in a hurry. He walked slowly, talked slowly. He gave a new dimension to the word *easygoing*. Tyler thought it ironic that a man who often seemed to live life in slow motion earned money in a sport where an eight-second ride brought the spectators to their feet.

"Isn't our guest of honor here yet?" Cal asked.

Tyler shook his head. "Daddy's gone to get her."

Lynn made some sort of disdainful sound. "Frankly, I'm going to be embarrassed to death tonight. You know she's going to be a shock to everyone here. Better she should be marrying Tyler."

"They're not getting married yet," Cal said. "And I don't know why you let her age bug you so much."

"It's just that I don't want Daddy to seem... foolish... like Bubba."

A minute of heavy silence followed. Bubba and Mary Gibson had been friends of the McKinneys for years, greatly liked and respected by all of J.T.'s children. The Gibsons were more like an aunt and uncle than mere friends. Now Bubba's affair was something they were all aware of but didn't want to talk about. "I guess Bubba will be here tonight," Cal said.

Tyler nodded. "Yes, he and Mary are coming."

"Thank goodness," Lynn said. "From what I've heard about how open he's being about it, I wouldn't have been surprised if he'd brought Billie Jo. What is it with older men, anyway? Why do they always go for the young ones? I mean, when was the last time you heard of a fifty-five-year-old man taking up with a woman his own age? I'm really disappointed in Daddy."

"Hush," Tyler admonished. "I think I heard the door opening."

The words were scarcely out of his mouth when J.T. and Cynthia appeared at the threshold. Three pairs of eyes fastened on them intently, and the room grew instantly and heavily silent.

To Cynthia J.T.'s kids looked like three students who had been sent to the principal's office. Their conversation had been terminated so abruptly that she rightly suspected she and J.T. had been its subject.

"Good evening," she said brightly, and they murmured acknowledgments.

"Have a seat, Cynthia," J.T. said. "I'll get us a drink. You want vodka and tonic, right?"

"Yes, thanks."

J.T. walked to the bar at the far end of the room and gave his order to the young man who'd been hired as bartender. Cynthia took a seat in the nearest chair, crossed her legs at the ankles, folded her hands in her lap and flashed what she hoped was her warmest smile. Everyone seemed to be trying to think of something to say.

"This has been a long day for you," Cal finally commented.

He alone, Cynthia noticed, had not gone to any great pains to dress for the party. He wore a plaid shirt, jeans and working boots. Lynn, on the other hand, looked fresh and pretty in a jade-colored float dress with a scoop neckline. Tyler was dressed much as his father was, except his trousers were dark blue, his shirt white. Cynthia wondered how long it would take her to stop being almost struck dumb by the sight of J.T.'s clone. "Yes, it has," she said in response to Cal's remark. "It's hard to believe it began in Boston before dawn."

"Have you always lived there?"

"Yes, always. According to my mother, a member of her family was in the Boston Tea Party. I can't vouch for that. She sometimes gets a little carried away when talking about her ancestors."

Cal grinned. "Tell me, just exactly what does an investment banker do?"

Bless him, Cynthia thought. He was doing his best to make her feel at ease. She gave him a brief job description—very brief since she didn't think he really was interested; then J.T. rejoined the group. Cal stood and headed for the bar. "I'm going to get a beer. Anybody want anything?"

"I'll take a Scotch on the rocks with a splash," Tyler said.

Exactly what his father drank, Cynthia noted. And the way he was standing with his hands clasped behind his back, head slightly lowered—she'd seen J.T. stand that way when he was deep in thought. She wondered if Tyler made a conscious effort to be like his father or if it came naturally. Father and son certainly were two peas out of the same pod, except that ranching was J.T.'s passion, a passion Tyler apparently didn't share. Or did he just want to do something different? They were so alike; perhaps Tyler was searching for something that would give him an identity of his own. At that moment the doorbell rang. J.T. set his drink on a table and turned. "That'll be Carolyn and Beverly. I'll let them in."

While he was gone, another uncomfortable silence descended. It occurred to Cynthia that neither Tyler nor Lynn had said a word to her, but she couldn't blame them solely for the strained quiet. She couldn't think of anything to say to them, either. Well, she had half expected this, hadn't she?

J.T.'s absence was mercifully short. When he returned he had his arm around the waist of an attractive blond woman of about forty-five, and right behind them was another blond woman, this one around Lynn's age. The younger woman was astonishingly beautiful. Cynthia got to her feet and waited for the introductions.

"Carolyn," J.T. said, "this is Cynthia Page. Cynthia, my sister-in-law, Carolyn Townsend."

Carolyn stared at Cynthia. It was only for a second, over so quickly no one else would have noticed, but in that split second Cynthia read stunned surprise on the woman's face, even shock. What had she been expecting? she wondered. Carolyn recovered quickly and offered her hand. The two women shook hands and acknowledged the introductions graciously, but Cynthia had the feeling she was being placed under a high-powered microscope by Pauline's sister.

Carolyn then stepped back to allow J.T. to introduce the other woman. "And this is Carolyn's daughter, Beverly."

For the first time since arriving at the ranch, Cynthia was introduced to a stranger who didn't look at her as if she had two heads. By any standard, Beverly was a beauty. In contrast to the conservative attire worn by the other women in the room, her dress was a vivid red with bright gold buttons. On its lapel was a gold pin shaped like a dagger. Beverly's earrings were oversize and dangling. Cynthia suspected the young woman deliberately dressed to call attention to herself, but she would have been noticed dressed in sackcloth.

"I'm really glad to meet you, Cynthia," Beverly gushed. "I love that blouse."

"Why, thank you, Beverly. And it's very nice meeting you, too."

"Living in Boston must be so exciting—the theater and museums and restaurants and shopping—all the really great things there must be to do in a city like that. I hope you'll find time to tell me all about it."

"I'll make sure I do."

Tyler stepped up to his aunt, placed a light kiss on her cheek and said, "Hello, Aunt Carolyn. Let me get you a drink."

"Thank you, dear."

"Get me one, too," Beverly said as she sailed across the room to sit by Lynn.

The new arrivals effectively caused the conversation to pick up, and though none of it was directed at her, Cynthia was grateful for anything that eased the mood in the room. Within minutes, the doorbell rang again. To her enormous relief, J.T. asked her to join him in greeting their guests. Maybe his friends would receive her more warmly than his family had.

HOURS LATER, Cynthia's head spun with names. During the lull between the time the dinner plates were whisked away and dessert was served, she activated the computer in her brain and tried to put names to faces.

On her right was Martin Avery; on her left was Cal. She now knew that Martin was a bachelor, an attorney and Crystal Creek's mayor, and he had known J.T. "forever." He was open, warm and chatty; Cynthia felt she could count on him to be a friend.

Next to Martin sat Mary Gibson, the wife of J.T.'s friend Bubba. She was a sweet, gracious woman, but there was something rather sad about her. It was in her eyes, a fatigue of long standing. But she must have been unusually well liked since all the women present went out of their way to be especially nice to her. Cynthia made a mental note to make friends with Mary, even though there was something about Bubba that put her off. However, she thought with an inner smile, she would have been terribly disappointed had she come to Texas and not met at least one person called Bubba.

Beverly was seated next to Cal, and they took turns trying to outflirt each other, even though they were cousins. Like Cal, Beverly flirted with every member of the opposite sex she encountered. It was as much a part of her personality as all that bubbly enthusiasm. She seemed to be the kind who loved being the center of attention, and since Cal had a lot of that quality in him, it was fun to watch them try to outshine each other.

At some point during the evening Cynthia had learned that Beverly was a former Miss Texas who had placed high in a Miss America pageant, which made her something of a local celebrity. It figured. What didn't figure was that she and shy, quiet Lynn were such fast friends. Perhaps it was simply the same unexplainable attraction of opposites that existed between herself and Sally.

Beverly's my real ace in the hole, Cynthia thought. She realized that J.T.'s niece was taken with her, if only because she came from a big eastern city and held an important position with a prestigious institution. If she won Beverly over perhaps it would help her with Lynn.

The man seated next to Beverly was Ken Slattery, the Double C's foreman and obviously a chum of Cal's. "My right hand," J.T. had called him when introducing him. Again Cynthia was struck by the lack of polarity between the McKinneys and those who worked for them. Like Virginia and Lettie Mae, Ken was treated like a member of the family. And Cynthia thought she had read approval in Ken's eyes earlier. Another possible friend?

Cal, as she had expected, wouldn't be a problem. She wouldn't go so far as to call him an ally, but she did sense a certain acceptance on his part. Or perhaps neutrality was a better word. Her eyes moved to the end of the table where Tyler sat talking to Carolyn and her cousin, a lovely woman named Lori Porter. Tyler was Cynthia's real problem. What there was about her that made him so skittish she couldn't imagine, but all evening, whenever she joined a group that also included Tyler, he had quickly excused himself and moved away. It was as though...well, as though he were afraid of her, as ridiculous as that was.

Cynthia quickly scanned the rest of the guests. The distinguished gentleman with the gray mustache was the family's doctor, Nate Purdy. His wife, who was at the other table, was named Rose. She was wearing a rose-colored dress, so that had been an easy word association. Also at the other table were Vernon Trent, real estate agent and justice of the peace, Bubba and

Wayne Jackson, county sheriff. It never hurt to have good friends in law enforcement.

So that left the Baptist minister and his wife. They were . . . the Blakes. Howard and Eva. Eva was so vivacious that it had come as little surprise to learn she had once been in show business, though that seemed a rather unusual background for a minister's wife.

Cynthia relaxed. Now she was confident that as the guests departed later, she would be able to call each one by name. Nothing, she had discovered through the years, pleased people as much as having a stranger remember their names.

"WELL, YOU WERE a hit," J.T. said as he closed the door.

"Do you really think so? I was awfully nervous," Cynthia confessed.

"It didn't show, I promise. Tired?"

"A little."

They were standing in the foyer, having just said good-night to the last of the guests. From that vantage point, Cynthia could look into the living room. Lynn had gone upstairs, but Cal and Tyler were still there, as though waiting to have a word with their father. Or perhaps they were waiting to see who was going to sleep where. She lowered her voice. "I think I'll go on to the guest house now."

"Fine, I'll walk you over."

Smiling, J.T. put his hand on the small of her back and guided her through the door. At the entrance to the guest house, he kissed her tenderly. "Don't lock up," he whispered.

"I wasn't planning to."

"I won't be long."

J.T. opened the door; she slipped through it, and he closed it behind her. Then he returned to the living room. "Are you guys hitting the sack anytime soon?"

Cal uncurled from the chair he was sitting in. "I told Ken I'd come out to the bunkhouse and have a nightcap with him."

"Don't keep him up until all hours. This still is a working ranch, you know."

"Right," Cal said with a grin and sauntered out of the room.

"Are you turning in, Daddy?" Tyler asked.

"Pretty soon."

A minute of silence followed. Then Tyler made a move to leave. "See you in the morning then."

"Good night, son."

Tyler took the stairs two at a time and soundlessly walked to his room at the far end of the hall. Only when the door was closed did he relax for the first time that evening. For him, the party had been miserable from start to finish.

She's too perfect, he thought morosely. *Too goddamned perfect.* Not one slip or gaffe all evening, the picture of poised elegance, smiling and showing all those perfect teeth, saying the perfect things. She'd had Martin eating out of her hand. Ken had just about yes-ma'amed her to death. Beverly had fawned over her. Bubba had almost drooled when he was introduced to her. From the remarks Tyler had heard, the collective opinion of the women guests had been, "Isn't she wonderful?" And, of course, none of the men had been able to take their eyes off her.

Not even me, Tyler thought, appalled at his reaction to his father's lover. It was the most unsettling experience of his life.

During his lifetime he had met a lot of women. Some he had liked a great deal. But unlike Cal, though he did enjoy their company, he didn't pursue them with the single-minded determination of Coronado searching for golden cities. He had always felt that most of them found him reasonably intelligent and attractive. He liked to think he possessed a certain sophistication and finesse with the opposite sex.

But he had only to step into Cynthia Page's presence to feel like an inept schoolboy. Whenever she was near, he was seized by the strangest feeling that if he opened his mouth, gibberish would come out. So he kept it shut. He had expected to dislike her, had wanted to dislike her, but all he could think about was how she looked, how she smelled, how she filled up a room. He had decided that the only way to handle such a forbidden attraction was to stay the hell away from her.

Tyler ran his fingers through his dark hair. Then he whipped off his belt and unbuttoned his shirt. Without bothering to turn on a light, he crossed the shadowy room to stand at the open window. He had to get away before he said or did something . . . unthinkable. California was the logical place to go. Tomorrow, regardless of what his father had to say about the winery, he would call Don Holden and tell him he was on his way.

Tyler's attention was diverted by some movement below. Looking down, he saw the unmistakable figure of his father crossing the moon-dappled lawn, heading in the direction of the guest house. A knot formed in the pit of his stomach, and he turned from the window, aware that his face was flushed.

Dear God, he thought, horrified. *I'm jealous.*

CYNTHIA WAS BRUSHING her teeth when she heard the door open and close. Rinsing quickly, she wiped her mouth and left the bathroom, turning off the light as she did. The only remaining illumination came from a small bedside lamp. J.T. stood in the center of the room, looking at her and grinning his lopsided grin.

For a minute they simply stood smiling at each other; then he closed the space between them. As he fingered the lace at the neckline of her gown he asked, "New?"

"Yes, I bought it especially for the occasion."

"Pretty." His arms went around her, and he kissed her soundly, deeply, gathering her into the niche of his body that seemed made just for her. Lifting his head, he smiled down at her. "Mmm, it's been too long."

She nodded. "Three weeks. Phone calls are so unsatisfying."

"Well, the waiting's over. Don't think this minute hasn't been on my mind most of the day." Taking her face in his hands, he kissed her again.

Cynthia sighed and snuggled against him. She loved the way he felt. There was something about J.T. that was so... solid. It often amazed her that twenty years separated them. He was as hard and muscled as a man half his age. For a few wordless minutes they held on to each other, stroking and petting, otherwise not moving. They both enjoyed the physical touching.

J.T. pressed his face into her hair, inhaled its fresh scent and felt intoxicated. The way he felt when he held Cynthia still amazed him. He recalled the first time he'd made love to her he had been afraid—afraid he'd forgotten everything he'd ever learned about lovemaking, afraid of his performance, afraid he wouldn't please her. She was young and so beautiful, and he was middle-aged. But she must have inspired him, for it had been so easy, as though they were longtime lovers. When it was over he had realized the only things he'd forgotten was how wonderful intimacy could be. Before the night was over he had known he was falling in love.

Now Cynthia stirred in his embrace. He released her and stepped back to unbutton his shirt. "Allow me," she said and proceeded to swiftly and expertly strip him. As she admired the body she now knew as well as she knew her own, she realized there wouldn't be a need for prolonged foreplay tonight. It had been a long time. She was hungry for him, and he was ready for her.

He led her to the bed and with one fluid motion removed her gown. Sliding into the bed beside her, he drew her to him. The touch of his hand on her bare flesh activated all the switches in Cynthia's body. While he kissed and stroked her, her arms moved restlessly across his back, her hips undulated, and her legs imprisoned him. For what seemed forever, J.T. nipped and sucked and murmured hot words of love in her ear. Impatient, Cynthia cupped his buttocks and held him firmly on top of her, forcing him to enter her. Moving together rhythmically, they sought the release they knew soon would be theirs.

IT WAS SOME TIME before either of them stirred. Cynthia rose on one elbow to look at the bedside clock. It was past midnight. She snuggled back under the covers. J.T. was lying on his side looking at her. She ran her fingers lightly over his arm, playing with its fine covering of dark hair.

"Does this arrangement suit you, sweetheart?" he asked. "Would you rather stay in the main house?"

"Where do you and I stand the best chance of being alone?"

"Here."

"Then this arrangement suits me."

"But I do want you to spend a lot of time with the family and the staff, to get a feel for our routine and see if there are any changes you want to make."

"Oh, I'll make a perfect nuisance of myself." Cynthia meant it to be a lighthearted remark, but somehow it didn't come out that way. With certain people, notably Tyler, her very existence seemed to be a nuisance. "And do you suppose Ken would object to my hanging around and asking questions about the ranch?"

"Of course not. Ken wouldn't dream of objecting, though why you'd want to is beyond me." He paused a moment before saying, "First impressions, please. What did you think of the people you met tonight?"

Cynthia gave it some thought. "Well...your friend Martin is a nice man...or seems to be."

"Steadfast, that's Martin," J.T. said.

"It's a wonder a man like that never married."

"He was in love once. She married someone else."

"Isn't that carrying steadfast a bit far?"

"Oh, he was badly burned, and by the time he got over it, maybe his opportunities were gone."

"Sad."

"What about Bubba?" J.T. asked.

Cynthia knew she had to tread carefully and remember that Bubba was a friend. "Well...I really didn't get to talk to him much," she hedged. "But his wife Mary...is she a celebrity of some kind?"

"Mary? A celebrity?"

"Yes, you know, like well-known or old family or old money or something. Or is she just popular? I noticed all the women cozying up to her."

J.T. pursed his lips. "No, Mary's not exceptional, not in the way you mean. What you saw tonight was a show of sympathy, a rallying of the sisterhood. You can't be around here long before hearing about this, so I might as well tell you. Bubba's taken up with a woman named Billie Jo Dumont. Billie Jo's in her twenties and is very pretty in a flashy sort of way."

"And Mary knows about this?"

"I don't see how she can help knowing. Bubba's doing nothing to hide the relationship. On the contrary, he seems rather proud of it, and Crystal Creek being the kind of town it is . . . I just don't get it. Bubba's acting like a jerk."

"No wonder that look of long-suffering in Mary's eyes." Cynthia's mouth set in a tight line. It was going to be very, very hard to be nice to J.T.'s friend. "I wonder why Mary doesn't leave."

"I've wondered the same thing myself, many times."

"I would . . . leave, I mean."

J.T. grinned. "I don't doubt that." He reached out and tucked a strand of hair behind her ear. "Listen, sweetheart, as nice as this setup is, in a week or so I think you should move into the house and start making your influence felt. Cal will be gone by then, so you can have his room. It's next to mine, and the rooms share a bath. Connecting doors."

"Handy," she said with a smile. "Does Cal just drift in and out as the mood strikes?"

"Pretty much. I never know when he's coming until I see the whites of his eyes."

"How do you feel about his following the rodeo?"

"I don't like it worth a damn. For one thing, it's dangerous. For another, he's not learning anything that will help him later in life."

"Then why don't you put a stop to it?"

"Cynthia, Cal is thirty. The best I can do is give him advice. He listens to it, then goes out and does what he wanted to do in the first place. I guess it's always that way with parents and kids. Maybe it's the way things should be, I don't know. I'll confess that if I had my way, the kids would all be in the cattle business, but they've decided to take other paths. I've always believed you have to let your children make their own decisions and mistakes."

Cynthia rolled over and stared at the ceiling. "That's so different from the way I was raised. I've always been structured to a fault. I grew up with an enormously long list of things to do, things I should do, things I must never do. To some extent I still follow them. I wouldn't dream of dropping in on my mother without notice. I phone her secretary to see if it's convenient . . . and if you wonder why my mother needs a secretary, it's because her mother had one and her grandmother had one. Nothing must be allowed to change. Mother's never actually said anything, but I know she thinks there's something unseemingly—one of her favorite words—about my having my own apartment and going off to work in an office. And I know she would drop dead if anyone in her employ ever called her by her first name.''

J.T. smiled at her fondly. "You're right, this is a whole new world."

"I've been here almost thirteen hours. Are you having some doubts?" Her look was earnest.

"It's *your* doubts I'm concerned about. That's why I wanted you to stay here awhile, to see firsthand what you'd be getting into. After all, I'm not the one making a major change in my life."

Cynthia snuggled up against him, drawing on his strength. "It's odd—I'm not worried that you and I won't adjust to each other. I just know we will. But I'm not so sure about...others."

"The family?"

"Uh-huh."

"If the idea's hard for them to get used to at first, they'll come around in time." He leaned over and kissed her. "Go to sleep, sweetheart. You must be dead."

She nodded. "Are you staying?"

"I'll stay right here until I'm sure you're asleep, but then I'll go back to the house. For appearances' sake." His smile was almost sheepish. "If I sometimes seem old-fashioned to you, it's because I am."

"You're also wonderful," she murmured sleepily. "What time is breakfast served?"

"Seven-thirty, but you sleep in if you want. Lettie Mae will be glad to fix you something whenever you want."

"No, I'll be there. I hardly ever sleep in." She had enough of an image problem without giving his family and servants the impression she was a lazy socialite who slept the morning away.

Her eyes closed, fluttered open, closed again. She felt J.T. lean over her to turn off the lamp; then he settled back beside her. Nestled in the warm cocoon of his arms, she was sound asleep within seconds.

CHAPTER FIVE

TO HER UTTER CHAGRIN, Cynthia overslept the next morning. By the time she struggled out of bed, took a quick shower and dressed, it was after eight-thirty. Talk about lousy first impressions! She debated whether or not to just do without breakfast altogether, but she was starved. Toast and coffee wouldn't be too much trouble, would they?

She hurried across the expanse of lawn separating the guest quarters from the main house and entered through the back door. The kitchen was spotless, and Lettie Mae was standing at the sink washing out the coffeepot. The cook turned when the door opened.

"I'm so sorry," Cynthia said. "I overslept, and I never do that . . . or almost never."

"No problem," Lettie Mae said. "I'll fix you something. What would you like?"

"No, no, please don't fix anything. Do you have cereal and maybe instant coffee?"

Lettie Mae frowned. "Well, yes, ma'am. I keep instant for Virginia and myself. Pauline insisted on brewed coffee, so that's what the family gets. Are you sure you only want cereal?"

"That's fine, really. That's what I have almost every morning back home...er, back in Boston. I usually eat on the run."

The cook shrugged. "Okay, if you're sure. I'll set a place for you at the dining table."

Cynthia disliked the thought of eating alone in that huge dining room. And this might be a good time to talk to Lettie Mae and perhaps find out more about the family. "Oh, don't do that," she said. "What's wrong with here?" She gestured toward a round oak table with four chairs that stood in the center of the big kitchen. Alicia would have been horrified.

Lettie Mae looked startled. "You want to eat in here?"

"If it's all right."

"Well...it's just that none of the family except Mr. Hank ever eats in the kitchen. I'm not too sure how this would sit with J.T."

"Then I won't tell him. Guests who can't show up at mealtime should be grateful they get anything at all to eat." Cynthia sat in one of the chairs and waited until the food was put in front of her. Lettie Mae seemed embarrassed to be plunking a box of cereal and a carton of milk on the table for a guest. She went back to the sink and finished washing and drying the coffeepot.

"How long have you been working here, Lettie Mae?" Cynthia asked after she had taken a few spoonfuls.

"A long time, ever since J.T. and Pauline got married. You see, Virginia and I used to work for the Randolphs—that's Pauline's family. We were sort of a wedding present, I guess."

"Then you and Virginia have watched J.T.'s children grow up."

"That we have. I feel almost like they're my own, except I didn't have to raise them myself. Pauline took care of that. She was a wonderful mother, a wonderful woman."

"So I understand."

"She saw to it that those kids knew the value of an education, and it took with everyone but Cal. She also saw to it that they were in church every Sunday. That they don't go so faithfully anymore is no reflection on her."

"Of course not."

"It was awful when she died, just awful. For a time I was afraid we might have to bury J.T., too. Virginia and I've worked awfully hard to keep the household humming along. If Pauline could come back, she'd find not a single thing has been changed."

Cynthia ate in silence a few minutes. She had a feeling she'd just been given a message. She watched in silence as Lettie Mae scurried around the kitchen, apparently making preparations for lunch. There was such efficiency in her work; not a movement was wasted. And she seemed to be able to do three things at once. Finally Cynthia asked, "How long has J.T.'s grandfather been here?"

"About thirteen years."

"Was he close to Pauline?"

"I guess...as close as Mr. Hank gets to people. Lynn's his favorite. He wouldn't admit that, but she is. He says she's got spunk. But he puts the boys down every chance he gets." Lettie Mae paused and frowned, as though wondering if she was saying too much.

Cynthia noticed, so she changed the subject. "Where's J.T.?"

"Reckon he's out in the bunkhouse office talking to Ken," Lettie Mae said. "That's the way he usually starts the day."

Cynthia nodded, finished her cereal, drained her coffee, then stood and carried her dishes to the sink. "Thank you, Lettie Mae. I promise not to be late for meals again."

Leaving the kitchen, she entered the dining room, stopped and listened for sounds. She heard nothing, and she decided it wouldn't be wise to go snooping through the house on her own, though she was dying to see the rest of it. To the left of the dining room, however, was a sun room she had noticed the night before. On a bright morning like this one it looked like an inviting spot. She strolled out to the cheery room, noticed a copy of the Austin paper on a glass-topped table and sat down to read it.

She had been reading perhaps ten minutes when she got the distinct feeling she was being watched. Twisting toward the doorway, she hoped to see J.T. Instead, she saw Tyler. He gave a start when their eyes met. "Good morning," she greeted him brightly.

"Good morning. I was...er, looking for Daddy."

"And I'm waiting for him. Lettie Mae says he's probably with Ken."

"Probably." Tyler took a backward step. "Well, I'll catch him later."

"Come on in and sit down."

"No, I... Sorry, I'm in the middle of some work. I'll see you later."

"Yes, of course." Cynthia stared after him, utterly dumbfounded by the effect she had on the man. *My God, one would think I'm a snapping turtle,* she thought irritably as she returned her attention to the newspaper. How was she going to get close to J.T.'s children if they wouldn't even talk to her?

A few minutes passed; then the front door opened and closed. She got to her feet, hurried through the dining room and encountered J.T. in the foyer.

"Good morning," she said.

His face broke into a smile. "Good morning, sleepyhead."

"Sorry. I'm used to an alarm clock, and..." She shrugged.

"Did Lettie Mae get you something to eat?"

"Yes."

He took a step toward her, but just then Tyler appeared, seemingly from nowhere. "Daddy, I'd like to talk to you."

"Good," J.T. said. "I want to talk to you, too." He turned back to Cynthia. "I'll be with you in a bit, sweetheart. Duty calls."

"Sure." Cynthia swallowed her disappointment as she watched father and son disappear down the hall. There didn't seem to be a thing for her to do, and somehow she had envisioned being busy from waking till sleeping.

But the Double C was a business, after all, she reminded herself. It couldn't just stop while she learned the ropes. She opened the front door and stepped out onto the porch. It was another beautiful day. She was restless, imbued with energy... and a little bored. She didn't suppose anyone would object to her wandering around and looking things over. Stepping off the porch, she rounded the house and headed for nowhere in particular.

From his cowhide rocker on the front porch of his house, Hank watched her. She reminded him of an oil-patch boll weevil, someone green as grass who didn't know nothing about nothing. Some weevils turned out to be pretty fair hands, but he couldn't see that happening with the Boston society gal. Not that it mattered. She wouldn't be around long. Last night he'd had one of his dreams, and he'd seen the Bostonian packing her bags and heading back where she came from.

Hank had been "seeing" things for as long as he could remember. Folks who believed said he was clairvoyant. Those who didn't said he was just a crazy old man. He knew better. He could see things that were going to happen, and he was never wrong. The Boston gal was going to leave one of these days, and that made him feel a heap better. To his notion, J.T. had pulled a boner tying up with that gal.

IN THE STUDY, J.T. settled into his swivel chair behind his desk and waited for Tyler to be seated across from him. "So," he said, "what do you want to talk to me about?"

"You know."

J.T. pursed his lips and drummed his fingers on the desk. "Tell me something, Tyler. How big do you want this thing to get?"

"How big? Well, if we're successful, I'm talking major."

"I see. So that means more land."

"Sure, someday."

"What about the ranch?"

Tyler frowned. "What about it?"

"The Double C is in the business of raising cattle. That takes land, too. I'm not inclined to use much of it for any other purpose. Say we plant vineyards, and say you start turning out good wine. Next thing I know you'll be wanting a tasting room and guided tours." He tried to remember everything Cynthia had mentioned.

Tyler uttered a little laugh. "Daddy, I'm a hell of a long way from a tasting room and guided tours. I'll be starting from scratch."

"Which brings up something else. More and more it's beginning to sound like I'll lose your services around here if I give this wine-making thing a go-ahead."

"I'm nothing but a glorified bookkeeper. You can easily hire someone to do what I do. Besides, you have Ken."

"True, and he's invaluable to me, but he isn't family. I've never given up hope that Cal will lose those itchy feet of his and start taking an active interest in this ranch. I've even gone so far as to hope Lynn will marry a man who wants to come into the family operation. It's always been my dream that there will be McKinneys on this ranch for as long—"

"As the pharaohs ruled Egypt, I know," Tyler interrupted. Getting to his feet, he walked to the window, clasped his hands behind his back and stared out for a minute. Then he turned. "I know you don't like to hear this kind of talk, but ranching as a way of life is going the way of the dinosaur. If you want the Double C to stay in business, you're going to have to diversify."

J.T. scowled. "That's what I get for sending you to Rice. I should have made you go to A&M."

"Daddy, the Texas wine industry is young and exciting. I honestly think that in twenty years it'll be where the Napa Valley is now. As for expansion, new land wouldn't have to be contiguous to the ranch. Let me go out to California and stay with Don awhile."

J.T. lapsed into thought and said nothing for a minute or two. When he did speak, it wasn't to say anything Tyler wanted to hear. "Son, you're a good hard worker, but you're impatient, always have been. When you want something you want it yesterday. But I don't do anything impulsively. The only reason I'd even consider this wine making is if I thought it was good business, that it'd make us some money. Now you're going to have to give me more time to study on it."

Tyler crossed the room and sat down in the chair he had just vacated. "What started all this?"

"What?"

"Who put this bee in your bonnet? You've done a complete one-eighty from the way you were talking a week ago. Was it the banker?"

J.T.'s eyes narrowed. "Are you referring to Cynthia?"

"Yes." Tyler almost hissed it.

"She asked me some questions I couldn't answer. And I realized that the reason I couldn't was because I hadn't asked enough of my own. She's savvy when it comes to business." J.T. stood up and reached for his Stetson, a sure sign that the meeting was over. "And speaking of Cynthia, I've left her to her own devices long enough. See you later."

Tyler sat fuming long after his father was gone. The one thing he couldn't tolerate was having his plans thwarted. He supposed that was a failing in his character, but that was the way he was. He and his father had locked horns on many past occasions, and J.T. usually won because . . . well, because J.T. was his father. But this time Tyler couldn't shake the notion that his plans would have been proceeding nicely by now if it weren't for Cynthia.

Damn, he couldn't even think her name without his equilibrium teetering precariously. He didn't begin to understand his emotions concerning her. On the one hand, he hated the thought of his father's remarrying. On the other, he couldn't get near Cynthia without wanting her himself. He slapped the desktop. And he couldn't go running off to California. That would leave his father under her sole influence.

Tyler passed a hand over his eyes. He supposed all he could do was hope she left, and he could certainly envision that happening. She didn't fit in; that had been obvious last night. She had stood out like a hybrid rose in a briar patch—an elegant, patrician lady who had stumbled into a macho, slightly sexist society. She didn't have the first idea what living in it was like.

Yes, God, please let her leave. That would solve his problems concerning his ambitions . . . and another problem too dangerous to think about.

CYNTHIA CLIMBED to the top rung of the corral fence and perched there. "Good morning," she called.

Ken Slattery turned. His face broke into a smile, and he came to stand in front of her. "Mornin', ma'am. Nice day, isn't it."

"It certainly is."

He hoisted himself up to sit beside her...but not too close. He was slightly in awe of the boss's lady friend.

Cynthia gestured toward an animal standing in the center of the corral. "Yesterday J.T. took me on a tour of the ranch, and I saw a lot of livestock, but that doesn't look anything like the cows I saw then."

"That's because the cows you saw yesterday were Brangus. That fella there, ma'am, is a genuine Texas longhorn."

Cynthia stared at the animal. "Yankee that I am, I would have guessed that the longhorn didn't exist anymore."

"Almost didn't," Ken said. "They were just about extinct until some preservation groups got busy and saved them."

"Why is he here? For the fun of owning one?"

"No, J.T.'s going to do a little crossbreeding with some of our cows."

"Why? Is there something wrong with the kind of cows you raise now?"

"No, not at all. The Double C raises mighty fine beef cattle, but the longhorns...well, ma'am, people in this part of the world tend to get all choked up about them—nostalgic, you know. There's sort of a mystique about them because they were such a big part of the history of the Old West."

Cynthia digested that. "J.T. doesn't strike me as a man who would go into a business venture out of nostalgia, mystique or not."

"You're right, he wouldn't, but the longhorns have a lot of other things going for them. They're hardy. They calve easily and make great mamas. They live a long time. Some of those old cows have a calf every year for... oh, twenty, twenty-five years. And when they're crossbred, they produce lean beef, which seems to be the ticket nowadays."

"And all this fiddling around with genes and things doesn't ruin the Brangus breed?"

"Brangus is a crossbreed to begin with. Yes sir, it's going to be downright interesting to see what kind of beef we come up with. Then J.T.'ll decide if the project moves ahead or not. He doesn't do things in a hurry. He likes to ponder on them a spell."

"That's right," another masculine voice said, "and for the past few minutes I've been pondering on where the hell Cynthia could have gotten off to." J.T. climbed up on the fence to join them, giving her an affectionate nudge. "What have you been doing to keep yourself busy?"

"I think I've been getting a crash course in animal husbandry."

"Well, you couldn't have a better teacher than Ken. He knows the cows inside and out."

Ken slid off the fence. "Guess I'd better get back to work. Looks like the boss caught me goofing off."

"Thanks for giving me a few minutes of your time, Ken," Cynthia said.

"You're welcome, ma'am. Enjoyed it. Anytime."

"And I think it would be nice if you called me Cynthia."

"Yes, ma'am." Ken turned to J.T.

"Larry will be out tomorrow," he said.

"Oh. Good," J.T. said. "We'll have a meeting in my study when he gets here."

Ken nodded and sauntered away. J.T. put a possessive arm around Cynthia's waist, and she put her head on his shoulder. "Who's Larry?" she asked.

"My cousin. He's an investigator. We've been losing some cows. I think we've got some cattle rustlers running loose."

Cynthia straightened to look at him. "Are you serious? Cattle rustlers? Shades of John Wayne!"

"Hey, it's not the movies, it's a real problem."

Just then the sound of a horse's hooves caused them to turn. Lynn cantered by, waved and continued on toward the stable.

"She sits a horse beautifully," Cynthia commented.

"She should," J.T. said. "She's spent half her life in a saddle. She's always had horses around. Dogs and cats, too, when she was younger. She was just crazy about animals, all kinds. I used to raise goats, and Lynn loved that."

"Goats?" Cynthia asked with a little laugh. "What on earth for?"

"Because they're great things to have in this hilly country. They keep the brush from taking over. And goat cheese is wonderful, to say nothing of barbecued kid. Trouble was, Lynn had the unfortunate habit of giving the baby goats names like Cottonball and Sugarplum. Things got a little testy come barbecue time, so I sold all of them. I sure miss those barbecues."

Jumping off the fence, J.T. held out his hand to Cynthia. "I've got some errands to run in town. Come with me. I might as well start showing you off."

She swung her legs off the rail and hopped down beside him. "Should I change?" she asked.

He looked her over. She was wearing the kind of jeans that probably cost sixty bucks and a chambray shirt with fancy cutwork in the yoke. The clothes doubtlessly passed for Western wear in Boston, but they were pretty fancy duds for Crystal Creek. "Naw. Every other woman you'll see will be wearing jeans."

Arm in arm, they strolled across the grounds in the direction of J.T.'s Cadillac.

BEVERLY SIGHED. From her vantage point seated on a bench in front of the stable she watched J.T. and Cynthia. "They make such a handsome couple."

Lynn paused in giving the horse its rubdown. She saw her father open the car's passenger door to let Cynthia slide in. She averted her gaze, made some sort of unintelligible sound and began rubbing again.

Beverly looked at her with a frown. "Don't you think so?"

Lynn shrugged. "What I think doesn't matter."

"Come on, you've got to admit they look wonderful together. J.T. is one of the best-looking older men

I've ever known, and Cynthia is beautiful. How could they not look good together?''

"If you must know, I think it looks as if Daddy's squiring his niece around . . . or his daughter."

"God, you sound like Mama," Beverly said.

That got Lynn's attention. "Aunt Carolyn doesn't approve of the age thing, either?"

"It's so dumb. If they're in love, what difference does it make?"

Lynn winced at that one.

"Now, I'll admit it would be different if your dad had taken up with a piece of fluff like Billie Jo Dumont, but Cynthia is such a class act."

"How can you possibly know that when you met her once?"

"You can tell," Beverly insisted. "She probably hasn't had an inelegant thought in her life. You've been around her. Isn't she almost perfect?"

"I haven't seen much more of her than you have," Lynn said. "She didn't show up for breakfast this morning."

"So?"

"So nothing. I just said she slept in or doesn't eat breakfast or something. She didn't show up."

Beverly lost patience with the conversation. Getting to her feet, she stretched her arms over her head, then let them fall. "Hurry up and finish. I'm bored. Let's go shopping. Let's do something."

Lynn shook her head as she led the horse into his stall in the stable. Beverly was beautiful, bright and vivacious. She also was spoiled, fun-loving and a little wild. There were times when Lynn envied her cousin, but most of the time she just felt sorry for her. There was such a lack of purpose in Beverly's life.

Sometimes she thought that being Miss Texas was just about the worst thing that could happen to a person. Who remembered who Miss Texas of, say, 1984, was? Who remembered the second runner-up in a Miss America pageant? One year of fame and glory, and poof! Oh, Beverly was still a celebrity of sorts around Crystal Creek, but she had wanted the whole ball of wax. And it simply hadn't happened.

Closing the stall door, she rejoined her cousin outside the stable. "Want to stay for lunch?"

"Let's have lunch in town. Maybe we'll run into something—or someone—interesting."

The two women began walking toward the house. "Maybe you ought to get a job or something," Lynn suggested.

"Doing what?"

"Oh...I don't know. The way you love pretty clothes, maybe Stephanie Miller could use you in her shop."

Beverly pretended to be horrified. "You want me to be a salesclerk?"

"The last I heard, it was legitimate work."

"And very confining. Something fun comes along, and you're tied down to a job."

"Well, you've got to do something," Lynn insisted.

"I usually stay busy. I don't know why things seem so slow right now. No parties. Nothing much going on at the club. But for now, I'm going to have lunch in town. Are you coming?"

"I don't think so."

"Why not? Lynn, honestly, if it weren't for me, you'd be a hermit. Personally, I hope J.T. and Cynthia do get married. She'll be good for you."

"How on earth do you figure that?"

"She could draw you out of your shell. She seems so worldly and cosmopolitan. I'll bet she knows how to throw really grand parties. A woman like that could shake things up around here."

Lynn's eyes narrowed, and her mouth set in a pinched line. "That's what I'm afraid of," she said. "All right, I'll go tell Virginia and Lettie Mae I'm leaving."

DINNER THAT EVENING was a mostly silent affair. As usual, Hank had eaten earlier and was not present. Cal smiled affably at Cynthia and spoke directly to her, but Lynn hardly said two sentences, and Tyler said nothing at all to anyone but his father. It irritated Cynthia that J.T. did not notice and make an effort to draw her into the conversation, but he was preoccupied with the cattle thieves and half a dozen other things. She supposed she was being too touchy. She tried to simply enjoy Lettie Mae's incredible cooking and to not let her feathers get too ruffled.

After dinner J.T. asked Tyler to join him in the study to discuss business. Cynthia rather hoped that since it was business, he would ask her, too, but no such invitation was forthcoming, and she wasn't about to invite herself. Cal wandered off to find Ken, which left Lynn with the task of entertaining their guest. After five minutes, it became apparent to Cynthia that Lynn was terribly uncomfortable. Wishing to spare her, she pleaded a headache and went to the guest house to read a book she had purchased in town that afternoon.

Later, as she readied for bed, she reflected on the past two days. Yesterday's anticipation and exhilaration had given way to a feeling of disorientation. Here she felt cut off from the world, as indeed she was from any world she had known before. That afternoon in Crystal Creek had served to intensify the feeling.

It was much the kind of town she had envisioned, for J.T. had described it often enough. What he hadn't described—possibly because he didn't realize it existed—was the atmosphere, the aura of the place. A certain clubbiness predominated. In Boston she had been left alone to live as she chose, away from curious eyes. Here, everyone knew everyone else, knew what everyone was doing and talked about it. At all the places they had stopped—the coffee shop, the feed store, the bank—J.T. had run into someone or several someones he'd known most of his life. The conversations invariably had begun with what ol' So-and-so was up to. She was astonished that so many people were privy to such personal information about so many others. A private person, Cynthia shuddered at the thought of having her actions and motives discussed and dissected, yet they surely would be if she became part of the local scene.

However, she had known that gossip went with small-town living, and, if there was one thing she knew how to do, it was to conduct her life with decorum. But she wondered if she would ever fit in. Everyone had been so openly curious about her and the city she came from, as if Boston were some remote and exotic place. Even J.T., whom she had thought she knew so well, surprised her every ten minutes. A doting father one minute, a stern patriarch the next. A hail-fellow, back-slapping good ol' boy as well as a businessman who could spout facts and figures to the bank president with the ease of a Harvard economist. Several times that afternoon she had felt as though some stranger was showing her around his hometown. Who was he really, and was he compatible with the kind of person she was?

She had anticipated a period of adjustment with J.T.'s family, and she had known it would take time to get used to small-town life. But never had she envisioned having the slightest doubt about J.T. and herself. In Boston they had been so close. Now she sensed some distance between them. Putting down the hairbrush, she sighed. Maybe she was imagining things. *Give it more time. Be patient.*

The door opened and J.T. stepped into the room. Cynthia smiled, turned and went into his arms. The doubts vanished as his arms closed around her shoulders. She did love him so. She was going to do whatever was necessary to make this work.

CHAPTER SIX

"IT'S LIKE the measles," Larry Wendt told them the following morning. "Once a rash of thefts start, it's hard to get it stopped. You must've been the fourth to call in as many days."

The portly investigator faced three very solemn-looking men—J.T., Tyler and Ken. "Far as we can tell, they started working up in Concho County about a month ago," Larry went on. "They're moving with lightning speed."

"They?" J.T. asked.

"We figure we're dealing with an organized group. One cow thief couldn't do so much damage so fast. And when you get an organized group running, they can eat your lunch before you get 'em caught."

"We lost two more last night," Ken said.

"Well, if it's any consolation to you, the rustlers aren't going to hang around this area long. Least, that's my guess. They'll be moving on. The longer they work an area, the greater the chances of getting caught."

"Damned if it doesn't gall my butt to lose even one cow to a thief," J.T. growled. "I don't understand how they get away with it. Brands are checked at market.''

"Yeah, but a smart thief won't try to sell at market. He'll sell to an individual who'll slap on his own brand. And I'll tell you something else—unlike fencing jewelry or electronics, the livestock thief can sell his merchandise for full value. I know one thing— rustling's a lot worse now than it was when I started as an investigator thirty years ago. A lot worse.''

"It's damned frustrating," J.T. said.

"That it is. You ought'a be looking for 'em all over the state like I am." Larry got to his feet. "Wish I could be more optimistic, but rest assured that we're doing everything we can.''

J.T. also stood and offered his hand. "Much obliged, Larry. I appreciate your getting here so quickly.''

"Don't mention it. I hate to run. I'd like to sit and visit a spell, but I have another call to investigate. Be in touch . . . soon, I hope. Good day, gentlemen.''

Tyler left to show their caller to the door. J.T. crossed his arms and frowned thoughtfully. "Well, Ken, we'll just keep on keeping on. Vary the men's routines. We might want to get a couple of them to ride fence all day. Nothing too obvious. Strange as it may seem, I'd prefer not to scare off the thieves. I'd like to catch the SOBs myself.''

"Right." The foreman touched the brim of his hat with a finger and left the room.

J.T. was right behind him. He had left Cynthia in the sun room when Larry arrived, and he expected to find her still waiting for him. But she wasn't there, and when a subsequent check of the other downstairs rooms didn't produce her, he went into the kitchen. Virginia was at the table sorting silver; Lettie Mae was at the sink.

"Where's Cynthia?" he asked.

"Went back to the guest house," Lettie Mae replied. "Looked to me like she was kinda miffed about something."

"Probably your imagination," J.T. said as he went out the back door.

Lettie Mae looked at Virginia and winked. They exchanged knowing smiles. "She won't last long," the cook predicted. "She doesn't understand the way things are done here."

CYNTHIA SAT FUMING in the guest house. She had been curious about what the investigator had to say and had planned to sit in on his meeting with J.T. Instead, she had been told—rather firmly, she thought—to "wait here." She wasn't accustomed being left out of important matters, and she didn't like it one bit.

It was beginning to irk her that at the Double C, men and women seemed to go their separate ways. She had come to the ranch expecting to be included in all its affairs. J.T. was simply going to have to understand that. She could never be contented merely to observe from the sidelines.

With a sigh she reached for the bedside telephone and dialed Sally's number in Austin. It rang three times before her friend answered.

"Hello?"

"Sally, Cynthia."

"You're here?"

"I'm at the Double C, yes. Got in day before yesterday."

"How're things going?"

"It's too soon to tell. Right now I feel as though I've been deposited in some strange, distant land where I don't know the language."

Sally laughed. "Remember how I felt when I got to Smith?"

"Can we get together?"

"Oh, hell! Ted and I have to be in Galveston tomorrow. It's a must. But we'll only be gone a few days, less than a week. I'll call as soon as we get back."

"Great. Here's the guest house number." Cynthia read the number posted on the phone. "If I'm out when you call, be sure to leave a message and I'll get back to you."

"Will do. So, how are you getting along with J.T.'s family?"

"Oh, I don't know. I'll talk to you when I see you. It's pretty complicated . . . or maybe it's just me."

"Doesn't sound good, Cyn. You've got to give it time."

"Yes, I know. Well, if you're leaving town tomorrow, you must have dozens of things to do. I just wanted to let you know I'm here and anxious to see you."

"Good, I'm glad you did. I'll call you the minute we get back. We'll have lunch and a nice long talk. It's going to be wonderful having you close. It's strange, you know. I have dozens of women friends but not one I can just sit and talk to for hours."

"Me, too. And believe me, I need a friendly face and a sympathetic ear."

The women said goodbye, and as Cynthia hung up the phone there was a knock at the door. "Come in," she said.

It was J.T. "I thought you'd wait in the sun room. What are you doing out here?"

"Sulking," she snapped.

He frowned and crossed the room to sit on the bed beside her. "Sulking? About what?"

"About being asked to leave the room like a good girl when the grown-ups have business to discuss. I came here to learn, J.T. How can I learn anything if I'm asked to wait outside when anything meaningful is discussed? I would have liked to hear what the investigator had to say. I would have liked to sit in while you and Tyler discussed business last night. So far the only person on this ranch who's told me the first thing about ranching is Ken." Her words were clipped and precise.

J.T. looked positively shocked at the outburst. "Okay, okay. I didn't realize that. I'll try to remember it. Pauline never wanted to..." He stopped. "As a matter of fact, I came out here to ask you to join me on a very important mission."

Her expression softened. "Where are we going?"

"To do a little aerial reconnaissance."

CYNTHIA WAS LESS than crazy about riding in the ranch helicopter. Even though she'd not complained about J.T.'s Baron, which was not considered small in the world of private aviation, she disliked flying in anything smaller than a company jet. When J.T. had offered to fly to Boston and bring her back to Texas, she had come up with a half dozen excuses, chiefly the unpredictable weather. But he handled the machine with the ease of a veteran pilot on familiar terms with its intricacies. Since he had made at least ten trips to Boston in it, she'd had to assume he knew what he was doing. Just as she had to trust him now with the helicopter.

"What are you looking for?" she asked. They had been scouting the area for thirty minutes, circling ever wider with each pass.

"Anything out of the ordinary. Those rustlers are holed up somewhere, and they have to have a trailer or truck for transporting their loot."

"Then I can't be of much help. I wouldn't know what was out of the ordinary and what wasn't."

"And this is a good way for you to get the lay of the land."

"It's such beautiful country, but I don't know how you expect to find something as small as a truck. Look, we passed right over a town, and I almost missed it, all nestled in the trees."

They flew on for another half hour. J.T. pointed out the town of Fredericksburg and LBJ Ranch and Lost Maples State Park, where, he said, he wanted to take her when the leaves turned. It was a glorious way to spend the morning once Cynthia got over her nervousness, but they spotted no dens of iniquity. Finally, declaring that he was starving to death, J.T. flew back to Crystal Creek Municipal Airport where he kept the helicopter.

"There's a café here at the airport," J.T. said as they crossed the tarmac. "They serve good, honest home cooking. Or we can go into town and eat at the Longhorn—makes no difference to me."

"Let's eat here." Cynthia knew, if yesterday had been the norm, that J.T. would encounter dozens of acquaintances at the Longhorn. Of course, he could run into someone he knew at the airport café, too, but most of its patrons were transients. For sure she was glad they weren't going back to the ranch for lunch. When she and J.T. were alone, things between them seemed as perfect as they had during those wonderful weekends in Boston.

The lunch specials were posted on a blackboard. Cynthia ordered chicken potpie and J.T. asked for meat loaf. She had noticed that when there was choice, he ordered beef. The food was excellent, as promised, but halfway through the meal, J.T. put down his fork and said, "Do you know what I wish we were eating?"

"What?"

"The beef curry you made that rainy Saturday night."

Cynthia smiled. "You really went for that, didn't you?"

"I've spent my entire life eating chile peppers. I do like spicy food. When I got home after that weekend, I asked Lettie Mae if she knew how to make curry. She said no... and in a way that implied she wasn't interested in learning, either. So that was that."

"J.T.," Cynthia said with a shake of her head, "you're the boss and she's the cook. If you wanted curry, you should have told Lettie Mae to find a recipe and make it. That's what I would have done."

"Mmm. That never occurred to me. I pretty much give Virginia and Lettie Mae carte blanche when it comes to the house."

"I have an idea—I'll make curry for you tonight. We can stop and get the ingredients on the way back to the ranch. I'd love to do it. It would make me feel useful. You know how much I like to cook."

Yes, he knew. During those lovely, lazy weekends in her Boston apartment, particularly when the weather was bad, she had turned out one delicious dish after another. "If I remember correctly, the curry was a pretty big production. You were in the kitchen an awfully long time.''

"A big production is the fun side of cooking. Anybody can open a can or shove something in the microwave. I'd really like to do it, J.T.''

"Okay. Yeah, sure, why not? My mouth's watering already." Winking at her, he returned his attention to his food.

After their meal they drove into Crystal Creek to a supermarket so Cynthia could buy the ingredients. There were a lot of them since she had no idea what the larder at the ranch would yield. That done, she and J.T. drove home.

Cynthia was in high spirits. She walked with J.T. to the cold cellar to pick out a large cut of beef. The curry would keep her busy for at least three hours, and maybe it would break the ice between her and J.T.'s family. Food, she'd noticed, often did that when all else failed.

She and J.T. were laughing when they walked into the kitchen laden with sacks. Lettie Mae turned at the sound. Seeing the grocery sacks, her brows knitted. "What in the world—"

"You can go put your feet up, Lettie Mae," J.T. said. "Watch your soaps and eat bonbons. Cynthia's fixing dinner tonight."

"She's what?"

"You heard me."

"I'll clean up, too," Cynthia promised. "Curry is a big event, and this will be my show from start to finish."

"Curry, J.T., you know Mr. Hank can't eat something like that."

"So?" J.T. said with a shrug. "You have to prepare something different for him half the time as it is."

"What if the kids don't like it?" Lettie Mae asked, her voice dripping with disapproval.

Cynthia set the sack she was carrying on the table. Lettie Mae was taking the wind out of her sails fast. "J.T. had never eaten it before I made it for him, and he loved it," she said in a measured voice. "He was the one who suggested it for tonight." That wasn't entirely true, but it was close enough.

Lettie Mae looked at J.T. as though he had committed some treasonous act, but he seemed oblivious. Setting two more sacks on the table, he gave Cynthia a light kiss on the cheek. "Have fun, sweetheart. I'm going to drive over to Carolyn's and give her the bad news about the rustling. She needs to have her people on alert. I won't be gone long." Turning on his heel, he left the kitchen.

Cynthia was fully aware of Lettie Mae standing with her arms folded, all but glaring at her. Taking a deep breath, she turned and faced the cook.

"I'll need a small pan for roasting the spices—a cake pan will do. And I'll need a Dutch oven and a griddle for cooking chapati," she said.

"For cooking what?"

"Chapati. It's an unleavened bread, sort of like a tortilla."

"Why don't you use tortillas? I have a bunch of those in the freezer."

Cynthia smiled thinly. "Chapati is more authentic. I want this dinner to be exactly as J.T. remembers. He enjoyed it so much."

Lettie Mae sniffed, but she grudgingly produced the requested items. "You know, Pauline hardly ever came in this kitchen. She certainly never came in it to cook."

"I know. J.T. told me. But cooking's something of a hobby of mine. J.T. really seems to like it when I cook for him."

"I see. Well, if you need me, I'll be in my room." Lettie Mae cocked her head toward a door on the left, then ambled off in that direction.

Why, Cynthia wondered, *does the simplest thing I do take on monumental importance?* That morning at breakfast she had casually mentioned how delightful it would be to have breakfast in the sun room when the weather was nice. Virginia had looked as though she'd suggested knocking out a wall. Meals, she'd been informed, were always served in the dining room.

J.T. had allowed the two women to come to regard this as their house. Well, when she was mistress of the manor, that would change. Cynthia might be able to accept the informality between family and servants, but at no time would she accept servants who had any doubt who was in charge of the household.

She slapped the huge chunk of meat on the cutting board and began cubing it. Oh, she knew the easiest thing to do would be to forget about the damned curry. That was exactly why she didn't intend to. Besides, she had promised it to J.T., and he was going to get the dish she had promised to make.

Cynthia had the spices roasting in the oven, sending out an intoxicating aroma, when Lynn came through the back door. "What is that heavenly smell, Lettie Mae? I—" She stopped, her eyes widening in surprise when she saw Cynthia at the stove. "Oh, I . . . what are you doing?"

"I'm preparing dinner, something special for your father."

"Is Lettie Mae sick?"

Cynthia smiled. "No. J.T. asked me to make a meal like one I once cooked for him in Boston."

"But...Lettie Mae never lets anyone but her helper do any of the cooking."

"So I've been told. Perhaps she gave in to your father this time. I believe she's in her room if you wanted to speak to her."

"Oh, no. I . . . I was going to tell her Beverly would be having dinner with us tonight, but we can do it some other time."

"Lynn, I would love to have Beverly. Really. There's no way I can make just a little bit of this. Please, have her, by all means."

Lynn cast a furtive glance around the kitchen, as if she were trying to think of a gracious way out. Obviously she came up with nothing, for she lifted her shoulders in a little shrug, and said, "Well, all right. The usual time?"

"I'll certainly try." If her preparing dinner was such a traumatic breach of family routine, heaven forbid she should compound it by serving the meal late.

Lynn left the kitchen after giving the pot on the stove a look of concern. Some minutes later, Hank came into the kitchen, saw Cynthia and did a double-take. They then had essentially the same conversation she and Lynn had had. Hank left, muttering something about Lettie Mae fixing him a hamburger steak and mashed potatoes.

Cynthia took a deep breath and turned her attention to the cooking pot. *I will adjust to them, and they will adjust to me,* she vowed. She suspected she could hasten the adjustment by talking to J.T., but that was something else she'd be damned if she'd do.

FROM HER OFFICE WINDOW Carolyn had spied J.T.'s car approaching the Circle T ranch house, and she was waiting on the front porch for him.

"Nice afternoon, isn't it?" she commented as he placed a light kiss on her cheek.

"Sure is. But I'm afraid I haven't come bearing tidings of joy."

"Oh? Something wrong?"

"You can say that in spades. I've had eight cows taken from my place this past week. You know my cousin Larry Wendt is an investigator for the breeders' association. He tells me they think there's an organized ring working the area.''

Carolyn bit her bottom lip. "It's been quiet for a while. I guess we have to expect this sort of thing to crop up every few years. Come on in, J.T. Can I get you something to drink?''

"No, thanks.'' He pulled off his hat as he followed her into the house. "You haven't lost any cattle?''

"No, not yet, but we'll be on guard.''

Carolyn led the way to her office. The wall behind her desk was covered with family photographs—several of her late husband, Frank, many of Beverly at various stages of her life and one of Pauline and Carolyn as teenagers. J.T. could never look at that one without experiencing a twinge, and today was no exception. As he sat down, he shifted his chair slightly so that the picture was out of his view.

Carolyn sat behind the desk and fastened her blue-green eyes on him. J.T. had always regarded Pauline's younger sister as more handsome than pretty. Pauline's beauty had been delicate, like Lynn's. Carolyn's was stronger, more commanding. She had what J.T. liked to call "presence,'' with a little bit of toughness thrown in for good measure.

He and his sister-in-law had been through a lot over the years. In earlier days, when Carolyn and Frank were struggling to make a go of the Circle T, J.T. had helped them financially. They had both lost their spouses and had suffered the pangs of being single parents. Their friendship was probably as solid as one could be.

"You should have brought Cynthia," Carolyn said.

"She's tied up fixing dinner."

"She's doing what?" Carolyn asked with a little laugh.

"Fixing dinner—something she cooked for me one night in Boston. She's a great cook."

"Oh, I bet Lettie Mae loves that."

J.T. frowned. "What do you mean?"

"Come on, J.T. Lettie Mae's as possessive of that kitchen as a mother superior is of her convent. She didn't want Pauline to come within a country mile of that stove."

J.T. wondered why he'd never noticed that. "I thought the reason Pauline stayed out of the kitchen was because she hated to cook."

"Well, of course that was part of it. And now Lettie Mae regards that as her bailiwick. Lynn used to grouse that when Beverly slept over, Lettie Mae didn't even want them coming in to make popcorn. She made it for them."

"That's pretty dumb, if you ask me, and she's going to have to get over it. Cynthia likes to cook. I imagine she'll spend plenty of time in the kitchen. Pauline had the right to stay out of it, and Cynthia has the right to practically live in it, if that's what she wants."

Carolyn's look was skeptical. "Then I hope you're prepared to deal with some hurt feelings. And I might as well tell you something else since you apparently don't have eyes. Virginia has made a religion out of keeping that house precisely the way it was when Pauline died. What happens if a new wife wants to move a potted plant or buy a different sofa?"

J.T. rolled his eyes toward the ceiling. "Women! By the way, what did you think of Cynthia?"

"She's beautiful . . . and young."

J.T. was sensitive to every nuance of Carolyn's voice. "Are you trying to tell me something?"

"No, but I was surprised, to say the least. You should have warned me."

"I didn't because, frankly, I never think about our ages." He did, of course, often, but he saw no reason to tell Carolyn that.

"How old is she, anyway?"

He hesitated, realizing that the truth embarrassed him a bit. "She's a year older than Tyler, but the age difference doesn't seem to exist, if you know what I'm saying. We get along like contemporaries." When Carolyn said nothing, he pressed the issue. "You disapprove."

"Oh, J.T., it's not my place to approve or disapprove. But I do wonder how the kids are taking it."

"Hard to say. Cal...well, Cal's Cal. Nothing fazes him. Tyler and Lynn? I have no idea, chiefly because they haven't said one word to me about Cynthia— good, bad or indifferent. I really hadn't thought much about that. I guess if they liked her they would have said something by now, right?"

"That seems reasonable. How about Hank?"

"Oh, God, who knows? Grandpa admits to liking maybe half a dozen people in the world, and two of them are dead. But I trust Cynthia to make them all come around."

"I hope so, I really do. If the kids are having a hard time with this, I doubt it has anything to do with Cynthia personally. They'd have a hard time accepting any woman."

"And you, Carolyn?"

"No, not so much. I know what being widowed is like, all those long, long days and even longer nights. I know how lonely you've been, and I'm glad you've found someone you care for. I just hope..." Carolyn paused, as if having second thoughts about what she was going to say.

"You just hope what?"

"I just hope you've found the right one. Cynthia seems so different from any of the women around here. Didn't you notice that the other night?"

"Maybe a little. Oh, I know she comes across as Miss Upper Crust at first, but that's the way she was raised. There's another side to her, the side that rose to a vice presidency in one of the biggest banks in the country. She didn't do that without learning how to handle people."

Carolyn sat back in her chair and looked at him thoughtfully. "Amazing that you went for a woman like that. Simply amazing. You're something of a male chauvinist, you know, just like most of the characters around here."

J.T. was slightly offended. "I treated Pauline as my partner, equal in every respect."

"Only because she didn't want to get all that involved in your affairs. You ought to try being a lone woman trying to make it in one of the most male-dominated businesses on earth. You'd find out soon enough how equal you were around here. I imagine Cynthia's used to doing business with men on a one-to-one basis, but the men around here really don't like doing business with a woman. They have to deal with me because I *am* the Circle T Ranch, but they don't like it. They'd much prefer I sent my foreman or one of the hands to take care of 'real' business. I'm afraid Cynthia has some surprises in store...more than she's already had, I mean."

J.T. fingered the crease in his Stetson. "Carolyn, that's precisely why I insisted she come here for a trial run, so to speak. I really do love her, but I want to make damned sure she's found the right one, too."

DURING THE DRIVE BACK to the Double C, J.T. thought long and hard about everything Carolyn had said. She had opened his eyes to a great deal. Yes, he guessed the house did still look exactly as it had when Pauline was alive, and, yes, Lettie Mae ruled over the kitchen like a czar. But he was accustomed to that, and certainly the kids were. Cynthia, however, could reasonably be expected to want a few changes, and she damned sure wouldn't want to give up something she enjoyed as much as she did cooking simply because Lettie Mae was possessive of her bailiwick.

At dinner that night, he was more observant than usual, hoping Carolyn had been exaggerating. He saw things he probably would have missed had he not been specifically looking for them. Lettie Mae was sulking, and Virginia wore a pinched expression, as though her shoes were too tight. Beyond that, though, everything seemed normal. Cal and Beverly were their usual exuberant selves, and they went to great pains to praise Cynthia's efforts with dinner. Lynn was quiet, as was Tyler, but with Cal and Beverly at the table, one had a hard time getting a word in here and there. Lynn, he told himself, was always quiet and became almost mute when she was around Beverly, perfectly content to let her cousin hog the spotlight. As for Tyler, any number of things could account for his silence. His was a complicated personality. When Tyler withdrew into his own thoughts, he became unreachable.

J.T. decided that Carolyn was an alarmist. Everything was fine. If Virginia and Lettie Mae had their noses out of joint, they'd get over it. Cynthia had turned out a superb meal, and she seemed to be having a good time. Everything was fine.

Later that night, in the privacy of the guest house, he hesitantly asked her if she was pleased with the way dinner had turned out.

She sat on the bed, placidly filing her nails. "Cal and Beverly were charming."

"And Tyler and Lynn?"

"They simply haven't warmed to me yet. Maybe they never will, J.T., but there's nothing you can do about it. I'll accept peaceful coexistence and bend over backward with your family. But your servants are another matter. If I want to whip up something in the kitchen, I don't like being treated like an invader."

"I'll have a talk with them—with all of them."

"I don't think that'll help. They'll only resent me more. You can order your cowboys to do what you want, and I suppose you can order your servants to give me some leeway, but you can't order your family to like me."

"I can't have you feeling you're being treated less than cordially."

"Give time a chance." She set down the nail file, buffed her nails on her robe, then beckoned to him with a smile.

Sighing, he went to sit beside her on the bed and take her hands in his. "Are you sorry you came?"

"Not a bit, but I'm anxious to get in on some of the inner workings of the ranch. I don't want my brain to atrophy."

"Well, this is the end of the month, the time to get caught up on my bookkeeping. That's as good as any to find out how the Double C is run."

Cynthia's smile brightened. "My specialty, facts and figures. What software system do you use?"

J.T. grinned. Dropping her hands, he tapped his temple. "This and . . . these," he said, holding up his fingers.

"What?"

"I keep ledgers."

"By hand? Oh, J.T., in this day and age?"

"It's the way I've always kept books. I'm comfortable doing it that way."

She chuckled and shook her head. "I can set you up a system that will enable you to do your book work in a third . . . a fourth the time it takes now."

"I hate machines," he growled. "I don't want to do the work in a fourth the time. On the last day of the month I expect to spend several hours in my study, and that's the way I like it." Leaning down, he slipped off one boot, then the other. They thudded softly as they hit the carpet. "There's something satisfying about the familiar. I'm not much of a man for changes."

Over his bent head, Cynthia stared across the room. She was beginning to realize that.

CHAPTER SEVEN

LIFE GRADUALLY FELL into a routine for Cynthia. For the next several days she followed J.T. almost everywhere he went—watching, listening, taking mental notes and keeping her mouth mostly shut. Mostly but not completely. She tried, but there was no way she could keep quiet about a bookkeeping system that was straight out of 1910. J.T.'s only concession to modern times was a small calculator he kept close at hand. He had no anwswering machine, his telephones lacked call-waiting, memory-dial or call-forwarding features. There was no fax machine. Watching him sift through piles of bills and invoices, write the checks by hand, then meticulously record the payments in a thick ledger exasperated her.

"J.T., this really is ludicrous. I have a marvelous system in my office at the bank. It's simple and efficient and does away with all this." Her hand swept out to indicate the clutter on his desk. "Most big stores will let you take a computer on a trial basis. Just let me show you what one could do for you."

"No," he interrupted, "I'm not the computer type."

"How do you know? Have you ever tried using one? The entire world is computerized now."

"Maybe that's why it's in such lousy shape."

Cynthia sighed and idly surveyed the study. It was a completely utilitarian room without frills. J.T.'s desk was the focal point. Three worn leather chairs sat facing it, and against the wall behind it stood several glass-enclosed bookcases. On top of one was a framed photograph of Pauline. *Sweet* and *serene* were the words that had popped into Cynthia's head the first time she saw it.

Her gaze went across the room to the long line of filing cabinets that occupied one entire wall of the study. They were old, very old, scuffed and scraped. J.T. had told her the cabinets contained information on every hiring and firing, every weather quirk, every bull, cow, calf, sale and purchase that had taken place on the ranch since he'd begun running it. Twenty years' worth of paper. Cynthia had taken a look in a couple of the drawers and had found them crammed so tightly one could hardly get a hand between the folders. "Think of storage alone," she persisted. "Everything in those filing cabinets could be put on disks that would take up maybe one shelf."

"And who would put it all on disks?"

"I would. Just let me bring a computer in and show you what it will do. I think you'll be surprised at how much it would simplify your business."

"I'm not interested. If it isn't on a piece of paper I can pull out anytime I want to, it doesn't exist as far as I'm concerned. I don't want a computer, Cynthia. I don't want to take the time to learn to run the damned thing. And I'll tell you something else—I went into the hardware store a while back, and their computer was 'down.' Hell, nobody could do a thing without that machine. Well, my head and my hands don't break down. I like doing things the way I've always done them.''

She opened her mouth to protest further, then thought better of it. It wouldn't do any good. It pained her to have to add *inflexible* to the more desirable adjectives that described J.T. He gave new meaning to the term *old-fashioned*.

Cynthia had been very observant during the past few days, and she had read many issues of the various publications J.T. subscribed to. She could see that much of the work done on the Double C was carried out by inefficient methods. Many of the cowboys still rode horses while they went about their chores. They still branded cattle out in the open instead of employing a chute that turned branding into an assembly-line operation. Some of the men liked to bed down under the stars with the herd and cook supper over an open fire, at least some of the time. It gradually dawned on her that what they were doing was keeping an archaic way of life in existence, as the preservation groups had done with the longhorn. It was ritual rather than efficiency they were after, and that was completely at odds with the way her own mind worked.

She gradually became aware of something else, too. J.T. stretched himself way too thin. He wanted to be all things—hands-on rancher who was on top of every single facet of the ranch's operation, an all-seeing, all-knowing family patriarch, a civic-minded citizen, a valued friend. His children expected and received his undivided attention whenever they wished it. Just let Carolyn hint that she could use some help with something and he went running. He made dozens of trips into town on errands that Cynthia thought others could easily have handled. Once there, he seemed to feel obligated to stop at the bank, the feed store, the drugstore—and always the Longhorn Coffee Shop, to press the flesh, he called it. Cynthia suspected—no, she knew—that if a winery was begun on the ranch, he would be in the thick of that, too.

"You know," she finally ventured to say to him, "what a good manager does best is delegate authority." That simple remark was met with a stony look that temporarily silenced her. But she never missed an opportunity to remind him that the reason one hired workers was so one person didn't have to do everything. That usually led to another argument, but she couldn't keep quiet.

How frustrated she felt. She was accustomed to getting things done. She also was accustomed to having her ideas and suggestions considered and discussed thoughtfully. Here she didn't feel she was doing a damned thing; for sure she wasn't making any decisions. Everything she mentioned to J.T. was dis-

missed as "not the way we do things around here."
She thought if she heard that phrase one more time,
she would scream.

Still, pretending she was learning the ropes and being useful was preferable to staying in the house and
trying to make her presence felt. Hank did little but
study her as though she'd just dropped in from Ura-
nus. Tyler, Virginia and Lettie Mae still treated her
with a cool politeness that made her uncomfortable.
She sensed that trying too hard with Lynn would be a
mistake, that she would have to let J.T.'s daughter
come to her, not the other way around. Cal was easy
to get along with, but that was due more to his easygoing manner than to any real interest and warmth on
his part. She could honestly say that since arriving at
the Double C she'd made only two friends—Ken and
Beverly. At least they always behaved as though they
were glad to see her. But she couldn't very well pester
Ken, and Beverly simply wasn't around all that much.
Most of the time Cynthia just felt shut out.

Yet whenever she telephoned her mother she was
careful to mask all her uneasiness and to declare she
was having the time of her life. She wasn't sure Alicia
believed her.

"But, Cynthia, what do you do all day every day?"

"I'm listening and learning, Mom."

But all she was really learning was the way J.T. did
things, the way he would always do things. The night
she met him at Sally's party, he'd told her that Pauline had been a full partner in the ranch's operation.

Now Cynthia knew that his idea of a full partner and hers were entirely different. He had set policy; apparently Pauline had just seen that his wishes were carried out. Perhaps his late wife really had been an apron-clad helpmate. *Perhaps that's what he expects me to be, too,* Cynthia thought in horror.

But she refused to believe they would remain at odds. After she'd had more time to study the business of ranching, she'd make him see that her ideas had merit, that she knew what she was talking about and that there was nothing wrong with modern efficiency. In the meantime, she would bite the bullet and her tongue.

When Sally finally called to make a date for lunch, Cynthia found the thought of getting away for a day and letting down her guard was irresistible. She was sure she had never grabbed at an invitation so eagerly.

"I ASSUME it's all right for me to take the day off," Cynthia said to J.T. after breakfast. "I don't seem to have made myself indispensable around here yet." She meant that to be a lighthearted remark. It came out tinged with sarcasm.

"No, that's fine, sweetheart. You picked a good day. The local ranchers' association is having its annual barbecue, so I'll be tied up all day. I damned near forgot about it. If Bubba hadn't called to jar my memory, I might have missed it."

"Mmm, that sounds like fun. Maybe I'd rather go to that. Sally and I can have lunch anytime."

J.T. smiled. "Don't change your plans. The association barbecue is strictly for the boys."

"You're kidding!"

"It's more of a stag party than anything. Oh, I suppose we get a little bit of work done, but very little. What we mostly do is eat a lot, drink a lot and swap tall tales."

Cynthia frowned. "What about ranchers like Carolyn?"

"What about them?"

"Aren't they included?"

"They understand. Several women attend the association's business meetings, but this annual thing . . . well, traditionally it's no women allowed."

"And God forbid that anyone should tamper with tradition. I thought that kind of thing went out when the first bra was burned."

J.T. chose to ignore that. "You'll need a car, so take the Cadillac. There are any number of things I can drive. I probably won't see you again today, sweetheart. The barbecue usually doesn't break up until the wee hours." He reached in his hip pocket and drew out his wallet. "I don't know how much gas is in the car. Here's my credit card if you need to fill up."

Cynthia looked at the card. "I have my own credit cards."

"I'd rather you use mine."

"Why, for heaven's sake?"

"It's my car.'

"But I'm going to be driving it and using the gas."

J.T. frowned darkly. "It doesn't sit right with me to let a woman put gas in my car."

"That's silly. I have money of my own."

"You can use it to buy personal baubles if you like, but around here I make the living."

"I'm used to buying things with my own money, and I enjoy it," she persisted stubbornly, up against another concept that was totally foreign to her.

He shot her a look of total exasperation. "Let's not have a summit conference over every little thing."

"I'm used to having conferences over every little thing."

"Take the goddamned card, Cynthia! Please!"

She stared at the card. Her instincts demanded she stand her ground, while common sense told her the card wasn't worth making a fuss over. In the end she took it. "All right, if you feel so strongly about it." Rounding his desk, she bent to kiss him.

"Be careful on the highway," he cautioned. "I can send one of the men with you, if you like."

"Why would you do that? Sally and I are going to have lunch and go shopping. I'm quite sure the poor man would be bored to death."

"I don't like having you out on the highway alone."

"I'll be fine. I guess I won't see you until breakfast tomorrow."

"Afraid not. Please get home before dark."

Dear God, she thought, *I feel like I'm seventeen again and listening to Mom.* "Right."

"Give Sally my regards, and you two girls have a good time."

The corners of her mouth twitched. "You *boys* do the same."

THE RESTAURANT Sally had chosen was a lovely Mexican place done in sun-washed pastels; its food was genuine Mexico rather than Tex-Mex. She insisted Cynthia start with tortilla soup. "Then we'll have a chorizo and cheese dish that's messy, loaded with calories and absolutely divine." They ordered, then sat back to catch up on each other's lives. But, of course, it was the relationship with J.T. Sally was most interested in.

Cynthia sighed. "It's so difficult, Sally, and I didn't expect it to be. Now I realize how naive I was."

"His family, right?"

"Well, they haven't exactly decided I'm their favorite person, but I never thought they would, not at first. Lynn, J.T.'s daughter, is a darling young woman but very quiet and retiring. I imagine it takes her a long time to warm to someone new. Cal, the middle one, is one of those devil-may-care types who's committed to no commitments. We get along all right because he doesn't seem to think about me one way or another. Tyler's a mystery. He treats me like I have a deadly contagious disease. And J.T.'s grandfather... well, he's eccentric, crochety, and he looks at me suspiciously, as if trying to figure out what I'm up to. But, like I said, I didn't expect to win over everybody in two days...or two weeks."

"Then I don't understand," Sally said. "You seem to be handling everything well. Why is it so difficult?"

"It's...J.T."

Sally looked startled. "Oh?"

"He's so different from the man I knew in Boston. There we just meshed, liked to do the same things, got along so beautifully. It was as though we were supposed to meet each other. I can't tell you how many hours we sat and talked about...everything. He seemed to think my thoughts and ideas were worthy of his attention. But at the ranch..." Cynthia's words trailed off. She was having a hard time explaining her feelings to Sally, mostly because she didn't understand them herself.

Sally, however, nodded sagely, as if she knew exactly what Cynthia was trying to say. She leaned forward, an earnest look on her face, as though dying to say something important. At that moment, however, their waitress brought the soup, effectively cutting off conversation for a few minutes. It picked up again when Sally said, "Let me guess. In Boston he was thoroughly charming, eager to please and almost gallant. At the ranch, he's overbearing, domineering, protective and possessive."

It was Cynthia's turn to look surprised. "Exactly. How did you know?"

"Because I know the men in this part of the world. My dad's a lot like J.T., and neither one of them is like any man I ever met on the East Coast. It's all tied to the frontier spirit or the code of the west or some such blather. All I know is, oilmen and cattlemen are the most fiercely independent breeds you'll find. They can't stand for anyone to tell them what to do, especially the government...or a woman. I don't think any one of them would come right out and say a woman's place is in the home, not in the 1990s, but plenty of them believe it in their heart of hearts."

Cynthia shook her head, mystified. "I never saw any of that in J.T. in Boston, but now I want to tear my hair out over his pigheaded determination not to change a thing they've been doing for the past twenty years. Would you believe he doesn't even own a computer?"

"I believe it."

"And he refuses to even give one a try."

"I believe that, too."

Cynthia looked away for a second, then back. "He's a mystery wrapped up in a puzzle. He runs that ranch with an iron fist, but when it comes to those children of his, he's as soft as warm butter. Get this— he won't put roads on his place because they take up valuable grazing land, yet he's thinking about giving Tyler a sizable chunk of property to grow grapes on, for no reason save that his son has this burning desire to be a vintner. Frankly, I can't see that it would be good business at all. And he allows Lynn to spend all her time with those horses of hers. At great expense, I might add—I've seen some of the figures. Then there's Cal. J.T. hates that Cal's still with the rodeo, yet he doesn't do a thing about it.''

"What can he do?" Sally asked sensibly.

"Put his foot down, for one thing. Have a no-nonsense talk with him. Tell him he's had twelve years of fun but now it's time to settle down and get serious about something, preferably the ranch. I think J.T. would be the happiest man on earth if his children were deeply involved with the Double C, and it sure would take some of the work load off his shoulders. As it is, he doesn't get much help from anyone but Tyler, and that might come to a screeching halt if that wine-making venture goes through."

"You know, Cyn, you probably should walk on eggshells where J.T. and his kids are concerned. I've heard from other women that being a stepmother requires a lot of keeping your mouth shut. They've all known one another a long time. You're new to the picture."

"J.T. asked my opinion about Cal, and I gave it to him," Cynthia insisted. "I only have J.T.'s best interests at heart. I think his kids take advantage of him."

"And you might as well accept that it's highly unlikely you'll change him at this late date, so..." Sally paused and frowned.

"So?"

"So I guess you're just going to have to decide if you can live with him the way he is."

Cynthia's gaze fastened on a bare spot on the pink stucco wall behind Sally's head. A whole gamut of emotions assailed her, many of them contradictory. Yet, sooner or later, they would all have to be dealt with one by one. For most of her adult life she had dreamed of being a part of a man's life and feeling she belonged there. But she knew her own nature; she would never subjugate her identity to anyone else's.

An involuntary sigh escaped her lips. She had come to Texas with such great expectations and the sure knowledge that she was finally on her way to happily-ever-after. Had she been following a pipe-dream?

THE BARBECUE was shifting into high gear. The event was always held at the ranch of one of the association's members. The Double C had hosted it two years earlier. This year it was being held at a picturesque little ranch near Johnson City. J.T. had only to look around to conclude that the owner didn't do much serious ranching, although there was some livestock around. The place was too pretty; it looked as if it had been built on a Hollywood movie lot. His conclusions proved to be correct when he learned that the ranch's owners mostly made a living renting rooms and cabins to city dudes with a hankering for fresh air.

J.T. was seated on a bale of hay, cold beer in hand, listening to two men engaged in a heated political discussion. Apparently the President had just made an appointment that one man thought brilliant and the other thought disastrous. J.T. considered himself to be apolitical, chiefly because he hadn't agreed with any agricultural policy out of Washington, D.C. in his adult lifetime.

"Hi, podnuh," he heard someone say. He turned to see Bubba Gibson approaching.

"Hi, Bubba. Pull up a bale."

"Ah, me," Bubba said, sitting down and folding his arms across his middle. "Great turnout this year, right?"

"Right."

"How's that gal friend of yours?"

"Cynthia? She's fine, thanks."

"She's sure a looker."

"Yes, she is."

Bubba gave his old friend an exaggerated scrutiny. "You're looking damned good these days, J.T."

"Well, thanks."

"The young ones will do that for you, eh? Stoke the fire in the old furnace."

J.T. blanched visibly, appalled that Bubba or anyone else would mention his own relationship with Cynthia in conjunction with Bubba's and Billie Jo's. He couldn't think of a thing to say.

It didn't matter. Bubba was feeling garrulous, having drunk just enough beer to loosen both his tongue and his inhibitions. He patted his belly. "I've dropped five pounds, can you tell?"

J.T. couldn't, but he said, "You're looking good."

"Yeah, and I feel good. I've been given a new lease on life, podnuh."

At the expense of someone I think the world of, J.T. thought regretfully. For months, ever since Bubba's affair with Billie Jo had become the favorite grist for Crystal Creek's gossip mill, J.T. had pondered the wisdom of trying to talk to his friend about it. As a rule, men butted out of other men's sex lives. It was a sort of unspoken code of the brotherhood. And if the truth were known, J.T. didn't think Bubba would take kindly to any criticism. He knew if he uttered one disapproving word, Bubba would take offense, their friendship would suffer and nothing else would really change.

But, damn, it was hard to keep quiet. Saying nothing was tantamount to condoning the affair. When J.T. thought back over the years to the camaraderie he and Pauline had shared with Bubba and Mary, he had to bite his tongue to keep from telling his pal he was making an ass of himself.

And there was more. Mary had been special to Pauline. Next to Carolyn, Bubba's wife had been her closest confidante. During the last year of Pauline's life, Mary had been a frequent visitor to the ranch, and during the final months her steady, unobtrusive presence had been a comfort to them all. No one could ever forget or repay such loyalty. If Pauline were alive, J.T. was certain she would have ostracized Bubba long ago.

Bubba's voice droned on, but J.T. heard little of what he was saying. He was too preoccupied with wondering why he was thinking about Pauline so much that day. Was it being around so many of their old friends, remembering all the good times?

Or was it the skirmish with Cynthia that morning? It hadn't been an argument or even an incident, just sort of a jockeying for position, an attempt to establish territories, a clash of wills. Pauline would never have allowed herself to be drawn into such silliness. She would have said, "Very well," and that would have been the end of it. Cynthia, J.T. was beginning to realize, was not the very-well type of woman. He had been left with a bad feeling, faced with a stubbornness and feistiness he'd never seen in Boston, and he wasn't sure he liked it a damned bit.

Or maybe what he really didn't like was admitting he had no idea how to handle a strong-willed woman. He was beginning to realize that what they had shared in Boston might have been the result of ideal circumstances. With no families or jobs to intrude, they had been free to concentrate solely on the strong emotional attraction between them. Perhaps if he had seen Cynthia in action at the bank, he would have recognized the independence she had displayed that morning.

"Yes sir," Bubba was saying, bringing J.T. out of his thoughts, "I sure can't fault your taste in women, podnuh. They don't come any prettier than Cynthia. But something kind of bothers me."

"Yeah? What?"

"How's living here gonna suit her? She's got big city written all over her. Somehow she and Crystal Creek don't jibe."

J.T. stared at the can of beer in his hand. "Bubba, you could have talked all day without saying that."

WHEN J.T. RETURNED to the Double C that evening, the first thing he noticed was the Cadillac, parked in its customary spot. Then he looked toward the guest house. A light shone from the front window, so he assumed Cynthia was there. He wasn't surprised that she was still awake. He had left the barbecue much earlier than he normally did. The festivities had begun to pall fairly quickly. In fact, he'd found himself wondering why he had ever thought all that he-man socializing was fun.

Parking the pickup, he got out and stood looking at the guest house for several long minutes. Then slowly, like a man resigned, he walked toward it. He tapped lightly on the door twice before pushing it open.

Cynthia was sitting up in bed reading. The minute he saw her, he melted inside. He forgot all their differences, forgot everything except loving her.

Seeing him, she glanced at the bedside clock. "So early?"

He pushed the door closed and crossed the room. "I must be getting old. The wee-hours-of-the-morning stuff just doesn't appeal anymore. How was lunch?"

"Oh, it's always fun to be with Sally." Patting the edge of the bed, she said, "I'm glad you're home early. There's something I want to talk to you about."

As he sank down, he leaned forward and dropped a light kiss on her mouth. She smelled wonderful; she always did. For all her big-city sophistication, Cynthia always managed to smell like sunshine and flowers. "So...what did you want to talk to me about?"

She gave him a small, self-satisfied smile. "Your birthday is a week from Saturday, right?"

"Right. I'm surprised you remembered."

"Well, I did, and I want to do something very special for it. I've thought and thought, but there's really nothing I can buy you, so...I'm going to treat you, treat both of us to a weekend in New Orleans. How's that?"

"New Orleans?"

"Yes. And don't tell me you can't get away. If you could get away to Boston every weekend for months, you can get away to New Orleans."

"Well, I..."

Cynthia slipped her arms around his neck and kissed him soundly. "Oh, J.T., it will be so wonderful. I've never been to New Orleans, but I've heard it's a perfect place for lovers. We can fly in on Friday night and leave Monday morning. Two days and three nights, just the two of us."

J.T. did not particularly want to go to New Orleans. He was not a man who liked to get away from it all. The Double C was the only place he wanted to be, and now that Cynthia was here with him, he saw no reason to ever leave it.

But the pleading he saw in her eyes was impossible for him to resist. And he was grateful there apparently would be no backlash from this morning's contrariness. "If you want to go to New Orleans, we'll go to New Orleans."

Relief swept through Cynthia. The idea had begun forming when Sally mentioned her own honeymoon in New Orleans and how romantic the city was. All during the drive from Austin back to the ranch, she had mulled it over. The more she had thought about it, the more appealing it had become. To get away from the ranch, just the two of them! Somehow she knew they would recapture the magic.

"You're staying here tonight, aren't you?" she asked.

J.T. grinned. "The thought crossed my mind."

"Wonderful. I thought I was going to have to fall asleep without you beside me."

She conveniently ignored the nagging inner voice trying to remind her they couldn't run away to romantic cities forever, that the differences between them couldn't always be settled by lovemaking. Sooner or later the problems would have to be met head-on.

CHAPTER EIGHT

LYNN WAS THE LAST ONE to arrive at breakfast the following morning. The others had been patiently waiting for several minutes. Cynthia's gaze wandered around the table. J.T., Tyler and Hank had their noses buried in newspapers. Cal looked as though he had a hangover and could use a cup of coffee. Lettie Mae kept popping in and out of the kitchen to see if Lynn had put in an appearance. Cynthia didn't know why she didn't just go ahead and serve the food, but there seemed to be some sort of tacit agreement that meals didn't start until everyone was at the table. She assumed that was another of Pauline's rules, just like every other thing that was done in the house.

Well, things were going to change. She was in a wonderfully jubilant mood, brimming over with self-confidence. J.T. had been so tender and loving the night before, taking great pains to reassure her that his love was as deep as ever. Her position was strong, so it was time to assert herself. No more hiding out in the guest house whenever J.T. wasn't around. Perhaps his family didn't accept her, but that was more their problem than hers. They would have to learn to deal with her. She felt a very weighty problem had been lifted from her shoulders.

Lynn bounded into the dining room with unusual exuberance. "Good morning, everybody," she greeted brightly.

Everyone mumbled something, even Cynthia, who assumed she was included in "everybody." The minute Lynn sat down, Lettie Mae appeared and began pouring juice and coffee. The McKinneys always ate hearty breakfasts, so the cook made several trips. Finally everyone settled down to the serious business of eating, and conversation was minimal.

At meal's end, J.T. was the first to make a move to leave the table, something that also seemed to be the custom. This morning, however, just as her father pushed back his chair, Lynn said, "Can you wait a minute, Daddy? There's something I want to tell everyone."

"Sure, hon. What is it?"

"Your birthday's coming up."

"So?"

"So, Beverly and I have been talking to Aunt Carolyn, and we want to throw a big barbecue to celebrate, the kind we used to have years ago. We've made all the plans. Virginia and Lettie Mae are going to—"

Cynthia's eyes flew to J.T. She attempted to telegraph him a message.

J.T. didn't see it and didn't need to. He had reached over and touched Lynn's hand to interrupt. "That's really sweet of you, hon, but I'm afraid I already have plans for my birthday.''

Lynn's face fell. ''You have? But...what?''

J.T. looked down the table and smiled at Cynthia. ''Cynthia is taking me to New Orleans that weekend.''

Lynn glanced at Cynthia, then back at her father. ''New Orleans? You never go away on your birthday. You've always spent it here with the family.''

''Maybe that's because no one's ever offered to take me on a trip before,'' J.T. said, giving his daughter a fond smile.

''Can't you go some other time?'' Lynn asked petulantly.

''Why don't you and Beverly plan the barbecue for another weekend?''

''It wouldn't be the same.''

''Sure it would.''

Cynthia was torn. She might have offered to change the date of the New Orleans trip if she hadn't felt it was good that J.T. was not giving in to his daughter's pleading.

J.T. got to his feet and looked at Cal. ''Don't disappear, Cal. I'd sure like to see you in the study.''

''Sure, Daddy,'' Cal said, but when J.T. had left the room, he looked around the table and affected a shudder. ''Why do I always get cold chills whenever Daddy wants to see me in his study?''

Lynn stood, shot Cynthia a cold look and left the room without a word. Tyler picked up his newspaper and followed her. Cal struggled to his feet and ambled out into the foyer. Hank also rose and, with some difficulty, limped out to the front porch.

Cynthia sat alone with her thoughts until Lettie Mae came in to clear the table. Pushing herself away, she got up and said, "That was delicious as usual, Lettie Mae."

"Thank you, ma'am."

Neither the housekeeper nor the cook ever called her by her given name, but she actually felt rather comfortable with that. It was easier to give instructions to people who treated one with a slight deference. Of course, J.T. gave the women plenty of instructions while being palsy-walsy toward them, but he had such a commanding presence he could get away with it. Cynthia felt she needed the leverage of a certain amount of formality.

She left the dining room, crossed the foyer and went into the living room. She found herself studying it intently. It was this room more than any of the others that she most wanted to do something with. Though nothing about the big house was actually formal, the living room seemed to her rather cheerless and uninviting. She wanted to scrap everything eventually and start from scratch, but for now, a bit more imaginative furniture arrangement would help.

At that moment, Virginia came into the room, carrying a feather duster.

"Ah, Virginia," Cynthia said, "just the person I want to see. Don't you think this room would look better if the sofa was moved over here and the two wing chairs were put over there, across from it? That would make the hearth the focal point of the room. The secretary desk could go in front of the windows, and those two chairs could be moved to the far wall, dividing the room into two conversation areas. It would be so much cozier.''

Virginia frowned. "But this is the way the room has always been arranged."

"So don't you think it's time for a change?"

"Does J.T. know about this? He's not much for changes. And I don't think the kids would like it a bit. This is the way their mother arranged the room. If the desk was in front of the window, where would we put the Christmas tree? It always goes there. If I were you, ma'am, I think I'd leave it alone."

"Well, it was a thought." And Cynthia was no fool. Until she became Mrs. McKinney, it would have to remain only a thought. But if she ever did get her hands on the house, to do what she wanted to with it, Virginia doubtless would go into shock.

THE MINUTE CAL ENTERED the study and saw J.T. standing at the window, hands clasped behind his back, head down, he knew his father had in mind more than a friendly chat. That stance was a dead giveaway that the discussion would be serious. He wasn't sure he was up to it, not with his pounding headache. "Daddy?"

J.T. turned. "Yes, Cal. Have a seat."

Sitting down, Cal experienced an uneasy sensation. He wasn't like Tyler, who had always been a chip off the old block; Cal's relationship with his father swung from warm and intimate to distant and strained. The source of the strain had varied over the years. As a youngster Cal had been less than enthusiastic about school, and his grades had reflected that. Every report card day had brought on a clash with his father. In high school he had been far more interested in girls than anything else. Womanizing, J.T. had called it; Cal just thought of it as having fun. His lack of any genuine interest in running the ranch had brought on more parental displeasure.

But nothing in recent years had colored their relationship as much as his chosen profession, and instinct told Cal that was exactly what his father had on his mind this morning.

J.T. was now seated in his chair, elbows propped on its arms, his index fingers forming a tepee while he regarded his son solemnly. "Cal, I think it's high time you quit the rodeo."

Cal expelled a labored breath. "You know how I feel about that, Daddy. It's the only thing I've found that I really enjoy."

"Yes, but there's more to life than enjoyment. You've been having fun since you got out of high school, and those are the years when most men are carving out careers for themselves. You have your priorities reversed, son. Work hard when you're young, then have a good time later. You're almost thirty, and you're not learning a thing that will do you a bit of good later in life. When I was your age, I could run this ranch single-handed.''

They had been through variations of this discussion many times before. Cal never knew what to say during these sessions. He had to guard against flip retorts, and he knew he couldn't launch much of a forceful argument because everything his father said was true. Rodeoing was not a lifetime career. The PRCA circuit was a training ground for nothing. But, God, how he loved it, and he hated the thought of giving it up while he was winning. In the past—usually after one of these run-ins with his father—he had given serious consideration to doing something else. But what? He couldn't picture himself as a full-time cowhand, and he had no training as anything else. "Look, Daddy, I know I can't ride forever, but—"

"And it's dangerous," J.T. went on, as though Cal hadn't spoken. "Every ride might be the one where you get hurt. You don't realize it, because thirty is pretty young, but your reflexes aren't what they were eight or nine years ago. You're not as supple. Do you want to go through life with a bum knee or bad back or worse? I'm telling you flat out that I want you to quit—now, while you're still hale and hearty. Not next week or next month, but now."

"Good grief, I'm leaving in the morning to rejoin the circuit. After this stint, we'll talk about it."

J.T. shook his head. "Not good enough. I want some assurances this time. I could use some help around here. The Double C will belong to you kids someday, and there's more to running it than riding herd on some cows.''

"Shoot, I know that, but—"

"And I'd like to see you give some thought to settling down and raising a family. I ought to have grandchildren by now."

"Well, I'm sure I will one of these days," Cal said weakly. Actually, having been so successful with women since he was old enough to date, he'd never given a minute's thought to the possibility of loving only one.

"You know, son, my daddy staunchly believed that if a man hadn't found his niche in life by the time he was thirty-five, chances were he never would. I agree with that, and I'm beginning to worry about you falling behind schedule."

The debate went on for some time. In the past, J.T. had terminated these discussions with something like, "Okay, you know how I feel," and that was the end of it. Not today. Today Cal was getting a good dose of Daddy's dynasty speech, mixed with a little McKinney family history. Why now? he wondered. Why had his father turned so damned adamant?

Then something occurred to him, something Cynthia had said to him just a few days ago. She'd asked him when he was going to start working on the ranch or "at least get a real job." She had implied that rodeoing was something for kids. He had bristled a bit at that, but since nothing bothered him for much more than a minute, he'd dismissed the remark. Now he wondered. If she felt that way, would she have mentioned it to J.T., thereby fueling his father's own feelings?

Since the day Cynthia had come to the ranch, Cal had not understood why Tyler and Lynn allowed the woman to bug them so much. They said she interfered, that she was a disruptive influence. Even his great-grandfather considered her a misfit. Cal had laughed that off, but he wasn't laughing now. She was meddling in his affairs, and he didn't like it worth a damn.

"I suppose Cynthia agrees with you," he said stiffly.

"I'm not sure that has anything to do with this, but as a matter of fact, she does. Why?"

"Do you think she has any business in my business?"

"Cal, there's a very good chance Cynthia will be a member of this family. Of course she's interested in you, in all of you."

Cal was tired of the discussion and could see it was going to end in a stalemate. "Well, I'll think about it long and hard while I'm out this time, Daddy," he promised halfheartedly. "That's the best I can do."

J.T. wasn't happy, Cal knew, and they parted on a cool note. He hated that. He wouldn't lose any sleep over it, but contrary to what Tyler thought, certain things did bother him, particularly going out on the circuit when loose ends dangled at home.

But more than anything, he worried that today's confrontation with his father might signal the beginning of the end of his rodeo career. J.T. had sounded very serious, more determined than ever before. Now his old man had an ally, someone who would keep his determination high. Cal had always managed to circumvent his father's objections to his career, chiefly because J.T. had so many other things on his mind. But now there was Cynthia. Why the hell didn't she just go back to Boston where she belonged and leave them in peace?

He was as upset as he had ever been. In the hall outside the study he made a fist with one hand and slammed it into the palm of the other. Then as he walked away he almost collided with Cynthia, who was coming toward the office. Her face broke into a smile when she saw him.

"Are you and your dad finished?" she asked.

Cal frowned darkly. "I'm afraid we've just started. Do me a favor, will you? Don't mention me to Daddy again. Just leave me out of your conversations altogether." Brushing past her, he headed for the front door.

Cynthia stared after him, her mouth agape. This was the first time she had seen Cal in anything but a sunny mood. Shrugging, she continued toward the study door, knocked twice and entered.

J.T. was standing in front of the window, hands clasped behind his back, head down. He turned when the door opened. "Come in, sweetheart."

"You and Cal must have had words."

"None we haven't had before."

"About quitting the rodeo?"

"Uh-huh." J.T. walked back to his desk and sat down. He looked rather tired, Cynthia thought.

"Do you think you made any headway with him this time?"

"Hard to say."

Cynthia thought of the uncharacteristic dark scowl on Cal's face and of what he'd said. "Did my name happen by chance to creep into the conversation?" she asked.

"Once. He asked if you agreed with me, and I said you did."

Cynthia sank into one of the chairs facing the desk. A sudden heaviness settled over her. Well, she'd certainly had a busy morning. She was sure Lynn was off somewhere licking her wounds and blaming Cynthia. She'd horrified Virginia by suggesting the sofa be moved. Now she had managed to alienate Cal. When one considered that Tyler looked right through her as though she weren't there, that Hank apparently disliked everything about her, and that Lettie Mae didn't want her near the kitchen, she was batting a thousand.

What if none of these things changed? Would J.T.'s love alone be enough to offset the others' hostility? If not, where did that leave her and J.T.?

"OH, I CAN'T STAND her!" Lynn exclaimed.

"You're just peeved over having your plans

changed," Beverly insisted. "We'll have the barbecue a week later."

"It's not just the barbecue. It's...everything. We always celebrate Daddy's birthday here at the ranch. Always. It just doesn't seem right not to."

The two women were in the stable, the place Lynn usually headed for when things weren't going right. Beverly had stopped by to see if Lynn wanted to go into town, and she'd found her cousin in the throes of a blue funk. She didn't know why a simple change of plans was such a big deal. "The barbecue will be just as much fun a week later. Personally, I think it's romantic of Cynthia to want to spirit J.T. away so they can be alone."

Lynn glared at her. "Why do you always do that?"

"Do what?" Beverly asked, puzzled.

"Take up for her. You always do, you know."

"Do I? Well...I like her. She's got class."

"She doesn't belong here," Lynn insisted. "She's too different."

"I'll give you that. She puts every woman for miles around in the shade."

Lynn wasn't in the mood for that kind of talk. She wasn't in the mood for one kind word about Cynthia Page. "I wish she would just leave so everything could return to normal. I'm surprised she's not already back in Boston. Unless she's incredibly dense, she must know that no one but Daddy wants her around."

"Maybe your dad is enough for her," Beverly said with an impish smile. "Did you ever think of that? Come on, Lynn. Loosen up."

At that moment Cal strolled into the cool, dim stable. He squinted to adjust his eyes to the changed light. "Hi, cuz," he said to Beverly. "What are you two up to?"

"Lynn's plotting ways to get rid of your wicked stepmother."

"She's not our stepmother," Lynn said quickly.

"Well, if you do think of a way to get rid of her," Cal said, "you can count on me for help."

Lynn looked surprised. "You? You've always been so nice to her."

"Not nice especially. Civil. But now she's turned into a buttinsky, and I don't need that, thanks."

His sister's interest was piqued. "What's she done?"

"She's been fanning the flames of Daddy's discontent with my chosen profession, and he's jumped on it like a dog on a bone." In a passable imitation of his father's voice, Cal related snatches of the father-son discussion.

"Who does she think she is?" Lynn asked in a huff. "Why doesn't she stay out of our affairs? Tyler says she's put all sorts of doubts in Daddy's head about wine making. That's none of her business. Can you imagine what it'll be like around here if she becomes Mrs. J. T. McKinney? She'll try to run everything."

Cal hooted. "That ought to be interesting—watching Daddy and Cynthia jockey for position. In case no one has noticed he likes to run everything, too."

Lynn's eyes widened, and she reached out to pinch his cheek affectionately. "You devil. You're a genius."

"I am?"

"You're right. Cynthia's an independent, take-charge type, and Daddy's overbearing, domineering and accustomed to having his word regarded as law. What eventually happens when two people like that come together? Why can't we use that to our advantage?"

Beverly had been listening to the exchange between sister and brother. Shaking her head in disbelief, she said, "You two slay me, you really do. Well, I'm off to town. Sure you don't want to come, Lynn?"

"I'm sure."

"Okay, I'll catch you later. Bye."

"Bye," Lynn and Cal chorused. A minute later they heard their cousin's sports car roar off. Cal sauntered over to a bale of hay and sat down. Lynn joined him, clasped one knee and hugged it to her chest. Cal studied her thoughtful face. "I don't think I follow you," he said. "How can we use their personalities to our advantage?"

"I'm not sure. It just doesn't seem to me that Daddy would like a bossy woman. Maybe he never sees that side of Cynthia. Maybe we ought to make sure he knows she butts in and how we feel about it."

"You're forgetting something," Cal said. "He's in love."

Lynn scoffed. "Are you sure?"

"Well, he's never come right out and said so in so many words, but he must be. Why else would she be here?"

Lynn chewed on her bottom lip and lapsed into thought. Finally she said, "I really do wish we could get rid of her."

"Rub her out, bump her off," Cal teased.

"Don't be funny. But why couldn't we make her life so miserable she'd want to leave?"

"I suppose that's possible. Don't ask me how, though."

"I think we'd be doing Daddy a favor. I can't imagine what he sees in her."

"Well, now, Lynn, in all fairness I must tell you I know what he sees in her. She's a damned good-looking woman."

"The world is full of pretty women. Daddy wouldn't stay interested in just a pretty face for long. What else about her appeals to him? She's not a bit like Mama."

"No, I'll grant you that. Maybe the difference is the attraction. Daddy's probably never known a woman like her. Who knows what attracts people to each other?"

"You're lucky to be leaving tomorrow," Lynn said wistfully. "I don't think living around here is going to be much fun if she stays."

Cal sighed and stood up. "This is getting a bit heavy for me. I want to try to find some fun my last day home." He reached out and rumpled Lynn's hair. "I'll leave you and Tyler to hold the fort and keep the home fires burning. Chin up, old girl. There's a good chance Cynthia Page will someday be nothing but a dim, distant memory. And if she isn't . . . well, I imagine we'll survive."

Giving her shoulder a pat, he ambled out of the stable into the sunshine. Lynn stared after him, wishing she possessed a tenth of her older brother's easygoing nature. Sure, Cal was miffed at Cynthia now, but that wouldn't last long. Lynn couldn't shake things off so easily.

She had done a lot of soul-searching lately, trying to come up with what it was about Cynthia that put her off so. Normally she didn't form quick opinions about people. The real problem was that she hadn't expected her father to ever become interested in another woman; it was that simple. He and her mother had been so close for such a long time, they'd gone together like bacon and eggs. Lynn, Cal and Tyler had grown up in an idyllic household, with a woman who thrived on motherhood and a man who epitomized strength and stability. With her mother gone, Lynn had increasingly turned to her father for reassurance, like a security blanket. Now that Cynthia had entered the picture, Lynn felt disoriented, as if she was floundering. She didn't think she could ever accept another woman's right to live in the house, sleep in her father's bed and direct the household activities.

Make her life so miserable she'd want to leave. That was an appealing thought, but how did one go about accomplishing it? For sure she couldn't do it alone, Lynn realized. She'd need an ally, an accomplice. Cal would be gone and, puzzling as it was to Lynn, Tyler wouldn't even talk about Cynthia. A pained expression crossed his face whenever her name was mentioned, but he never came right out and said how he felt about her. Lynn assumed he found the idea of his father's remarrying as distasteful as she did but considered himself above family squabbling.

She stood, shoved her hands into the pockets of her jeans, left the stable and looked toward the house. Virginia was hanging sheets on the clothesline. Lynn wondered if theirs was the only household left in America where sheets were still hung out to dry. Pauline had loved the smell of sheets dried in the sunshine, so Virginia still followed the outmoded practice. In fact, the housekeeper still did everything the way Pauline had liked it done. She had adored her mistress.

The thought no sooner formed in Lynn's mind than another joined it. Surely Virginia hated the idea of J.T.'s marrying again. And there was no doubt how Lettie Mae felt about Cynthia's penchant for cooking. What better allies could she have? Quickening her step, she walked on toward the house.

"Morning, Virginia," she greeted as she neared the housekeeper.

"Morning. Nice one, isn't it?"

"Did you hear? You and Lettie Mae can forget the birthday barbecue."

Virginia picked up the empty laundry basket. "Oh?"

Falling in step, the two women headed for the back door. "Yeah, Cynthia's taking Daddy to New Orleans that weekend," Lynn explained with a toss of her head. The tone of her voice left no doubt as to how she felt about it.

"Well, she certainly seems bent on changing as much around here as she can," Virginia said with a disgruntled sniff. "This morning she wanted to rearrange the entire living room. I told her I thought not, but I haven't heard the last of it, I'm sure. There's no telling what she'll do if she and J.T. get married."

"My thoughts exactly," Lynn said, "and I want to talk to you and Lettie Mae about just that."

CHAPTER NINE

DURING THE DAYS that followed, Cynthia was much too busy with preparations for the New Orleans trip to notice the deepening currents of hostility swirling around her. Had she been more alert she might have noticed a change of atmosphere, but to her it seemed nothing much had changed. Lynn remained unapproachable, as did Tyler. Cynthia attributed Lynn's behavior to the young woman's naturally aloof nature. Tyler was a mystery she was no longer interested in solving. She found it far easier to understand Virginia and Lettie Mae. They wanted her to be Pauline all over again. Maybe Hank did, too. Cynthia had no idea how close the old man had been to his grandson's wife.

Now that Cal was gone, J.T. had begun urging her to move into the main house, but Cynthia didn't think the time was right. When she moved in, she would be Mrs. McKinney, and they would all have to live with that. For now, the guest house was her refuge, a place where she and J.T. could be alone and talk freely. In spite of earlier vows, she headed for it like a port in a storm whenever J.T. was away from the ranch or otherwise occupied. She did not think of what she was doing as hiding or sticking her head in the sand. Rather, she was convinced she was keeping the peace. After all, she had made a major concession in deciding to wait until she and J.T. were married before imposing any of her own changes on the household. She stayed out of the kitchen, even when the urge to whip up something was all but irresistible. She thought they had achieved a cautious détente, and she frankly gave herself the lion's share of credit for that.

Still, it was all a bit nerve-fraying. Although Cynthia was convinced her patience would be rewarded one day, she could hardly wait to get on that plane for New Orleans.

"WELL, that *is* good news, Larry," J.T. said into the phone, a broad smile crossing his face. "Not a minute too soon, either. I'm leaving town on a little vacation tomorrow, and I hated going off with this hanging over my head."

"Yeah," Larry said. "It took us a while, but we finally got 'em. As we suspected, it was an organized gang. Half a dozen of 'em working out of San Antonio."

"Good work. My men will be glad to hear it."

"You know there's something that puzzles me about the bunch, though."

"What's that?"

"They 'fessed up to thieving on a lot of ranches, but I never could get 'em to admit to stealing Double C beef. That bothered me for a spell, but then I figure they probably don't even remember all the folks they stole from. Or it could be they think an outfit the size of the Double C might have some influence with the law. They're the ones, though. Gotta be.''

"I appreciate all your hard work, Larry."

"Don't mention it. I'll swear if the judge only gives 'em a slap on the wrist this time, folks in downtown Dallas are gonna be able to hear me squall.''

J.T. chuckled. "I don't blame you. Good luck with an indictment."

"Thanks. Be talking to you, J.T.''

Cynthia walked into the study just as J.T. hung up the phone. "What put that cat-got-the-canary look on your face?" she asked.

"They caught the cattle thieves."

"Oh, good. I know you're pleased."

"More than just pleased. Now I won't have that on my mind while we're gone."

Cynthia impulsively rounded the desk and threw herself on his lap, locking her arms around his neck. She gave him a sound kiss. "I can hardly wait! Are you excited?''

"Yes, because you are." J.T. rubbed her jean-clad thigh and smiled at her fondly. Sometimes her big-city sophistication slipped enough to reveal a glimpse of girlish enthusiasm. When that happened, she was a delight.

He thought things couldn't have been going better. In the future he vowed not to blow their differences all out of proportion. Their chief difference, it seemed to him, was that Cynthia was a product of modern times. At thirty-five, she was eager to try every newfangled gadget and theory that came along. Maybe at thirty-five he had, too; he couldn't remember. If she couldn't understand why he wanted to do things the way he always had, it was because she hadn't lived long enough to know how comforting the tried and true could be.

Thinking that prompted him to dwell on the one difference that did trouble him from time to time—their ages. He often brooded about that, wondering if he would be doing her a disservice by marrying her. She was so young and vital, and by becoming his wife she would almost surely sentence herself to a relatively young widowhood. The thought always took him aback because it forced him to think about his own mortality. Then he would be reminded that Pauline had left him a relatively young widower, and, painful as that had been, the world had not stopped.

Increasingly, J.T. knew he wanted to marry Cynthia. She was the only woman since Pauline he wanted around all the time. And all couples had their differences. He had come close to asking her to set the date last night, but as she had chattered away happily about their upcoming trip, he'd decided to formally propose while they were in New Orleans. She wanted a romantic weekend, and what was more romantic than a marriage proposal?

Now he said, "I suppose you have our itinerary worked out to the last minute?"

"No, not down to the last minute—there has to be room for spontaneity. But there are some musts. The hotel is supposed to have this great restaurant, so I thought we could have dinner there tomorrow night. Then Saturday we ought to get in some serious sight-seeing. There are a few restaurants we simply mustn't miss, but other than that..."

The door to the study opened, and Tyler entered the room. "Daddy, I—"

He stopped and looked struck dumb by the sight of Cynthia perched on his father's lap. For what could only have been a second but seemed much longer, J.T.'s son simply stared at them. Then he gave a start and looked at the floor. "I'll talk to you later," he mumbled, pivoted and hurried out of the room.

An involuntary sigh escaped Cynthia's lips. She glanced at J.T., an apology ready, but to her surprise, he was grinning. "I guess it was a shock for him to see his old man with a nubile nymph on his lap."

"I guess. And I'm nubile but no nymph," she said. She wondered whether he really didn't see how hostile his children were toward her, or whether he saw it and chose to ignore it. But if there weren't some marked changes in their attitudes soon, détente was going to crumble right before their eyes.

BY FRIDAY EVENING, Cynthia couldn't stop congratulating herself. Now that they were actually there, the trip to New Orleans seemed like a brilliant, almost inspired idea. The flight from Austin had been smooth and as uneventful as airplane rides were supposed to be. Their hotel was perfect, an older place in the heart of the French Quarter, where law limited the size of buildings. What their accommodations lacked in glitz was more than made up for by charm and coziness.

The only tense moment came when she marched up to the registration desk, produced a credit card and said, "I'm Cynthia Page. I have reservations for a double." J.T. blanched, backed off a few steps and pretended to study an array of brochures in a nearby rack. She supposed he was trying to give the impression he wasn't with her, but at least he said nothing. She considered that a real plus. Obviously he was as committed to the weekend as she was.

"Do you like it?" she asked eagerly after they had had time to inspect their room.

"It's delightful," J.T. told her. "How did you know about this place? You said you've never been to New Orleans."

"Sally told me about it. She and Ted spent their honeymoon here, and they try to come back every year on their anniversary. Isn't that a delightful custom? She said that staying here is like visiting a wealthy relative who wants to pamper you."

The evening turned out to be a study in perfection. Cynthia detected a noticeable relaxation overtaking J.T. Free of the constant demands on his time that he experienced daily at the ranch, he seemed much younger, looser, freer. That only reinforced her belief that he let his family, friends and staff take advantage of him. Her mission in life, she decided on the spot, would be to give him more such carefree weekends. It was Boston all over again, only more exciting because the city was new to both of them.

That first evening, however, they stuck close to their hotel. After drinks in their room, they went down to dinner. The restaurant was everything Sally had promised—exquisite decor, superb food, efficient but unobtrusive service. Afterward, they strolled outside and dropped into a nearby jazz spot to listen to Dixieland jazz for almost an hour. Cynthia felt the magic returning. Tyler, Lynn, Hank, Virginia, Lettie Mae and the ranch all seemed very far away and very, very unimportant.

The following day, J.T.'s birthday, they did all the things affluent visitors to the city normally did—breakfast at Brennan's, dinner at Antoine's, and plenty of sight-seeing and shopping. They even managed to work in an afternoon river cruise before hurrying back to the hotel to dress for dinner. It was almost midnight when they returned to their room, exhilarated and a trifle giddy from the day's whirlwind activities.

"Tell me something," J.T. said as he shed his jacket and tie, "what's all this costing you?"

"Let me worry about that," Cynthia admonished.

"No, I want to know. You won't let me pay for a thing, and I'm curious. For instance, what did breakfast cost?"

She decided to tell him. "Thirty-five dollars."

J.T. looked stunned. "You paid thirty-five dollars for us to have breakfast?"

"No, I paid thirty-five dollars for me to have breakfast. I also paid thirty-five dollars for you to have breakfast."

He made a show of clutching his heart. "Seventy dollars for breakfast! I'm glad I didn't know at the time. I wouldn't have been able to digest my food."

"But wasn't it glorious food? When was the last time you had a three-course breakfast? Confess now, was today a birthday to remember or what?"

J.T. took her hand and gallantly lifted it to his lips. "It was wonderful. I don't know how to thank you."

"You don't? Well, I'll bet I can think of something."

She was wearing a slender black sheath, a mere slip of a dress that exposed her smooth shoulders, arms and a wide expanse of her back. Its only adornment was an opera-length strand of pearls. Not many women could get away with that dress, J.T. thought admiringly. He watched, fascinated, as she deftly lifted the necklace over her head and placed it on a nearby table before effortlessly wiggling out of the dress. It fell in a puddle around her ankles. She stood before him in a black lace undergarment that was skimpier than most swimsuits. Her eyes twinkled merrily, almost mischievously.

J.T. sucked in his breath. She was without question the most alluring woman in the world. He did not think he was dishonoring Pauline's memory by considering Cynthia the most beautiful woman he had ever known. Drawing her to him, he covered her mouth with his, burrowed his face in the curve of her neck, held her and stroked her until he felt her tremble. It pleased him, and sometimes amazed him, that he could arouse her so readily. He stepped back and looked at her clad only in the filmy lingerie and black high heels, her golden hair shimmering like waves of wheat in sunshine. She was part vixen, part goddess, and wholly desirable.

"I love you, Cynthia Anita," he said solemnly, like a man taking an oath. "I have from the moment I met you."

That declaration sounded more profound than it ever had before, so much so that Cynthia felt her throat clog with emotion. "And I love you, John Travis. More than I know how to tell you."

Kicking off her shoes, she turned and went to the bed. During their absence that evening, it had been readied for them, its thick spread folded neatly at the foot, pillows plumped, sheets turned back. In a fluid gesture, she stripped off her remaining piece of clothing and her pantyhose, slid between the sheets and waited for J.T. to undress.

When he joined her under the covers, he immediately began the sensitive, tactile exploration of her body that usually preceded their lovemaking. Her smoothness and firmness so pleased him that he could never get enough of touching her, and the caressing usually went on for some time. Tonight, however,

Cynthia was impatient. Her body twisted and turned into his, making silent demands. Her very impatience inflamed him, imbued him with strength and delight. He felt young and vital, like a man at the very height of his sexual power. Pulling her to him, he stroked and petted her, felt her body's heat seep into his veins. He held off as long as he could, then entered her. They caught the rhythm of longtime lovers. When at last, in a violent burst of passion, they completed each other, J.T. was sure he was living out every romantic fantasy he'd ever had.

For a long time they lay still, wrapped in each other's arms. Finally he broke the silence. "You're wonderful," he whispered.

"You're pretty special yourself."

He kissed her and brushed her hair away from her face. "This has been a memorable day."

"Better than a barbecue at the ranch?" she teased.

"I'm afraid I have to say yes. And to cap it off, I have a question I'd like to ask."

"Ask away."

"Will you marry me? Soon? Right away?"

Cynthia bolted straight up in bed. "Are you sure, J.T.?" she asked breathlessly.

"Very sure."

"Then of course the answer is yes." She lay back down beside him. She had been so right to bring him here. Her dreams were coming true after all.

"I suppose you'll want to have the wedding in Boston," J.T. remarked.

Cynthia considered for a moment. If the wedding was held in Boston, Alicia would want the works, the to-do of the decade, requiring months of preparation. Cynthia had served as a bridesmaid in countless such society weddings, and she considered them largely a pain. When the big day finally rolled around, the bride was often more in need of a sanitarium than a church. "No," she said. "By the time my mother got through making her plans, it would be only slightly less opulent than a royal wedding. You'd hate it, trust me. I'll have my folks come to Texas, and we'll get married at the ranch. Is that all right?"

"Sounds great to me." His arm slid beneath her shoulder, and she buried her face against his chest.

J.T. was asleep within seconds, but Cynthia's mind spun with thoughts and plans. The wedding would be all her show. She would plan everything down to the last detail. She hoped Lynn, Virginia and Lettie Mae would accept the inevitable and join in. If they didn't, she wouldn't let it ruin her grand day.

There was more behind her decision to be married at the Double C than wanting to be spared a formal wedding and its attendant headaches. She wanted everybody—J.T.'s friends, his workers and especially his family—to actually see her become Mrs. John Travis McKinney. Then there would be no mistake about who the lady of the house was.

THE DOUBLE C RANCH was at its sleepiest on Sunday mornings. If there were no pressing matters demanding attention, most of the workers were given the day off. In the main house today, Lettie Mae bustled around the kitchen, preparing the usual lavish Sunday dinner, though only Hank, Tyler, Lynn, Virginia and herself were there to eat it. A feast served at one o'clock had been one of Pauline's cherished traditions, so it wouldn't have occurred to any of them to grab a bite and run. The sound of the cook's humming mingled with the clatter of pots and pans that echoed through the quiet house.

In his father's study, Tyler sat behind the mahogany desk and regarded his sister solemnly. "You want to know what I think? I think it's childish. It could backfire in your face. I hope you don't think I'm going to be a party to it. I would like to think you, Virginia and Lettie Mae have a lot more to do than think up ways of making Cynthia's life miserable."

"Do you want Daddy to marry her?" Lynn asked with a dark frown.

"If it's what Daddy wants..."

"I don't think Daddy is thinking clearly these days. Cal agrees with me. So does Grandpa Hank. She doesn't belong here. Our lives will never be the same if she stays. She's already spoiled your plans for the vineyard—"

"Not entirely," Tyler interrupted. "They've just been put on hold temporarily."

"Are you sure? And she's got Daddy all stirred up about Cal and the rodeo. All day yesterday I just felt sick. I can't remember a time in my entire life when

Daddy wasn't here on his birthday, when we didn't have some kind of celebration, even if it was only family."

"Lynn, you're resisting change," Tyler said gently. "I guess that's normal, but change is inevitable. Our lives changed drastically when Mama died."

Lynn's eyes wandered to her mother's picture on the bookcase behind the desk. "When I think of the kind of person she was...so sweet, so eager to please, so..."

"Willing to do what Daddy wanted without question," Tyler finished for her.

"Yes," Lynn hissed. "Cynthia's not like that at all."

"I don't think either of us knows what she's like because we haven't taken the trouble to find out."

"Since when did you become her champion? When did you join her side?"

"I'm not on anybody's side," Tyler insisted, "and I don't think you should be, either. But I've been doing some thinking. This is Daddy's business, not ours. Back off. If he marries her, try to make friends with her. That's the best advice I can give you."

Lynn opened her mouth to say something, then closed it, stood and left the room. Tyler stared after her, slowly shaking his head. Cynthia really got to Lynn, and Virginia and Lettie Mae gossiped about her all the time. Every word, every move, every mannerism came under their microscopic scrutiny. From what he could gather, they hadn't found much they liked. Even Grandpa Hank said Cynthia was "trouble looking for a place to happen."

They all assumed Tyler disliked her, too, but that wasn't the case, not any longer. True, in the beginning he had found it all but impossible to think of another Mrs. J. T. McKinney. And his initial physical attraction to Cynthia had been so unsettling, so frightening that he'd kept his distance, prudently, he thought. But now, thank God, he was past that or hoped he was, and it occurred to him he hadn't been quite fair. Maybe if, instead of staying aloof, he tried to show her his side of the vineyard issue, she might approve. He was persuasive, and she was bright. She also, as his father pointed out on every possible occasion, had a good business head on her shoulders. Since she did, he could show her in terms of dollars and cents that ranching was no longer financially viable, while wine making was quickly establishing itself in the state. Cynthia would be a powerful ally. Anyone with an open mind and eye could see she had made his father happy. Tyler thought it was time all of them gave the lady a chance.

He wondered what Lynn, Virginia and Lettie Mae had in mind when they said they wanted "to make her so miserable she'll want to leave." What could those three possibly do? The worst was make themselves look foolish. Cynthia was too smart to fall for anything they could come up with.

CYNTHIA AND J.T. FILLED every minute of Sunday. They toured the Garden District, lunched at Commander's Palace, and that night they dined aboard a wonderful Mississippi River steamboat. They both were in a lighthearted mood and had a wonderful time, but by Monday morning, J.T. was itching to get home.

He was standing in the bathroom, shaving. "Enough is enough," he said with a grin. "I can only stand so much fun. I want to get back to work."

But for Cynthia, it was over much too soon. She wouldn't have cared if they never went back. She no sooner thought that, however, than she scolded herself. The Double C was going to be home, so she had to start thinking of it that way. J.T.'s family and his friends were going to be her life.

She gave the contents of her suitcase careful scrutiny, then went into the bathroom to gather up her cosmetics and toiletries. As she picked up the case containing her birth control pills, she grinned. "When these are gone, I'm not going to refill the prescription. Being pregnant on my wedding day wouldn't bother me a bit." Winking at J.T., she left the bathroom, oblivious to the peculiar look on his face.

But he came into the room almost on her heels, wiping his face with a towel. "Cynthia, sweetheart, please tell me you were joking."

"Joking? About what?"

"The pills. You weren't serious, right?"

"Wrong," she said, tucking items into the pockets of the suitcase. "I've never been more serious about anything...except loving you, of course. There are four more pills in that case, and when they're gone, that's it. I want to conceive as soon as possible.''

J.T. sank down on the edge of the bed. He looked like a man who'd just received a severe blow to his stomach. "I'm too goddamned old to have a baby!"

Cynthia chuckled. "Don't be ridiculous. You are not. Men far older than you father children."

"I don't *want* a baby!"

He said it so vehemently that Cynthia looked at him. Her smile faded as she realized how serious he was. "Of course you do."

"Of course I don't."

"Well, I do, and I deserve one. Every woman does who can have one."

J.T. looked stunned. "Why didn't it even once cross my mind you might be thinking along these lines? I thought . . . I thought just the two of us . . ." Standing, he walked to her, took her by the shoulders and smiled down at her. "Please, sweetheart, just forget it."

Cynthia did not smile back. "That's not fair, J.T., and I think you know it."

"A baby will only clutter up our lives. I don't have the patience for small children."

"What about all those grandchildren you insist you want?"

"That's different. Please . . . forget it. Keep taking the pill, or use something else, or I'll use something, but let's not talk about having babies again. I'm not in the least interested in starting a second family. Good God, I'd be over seventy when the poor kid graduated from high school!" He walked back to the bathroom shaking his head.

Cynthia was speechless. She didn't want to end their lovely weekend with a quarrel, so she would force herself not to say anything else until they were back at the ranch. But he hadn't heard the last of this by any means.

Naturally, she was distressed that J.T. didn't want a child. It hadn't once occurred to her that he wouldn't. But she was even more distressed that he had handed down another unilateral decision and apparently expected her to accept it without question.

And she knew how J.T. could be when he dug in his heels. The upcoming clash of wills would not be a minor skirmish. And why, dear Lord, did he so often put her in the position of needing to win a battle or score a point? She closed the suitcase and placed it on the floor, her spirits plummeting. Why did nothing come easy with him?

J.T. came out of the bathroom and began putting his things in his garment bag. He couldn't have looked more unconcerned. Obviously he thought the matter was settled. He had spoken; that was that.

True to her vow, however, Cynthia said nothing more about having a baby, not during the ride to the airport, not during the flight to Austin, not during the drive to the Double C. But the subject was never out of her thoughts. She knew she could have "an accident." Those happened all the time. But that was dirty pool and not the way she liked to operate. She would bide her time and pick her moment. J.T. would come around.

But what if he didn't? What if this turned out to be a case like the computer or that damned credit card? Would she still want to marry him, knowing that childlessness was part of the bargain?

She knew that if she loved him—and she did—she should say yes unhesitatingly. Unfortunately, saying yes just wasn't that easy.

J.T. MADE SOMETHING of a production out of telling his family he and Cynthia were getting married. He waited until after dinner, then rose from the table and fastened his peerless smile on Tyler and Lynn. "I'd like both of you to know," he said, "that I have asked Cynthia to marry me, and she has accepted my proposal. We'll be married here at the earliest possible time. I don't want to drag my heels." He made a point of shooting Cynthia a look of utter devotion.

The silence following the announcement was brief, so brief J.T. might not have noticed it, but it momentarily stung Cynthia. She looked at Lynn, and for one awful second she thought J.T.'s daughter was going to cry. Tyler, however, reacted quickly. Getting to his feet, he went to his father and offered his hand. "Congratulations, Daddy." He then walked to Cynthia's chair and said, "I hope you'll be very happy. I mean that." And the curious thing was, he sounded sincere. When did we turn a corner? Cynthia wondered.

Lynn had gone to her father and put her arms around his waist. If she said anything, Cynthia did not hear what it was. She simply hugged J.T. ferociously, then mumbled her own congratulations and fled the room. The scene had hardly been one of unrestrained joy, but all in all, it hadn't been as bad as Cynthia had feared.

After dinner, she and J.T. holed up in the study to make plans. They tentatively selected the week before Christmas as the date. That would give Cynthia plenty of time to tie up loose ends in Boston, make arrangements for moving her belongings and get back to the ranch to plan the ceremony and reception. With that much decided, Cynthia went out to the guest house and called, first Sally, then her parents, with the news. Her father answered the phone, listened, said, "Well, well," then quickly put her mother on the phone.

"So you really are going to marry your cowboy," Alicia said. She didn't sound overjoyed.

"I really am, Mom."

"The week before Christmas? Dear me, I have so much to do. I suppose my first move should be to get in touch with Father Parker, then the florist and the caterer. Or perhaps I should order the invitations first. You can't start these arrangements too early, you know. Christmas? Goodness, the people I use for parties are booked up months in advance. I really wish you'd give me more time, Cynthia."

"Mom, you don't have to do a thing but make a list of people you want to invite and buy a plane ticket.

We're getting married here at the ranch. Everything will be handled from this end.''

Cynthia heard a gasp. "Cynthia Anita Page! You aren't getting married here...in the church you grew up in? How can you do this to me? Every Page since—''

"I know, Mom, but it would get out of hand. Those things always do. J.T. and I want to keep it small and intimate.''

"Since the day you were born, I have dreamed of the kind of wedding I would someday give you. This is unseemly...and unfair of you, too.''

Cynthia sighed. Alicia was a master at the art of guilt trips. "Please, Mom, I'm thirty-five and have been on my own for years. A wedding like you're thinking of would be in poor taste for a woman my age.'' That should do it, Cynthia thought. Alicia could forgive unseemliness, but never poor taste.

"Well...'' A sigh followed. "I don't know what the rest of the family is going to think about this.''

"They'll probably be thrilled to be spared having to attend yet another grand wedding.''

"I suppose you'll make me a grandmother one of these days.''

"I certainly hope so. I'm anxious for motherhood. And I thought you wanted to see the next generation.''

"Oh, I do, I do,'' Alicia said quickly. "I'm just not anxious to be...called Grandmother.''

"You'll love it once it happens. Listen, Mom, I'll be coming back soon to tie everything up."

"All right, dear. Just let me know when."

They hung up, and for several minutes Cynthia stood studying a fingernail. She thought a long talk with her mother might do her some good. There were tricks of the wifely trade, and her female parent knew them all. Alicia honestly believed a smart woman could have her way ninety-five percent of the time while making her husband think he was having his way all the time. And that certainly worked in the Page household. Alicia ruled the roost, but Joseph thought he was lord and master.

However, Cynthia conceded, her father was a quiet, studious man who bent over backward to avoid scenes. Hardly a J. T. McKinney.

But I'm going to get my baby, Cynthia decided. It would be interesting to see what happened when unyielding stubbornness came smack up against dogged determinaton.

WHILE CYNTHIA was talking to her mother, Lynn sat in Virginia's room, commiserating with the housekeeper and Lettie Mae. Her father's announcement had come as such a shock, even though they had been half expecting it. Nevertheless, she felt sick inside, as if she were standing on the sidelines, watching disaster in the making but powerless to intervene. "It was that trip to New Orleans," she said bitterly. "Now we're too late. It's going to happen."

Virginia flicked at an imaginary speck of dust on her bedside table, then glanced first at Lettie Mae, then at Lynn. "Maybe not," she said enigmatically. "There might still be time."

CHAPTER TEN

MARTIN AVERY HAD dinner at the Double C the next evening. He and J.T. had some legal matters to discuss afterward, and Cynthia was not asked to join them. For once she didn't care. There was only one thing on her mind now—her campaign to soften J.T.'s hard-line stand against fatherhood. She spent the evening in the guest house, shampooing her hair, doing her nails and making lists. When ten-thirty came, she glanced out the window and noticed Martin's car still parked in front of the house. J.T. almost certainly wouldn't be joining her tonight, so she turned out the lights and fell into a deep sleep. Perhaps tomorrow.

However, when she went to the house for breakfast the next morning, J.T. informed her he had a breakfast meeting with Martin in Crystal Creek and would be gone until lunch. Cynthia suffered through another mostly conversationless meal, though Tyler, for the first time, tried to liven things up a bit. Very cautiously, however, almost as if he didn't want to appear disloyal to Lynn. Cynthia couldn't imagine what had prompted the change in his attitude toward her, but she gratefully accepted it as one small victory.

After breakfast, she beat a hasty exit for her private retreat, since there were a number of things requiring her attention. Her mother had forwarded her mail; there were bills to pay and letters to answer.

But the guest house had no desk or anything that could serve as one. There was also no stationery. Cynthia was sure she could find anything she needed in J.T.'s study so she gathered her correspondence and returned to the big house.

The housekeeper was dusting the study. "Virginia, we really should put a small secretary desk out in the guest house. It would be a thoughtful gesture for guests. I have some work to do and nowhere to do it. I'll just do it in here, if that's all right."

There was a slight pause before Virginia said, "I . . . guess so."

"It's awfully cluttered," Cynthia commented. That was an understatement. There wasn't an inch of clear space on the entire desktop. "How does he work in this mess?" Setting her own things in the chair, she methodically began sorting through the papers.

In front of her Virginia watched, opened her mouth to say something but quickly closed it. Giving the study a final inspection, she left the room.

Cynthia's desk at the bank stayed pin neat at all times, and how she longed for it right now. She carefully sorted all the papers, putting them in orderly stacks around the perimeter of the desktop. Pencils and pens went in the drawer where they belonged.

Then when everything was nice and neat, she sat down to do her own work.

The task consumed almost two hours, but that still left her with an hour or more before J.T. returned from town. She wandered out near the bunkhouse, where she ran into Ken. They talked for a few minutes, but he had work to do. Cynthia thought how nice it would be to go to the stable and visit with Lynn, but their relationship simply did not invite visiting. J.T. was going to have to give her more to do around the ranch. She would go crazy trying to fill up idle hours.

Then something wonderful occurred to her, and as she walked back to the guest house where she could at least read a magazine, she smiled secretly. Once the wedding took place, she wouldn't have too many idle hours. She was going to go through that house like a whirlwind. No one would recognize it when she got through with it. She knew exactly what she wanted—color, lots of it, brightness, plants everywhere and a kitchen open and accessible to the dining room. She would even knock out walls if she took a mind to.

Then, hopefully, a baby would be on the way. Cynthia didn't think she'd ever find herself with an idle hour once she was a mother. Somehow she had to make J.T. realize how desperately she wanted this. She was full of feminine conviction. Once a baby in her womb was fact, J.T. would, of course, be thrilled. All her life she'd been told she had persuasive powers. If ever they were to work for her, let it be now.

"UNDERSTAND you two are gettin' hitched," Hank said as Cynthia and J.T. were sitting down for lunch.

"That's right, Grandpa," J.T. said.

Hank squinted over at Cynthia. He held a cigarette pinched between his thumb and forefinger. Cynthia passed a hand over her nose in an effort to fan away the smell, and he grinned. "Spose you'll be wantin' to make all kinds of changes . . . polky-dotted sofas and the like."

"Well . . . I really haven't thought too much about it, Mr. Travis," she lied.

"Remember, we all like the house the way it is. Don't go makin' a lot of changes. We're not much on changes."

Tell me about it, Cynthia thought wryly.

"Aren't you having lunch, Grandpa?" J.T. asked as Hank turned to leave the room.

"Nope. I had me a sandwich. I'm not one for heavy food in the middle of the day."

Once Hank was safely out of hearing range, J.T. told Cynthia, "He grazes all day. I don't think he ever eats what you and I would call a meal."

"I know his hip gives him a fit," she commented, "but other than that, he seems fairly healthy for a man his age. Those are his own teeth, aren't they? He still reads and watches TV."

J.T. nodded. "He's slipped badly in the past few years, but it's remarkable he's lived so long, all things considered. He still smokes those god-awful cigarettes. He still swigs bourbon instead of taking the pain pills Nate Purdy gives him. He once told me that when he was working a rig, he ate two bologna sandwiches and three chocolate cupcakes for lunch every day. I personally have never seen him eat anything green except guacamole. Wouldn't a modern nutritionist have a field day with him?"

"Should he be living alone in that house? Wouldn't he be safer here?"

"Probably, but he won't hear of it. That stone house is his last vestige of independence."

Since neither Tyler nor Lynn was home for lunch, Cynthia and J.T. had their first meal alone since New Orleans. He related all the gossip he had heard in town that morning; Crystal Creek's citizens lived off the stuff. Very little of his news meant anything to Cynthia, but she listened intently, realizing the little conversational tidbits would be helpful to her when she was part of the local scene.

Then they talked about the wedding. J.T. sounded enthusiastic when he told her she could do whatever she wanted, keep it small or pull out all the stops. Cynthia had one definite request, that it be an Episcopalian ceremony. J.T. thought about that, having assumed Reverend Blake would officiate. He finally agreed that Howard and Eva Blake could be honored guests, and they'd find an Episcopalian minister somewhere. He seemed to be in as affectionate and agreeable a mood as Cynthia had ever seen him. When they went into the study after lunch, she turned deliberately and closed the door behind them. Now, she decided, was as good a time as any to bring up the subject of the baby.

Suddenly, from behind her came a strange sound— as if someone were being strangled. Turning, she saw J.T. standing behind his desk, a look of utter horror on his face. "Who the hell has been messing with my desk?" he yelled.

"I straightened it up, if that's what you mean. I had some work to do, and there wasn't a clear surface anywhere."

His chest heaved. "Cynthia, no one is ever supposed to touch my desk. No one . . . ever! Everyone in this house knows that's rule number one."

Cynthia's eyes narrowed; she pursed her lips and crossed her arms under her breasts. "Everyone?" she asked.

"Yes, yes, everyone," he said irritably. "It'll take me days to find everything."

"Oh, that's ridiculous." She walked to the desk and gestured with an arm. "I sorted through everything carefully and made logical little stacks. All the invoices are there. Here are all the government reports. The pencils and pens are in the drawer where they belong. I don't know how you work in such a jumbled mess." She also didn't know where all the ridiculous rules around the ranch had come from. She had learned that no one would dream of sitting in Hank's rocker. Of course no one but Lettie Mae was ever supposed to go near the kitchen range. Now no one was ever supposed to touch J.T.'s desk.

"Just don't…ever touch my desk again!" he yelled.

"Stop yelling at me!"

J.T. sat down and heaved another sigh, collecting himself. "I'm sorry. I just don't like having my desk touched. But I suppose you had no way of knowing that. Now you do."

"Yes," Cynthia said icily. "Now I do." Her eyes fell on Pauline's picture behind his desk. The woman's serene countenance smiled back at her. *Did you ever have to put up with things like this, or did you instinctively know the right way to handle him?* Probably the latter, Cynthia decided. Early in their relationship J.T. had told her he and Pauline had literally known each other all their lives. His quick and sometimes irrational temper would have been no surprise to his first wife.

Of course it would have been easy to tell him Virginia had been standing right there when she began cleaning off the desk, but that would sound childish. But she did wonder why the housekeeper hadn't warned her that touching his desk would send J.T. into a rage. Had she hoped to foment discord? If so, she had succeeded. Wisely, Cynthia decided this afternoon was not the best time to talk about the baby.

A knock sounded on the door. "Come in," J.T. called.

The door opened, and Ken Slattery stepped into the room. "I got some bad news, boss," the foreman said.

"Wonderful," J.T. growled. "Just what I need. What is it?"

"More cows missing. Three this time."

J.T. slammed his fist on the desk. "Son of a bitch! Larry told me those thieves had been caught."

Ken scratched his head. "We counted the herd twice. There's no mistake."

J.T.'s expression, which had been none too pleasant to begin with, darkened further. He grabbed the phone, flipped through a rotary file, then dialed. "Let me speak to Larry Wendt," he snapped when his call was answered.

As he waited, he fumed. He hated his stormy moods, particularly when they were tinged with remorse. He'd had no business flying off the handle and yelling at Cynthia. She couldn't have known how he felt about his desk, and he imagined at her own desk she was a neat freak. He often wished he could curb his temper—to his notion it was his greatest fault—but diplomacy and restraint were not his strong suits. When he was unhappy, the world knew about it, and it was highly unlikely he would change much at the age of fifty-six.

"Larry Wendt," a voice on the other end of the line said.

"Larry? J.T. I thought you told me those rustlers were caught."

"They were."

"Then how come I've got more cows missing?"

"I don't know. It wouldn't be that bunch who did the taking, J.T. I'd make book on that. Those boys are waiting for the grand jury hearing, and they're plenty scared.''

"Could there be another gang working?"

"I haven't heard any reports." Larry paused. "You know, you might have some locals doing a little thieving, or... you might want to consider the possibility it's an inside job."

That brought J.T. up short. The thought that his own men might be stealing from him was all but impossible for him to accept. He scratched his chin thoughtfully. "Tell you what, Larry, let me think about this a spell, and I'll get back to you if I need to. Thanks."

"Don't mention it. Be seeing you."

As J.T. hung up, he looked at Ken. "Larry says we might have an inside job. Could that be, Ken?"

Ken let out a whistle and shook his head. "Lord, boss, I know those guys. We're practically like family. I just don't think so."

"Anybody been doing more than ordinary bitching?"

Ken thought about it. "Nope, not that I can think of. None of them would want to do harm to the Double C, boss. They like the ranch, they like their jobs, and they want to keep them."

"Well, keep your eyes open. I'll swear, if it isn't one thing, it's twelve others. Goddamn, if I don't hate this!"

Cynthia sighed. Now she was sure today wasn't a good time to mention having a baby.

By EVENING, however, J.T.'s mood had made a complete turnabout, and he was as placid as a lamb. The storm had passed and was forgotten. On a lark, he suggested he and Cynthia pass up dinner at the house in favor of going into town to eat. Naturally, she grabbed at the chance to be alone with him.

Crystal Creek didn't have much to offer in the way of good restaurants. The locals favored mom-and-pop operations—barbecue joints, Mexican cafés and German smokehouses. A pizza parlor and a drive-in catered to teenagers. Zack's was a real honky-tonk that served good food, but drinking and dancing were Zack's main draw. It was fun if one was in the mood for that sort of thing. What passed for posh dining in Crystal Creek was pretty well limited to the country club. Then, of course, there was the Longhorn Coffee Shop.

In the interest of softening J.T. up and getting him in the best possible mood, she suggested his favorite—the Longhorn. Actually Cynthia rather enjoyed the atmosphere there, too. Sitting on the sidelines and listening to the conversations was like studying a foreign language and culture. Plus, if one went in for home cooking, the Longhorn was the best.

"Good!" J.T. said, obviously pleased. "Wednesday night is all-you-can-eat catfish. Dottie makes the best. There'll be a crowd."

The coffee shop was packed. As J.T. and Cynthia stood near the entrance, craning their necks to search for a table, dozens of people called out to him. He slapped backs and pumped hands. Cynthia found it difficult to equate this amiable charmer with the raging bull who had found his desk "messed with." She adored this man. Her feelings about the other one were more complicated.

Martin Avery and Sheriff Wayne Jackson were seated at a table for four; they waved an invitation to join them, and J.T. and Cynthia did so. After the usual round of small talk, Wayne, who hadn't seen Cynthia since the night of her welcoming party, began quizzing her about growing up in Boston, and that in turn led the conversation around to the sheriff's childhood. He'd been born in Nevada but orphaned at an early age. As a result, he'd grown up in a succession of foster homes, something that seemed terribly sad to Cynthia. Wayne, however, talked about it as matter-of-factly as if he were telling her the color of his hair or his height. She sensed he didn't in the least mind talking about it.

"What was that like?" she asked gently and with interest.

"Oh, like just about everything in life, I guess. Some of those homes were great, others less so. But I was lucky. I never was treated badly. I always had everything a boy needs."

"What was the best home you ever were in?"

Wayne smiled. "You know, it's funny, but the best one was the one I originally had most doubts about. I was twelve, and I guess you know how rambunctious twelve-year-old boys can be. The social worker placed me with an older couple. They must have been near sixty. I took one look at them and thought, 'Oh, oh, this isn't going to work. They're old and set in their ways.' But they were wonderful, especially the man. He said he'd learned a thing or two raising his own kids and thought he could do a better job the second time around, that he knew how to sort the trivial from the important. We sure had us some good times together, and we kept in touch until he died."

Cynthia could have kissed Wayne, but she was afraid to even look at J.T. She just hoped what the good sheriff said had sunk into his incredibly thick skull.

"THAT WAS FUN," Cynthia said as they drove home. They had stayed at the Longhorn more than two hours, far longer than it took them to eat. People had kept stopping by the table for a word with J.T. Then after the dinner rush was over, a hard core of regulars lingered long over pie and coffee. The atmosphere was laid-back and convivial. Cynthia found the absence of pretense refreshing. No one was "on." No one was trying to impress anyone. She still felt like an outsider, though less and less like one with each visit to the popular establishment. It amused her to think of her so-proper parents meeting these salt-of-the-earth types.

When J.T. parked the car in front of the ranch house, she got out and cocked her head toward the guest house. "Coming?" she asked.

Smiling, he rounded the car, and arm in arm they crossed the lawn. Inside the guest house, he saw that a lamp had been left burning and the bed turned down invitingly. "Expecting someone?" he asked.

"Mmm. I'm having a tryst with my lover."

"Lucky fellow."

Smiling seductively, she went into his arms and kissed him, a deep, lingering, moist kiss. When he lifted his head, his eyes were dark with emotion. "He is, you know. Very lucky."

At that moment, Cynthia felt he would refuse her nothing. Digging deep into her fantasy grab bag, she pulled out every erotic move she could think of, taking the initiative, loving him into senselessness. And she felt not the least bit guilty about doing so. There were times when feminine wiles had to be employed. After all, she had loved him this way many times when she wanted nothing but love in return. And she wasn't going to deceive him; she was going to convince him he wanted a child.

When he was spent, she rolled off him and tucked her body beside his, throwing a possessive leg across his. "How was that?" she cooed.

Smiling with satisfaction, J.T. made a guttural sound. "Awful. Terrible. I don't know why I allow myself to be a party to such carrying-on."

She chuckled.

"You can be a real siren when you want to be."

"Um-hmm." She traced the outline of his profile with a fingertip. "J.T.?"

"Mmm."

"Did you hear what Wayne said tonight?" She felt him tense.

"Wayne said a lot of things tonight, but I'm sure I know what you're referring to. I saw the wheels in your head churning away."

"Didn't it make an impression on you?"

"Cynthia, please, let's not start that again." He rolled off the bed, slipped into his jeans and padded into the bathroom.

A less determined, and perhaps more prudent woman probably would have dropped the subject right then and waited for another opportunity. Cynthia, however, pressed on. Sitting up, she tucked the sheet around her breasts and raised her voice so he could hear her. "What makes you think it wouldn't be like that with you and a new son or daughter? I think you'd make a great father. Think of the wisdom and maturity you have to offer a child."

J.T. came out of the bathroom, wiping his hands with a towel. "I've done it, and I'm too old to do it again."

"But I haven't done it. Do you think it's fair to keep me from being a mother because of some silly notion you have about age? I do so want a child, and I'm running out of time."

He ignored that. "I'll tell you something else, Cynthia. I don't want you tied down to a baby."

She rose on her elbow and looked at him in astonishment. "Are you serious?"

"Very. There's no telling what all we might want to do. I want you free to do…well, whatever I want you to do."

She had to give him credit for one thing. He didn't waste time pretending he was anything but chauvinistic. "But women don't neglect their husbands when they have babies. I have little enough to do around here as it is, no duties that I can see. It's not as though I'd have to do all the housework and cook three meals a day. And the house comes equipped with babysitters. I would have all the time in the world for you and a child. It would enrich our marriage, not interfere."

J.T. sighed. "Why, oh, why must we argue over every little thing?"

"This is no little thing. We are talking about something very near and dear to my heart—a normal desire for a child. And I suppose we argue because you treat my wishes as irrelevant."

"Drop it," he said sharply, then softened his tone. "Please, sweetheart. I don't want a child. I like things the way they are. You'll have to accept that." He tossed the towel on the lavatory behind him, and when he turned around, he spied something on top of the tall dresser. It looked like a frame lying facedown. Curious, he turned it over, and the strangest expression crossed his face. Over his shoulder he glanced at Cynthia, his brows knitted tightly.

Puzzled, she asked, "What's that?"

Slowly he turned the flat object around and held it up. It was the photograph of Pauline that usually graced the top of the bookshelf in J.T.'s study. Now it was Cynthia's turn to look puzzled.

"You should have told me the picture bothered you," J.T. said quietly. "I would have put it somewhere else."

She gasped. "J.T., I didn't put that picture there!"

"Then how did it get here?"

"I have no idea," she said, but she thought she did. "It bothers me enormously that you would think I'd do something so...childish. If that picture bothered me, I would have told you so. I don't care if you paper the walls with Pauline's—"

She stopped, wanting to bite her tongue. "I'm sorry. I shouldn't have said that. The picture doesn't bother me."

"You're sure?" he asked skeptically.

"Very. I know how close you and she were, and I'm not the jealous type." The evening, she thought sadly, was deteriorating right before her eyes. Worse, she couldn't tell if he believed her or not. "Take it back where it belongs."

Cynthia morosely watched him set down the photograph, finish dressing, then tuck the frame under his arm. Walking to the bed, he bent to kiss her. "Sleep well. I'll see you in the morning."

"Yes, of course." For once she didn't want him to stay. She wanted to be alone with time to think. But when he reached the door, she detained him for a minute. "J.T.?"

He turned. "Yes."

"I want you to do a favor for me."

"All right, if I can."

"I want you to put that picture back where it belongs and not say a word to anyone about it, okay?"

He cocked his head and gave her a quizzical look. "Why?"

"If you must know, it's because I think someone wants it to become an issue."

"Cynthia," he said, shaking his head, "you're making a mystery out of something simple. If you didn't bring the picture out here, then...well, there are probably half a dozen ways it could have shown up here."

"Name one."

When he didn't come up with an answer, she said, "Promise me?"

"Yeah, okay, I promise, even if I don't understand. Good night."

"Good night."

Staring at the back of the door after he'd closed it behind him, Cynthia tried to marshal her thoughts, to make some sort of sense of things that made no sense to her at all. She pulled up her knees under the sheet, hugged them and stared into space.

So this was how it was to be. Somebody—maybe more than one somebody—wanted to make her look petty or foolish or both. Yet, surprisingly, that didn't bother her. She merely thought it silly, and whoever was behind it couldn't keep it up forever.

J.T., however, did bother her. *I like things the way they are. You'll have to accept that.* Maybe she should have that written into their marriage vows. I, Cynthia, accept that thee, J.T., likes things the way they are. I, Cynthia, won't argue with thee, J.T. I, Cynthia, won't do one damned thing that thee, J.T., doesn't want me to do.

She sighed and raked her fingers through her hair. He was so rigid, so immovable in his thinking that she couldn't imagine an argument forceful enough to change his mind about having a child. She felt utterly helpless. Of course he was being unfair. Of course he was cheating her out of something. But that was J.T. He'd already had everything she wanted—a spouse, children, work he loved. Now he wanted a young wife who was free to be at his beck and call. Talking to him was like beating her head against a wall. Again they had clashed; again she had backed off. Or rather, what she wanted had been dismissed as unimportant.

Each time he did that, her commitment to him slipped. Perhaps not precariously, but slip it did. Less and less did he seem like that wonderful man who had courted her so assiduously in Boston. And that frightened her. She was afraid she might forget he was the only man she had ever truly been in love with.

CHAPTER ELEVEN

CYNTHIA'S PLANS the following morning included some shopping—browsing, really—in Crystal Creek to find out what was available locally and what she'd be better off buying in Boston. She looked at invitations at the print shop, thumbed through florist catalogs and fingered every dress in the bridal shop. But she neither bought nor ordered a thing. Nothing grabbed her, and she found it impossible to make a decision. Finally telling herself she just wasn't in the mood for shopping, she left the bridal shop and almost collided head-on with Beverly on the sidewalk.

"Beverly!" she exclaimed with delight. Stepping back, she studied J.T.'s niece. As usual she looked spectacular. Beverly wore jeans just like everyone else did, but hers were never just jeans. The ones she had on this morning were of dark suede, and they hugged her curvaceous figure as if they had been painted on. With them she wore an oversize orange silk shirt that plunged almost to her bra line. No one could not notice her. "It's so nice to see you."

"Thanks, Cynthia. It's nice to see you, too. Oooh, if you're coming out of Pamela's, does this mean what I think it means?"

"Well..." Cynthia smiled. "I was just looking. We haven't set a date."

"I think it's really great about you and J.T., I mean that."

That makes you a minority of one, Cynthia thought. Then she qualified the thought. Tyler, while not exactly overcome with joy, at least seemed to have made peace with the idea of a stepmother. She glanced at her watch. She was in no hurry to get back to the ranch, and she'd never had a chance to really talk to Beverly because Lynn was always around. "If you have time, why don't we have coffee?"

"I'd like that, thanks."

"The Longhorn?"

Beverly shrugged. "I get so tired of that place. Same old faces, day after day. The bakery around the corner has wonderful coffee and pastries. Would you like to try that?"

"Sounds fine."

The bakery was a charming shop, and like so many of the business establishments in Crystal Creek, it had received a facelift during a town-renewal project some years ago. A small area inside had been set aside for tables and chairs, and the aroma was irresistible. Cynthia couldn't imagine walking into the bakery and not buying something.

She ordered only coffee, but Beverly also took a pastry that looked like a Danish, but since the bakery was a German one, the pastry was probably called something else. The two women sat at a table in front of a window, commented on the fine weather, the clothes in the window of a shop across the street— Beverly adored shopping almost as much as she adored flirting—and then Cynthia inquired about Carolyn.

"Mama's fine, thanks," Beverly said. "Mama's always fine. She's the strong type, you know."

"She and J.T. seem very close."

"J.T. has been a big help to Mama many times, and she returned the favor when he just about cracked up after Pauline..." Beverly hesitated. "Should I be talking about these things?"

"That's perfectly all right, Beverly. J.T. has told me a lot about Pauline."

"Well, Mama and Daddy, J.T. and Pauline were...it's hard to explain. They were family, of course, but they also were best friends. When Pauline and Daddy died it was like...like they had no business going off and leaving Mama and J.T. to get along without them."

"Tell me about Pauline," Cynthia said gently.

Beverly lapsed into thought for a second or two before saying, "She was so dignified and graceful. She seemed delicate, but she was anything but that." She rambled on and on about J.T.'s late wife. It was obvious to Cynthia that Beverly had thought the world of her aunt. The young woman concluded with, "And one thing was for sure—J.T. was the center of her universe. He was the sun and she just orbited around him. You see a lot of that in this part of the world. If hubby's around, he's what counts. He leaves town, and she steps forward to take over. He comes home, and it's back to the shadows for her.''

"What does she get in return?"

"Hard to say. Security, I guess, and as much comfort as the husband can afford. She gets put up on a pedestal. Sounds pretty awful to me, but that's the way most of that generation operates.''

The words were no sooner out of Beverly's mouth than the bell over the door jangled, and Mary Gibson walked into the bakery. Bubba's wife did not see them at first. She walked to the counter and placed an order for a dozen glazed doughnuts. Only when she'd paid for the purchase and turned to leave did she notice Cynthia and Beverly. She stopped and exchanged small talk with them for a minute or two before leaving the shop. Cynthia's eyes followed her departure, and she shook her head sadly.

Beverly noticed. "I take it you've heard about Bubba's philandering,'' she said.

"Why doesn't Mary leave the man?"

"He's a husband," Beverly said simply.

"Tell me, Beverly, what kind of man would you want to marry?"

"Someone who's fun," the young woman replied without hesitation. "Someone who likes to do things, go places. Someone who understands I want pretty things. For sure I don't want someone who expects me to stay home and cook for him . . . like the generation I was just telling you about.''

J.T.'s generation, Cynthia thought. Once more she was up against a concept that was totally foreign to her.

She and Beverly sat talking in the bakery for more than half an hour, mostly about Boston, but finally Beverly had to leave to keep an appointment for a haircut. Cynthia bought a dozen lemon tarts, left the bakery and went to the Cadillac parked in front of the bridal shop. During the drive back to the Double C, she considered everything Beverly had said, and again she felt as if she were studying the customs and habits of some exotic civilization. *Nothing about me fits in here,* she thought in dismay. *It must have been obvious to J.T. What attracted him to me in the first place?*

She drove through the front gate and parked the Cadillac in its customary spot. Carrying the box from the bakery, she walked through the house, straight for the kitchen. Lettie Mae looked startled, as she always did when Cynthia entered her domain.

"I was at the bakery," Cynthia explained as she set the box on the counter, "and these looked so good. I know J.T. likes anything lemon, so I thought perhaps we could have these for dessert tonight."

Lettie Mae peeked inside the box. "I'm not much of a one for store-bought things. I already made tonight's dessert. Chocolate pudding."

"Well, then perhaps everyone can have a choice." Smiling as sweetly as she could manage, she left the kitchen and went in search of J.T. Something told her that was the last she would ever see of the lemon tarts.

THEY WERE SERVED chocolate pudding for dessert that night. Cynthia didn't inquire about the fate of the lemon tarts, and Lettie Mae offered no explanation. Perhaps the cook had hoped she would mention them, maybe demand to have one for her own dessert, cause some kind of little stir over the damned tarts. If so, it delighted Cynthia to disappoint her. To hell with Lettie Mae.

Oh, she was bitchy tonight! Her mood had been building like a summer storm ever since her talk with Beverly. Working hard to fit in and win acceptance was tiring, particularly when she seemed to be getting nowhere. It seemed for every step forward, she fell back two.

At the other end of the table J.T. was in high spirits. She hoped his good humor lasted; one never knew with J.T. She could use a good dose of those spirits tonight, along with some gentle reassurances from him. When they were alone later, she vowed, she wouldn't so much as whisper the word *baby*. They would talk only about the two of them and the future.

But she was destined to be disappointed. When J.T. rose from the table he looked at Tyler. "Poker in the bunkhouse tonight. Want in?"

Tyler placed his napkin beside his plate. "Yeah, that sounds great." However, he made no move to get to his feet.

"Ladies, if you'll excuse us," J.T. said, rounding the table and giving Cynthia a pat on the shoulder. "A deck of cards awaits."

Run along, girls, Cynthia thought sourly. *We boys have something important to do.*

Lynn, of course, left the room the minute her father did, but Tyler surprised Cynthia by remaining seated. He reached for something in one of the empty chairs. Standing, he walked to her and handed her a manila envelope. "If you have time, I'd appreciate it if you'd have a look at this."

Time was what she had more of than anything. "Of course," she said, puzzled and curious.

"I'd also appreciate it if you didn't tell Daddy I gave it to you, not right away, at least."

"All right, I won't."

"Thanks." Tyler then hurried out of the room to catch up with his father.

Cynthia stared after him. *My lone success,* she thought and had no idea what she had said or done to win him over.

Pushing herself away from the table, she stood and gathered the folder to her chest. Wonderful! Another solitary evening in the guest house. The prospect was positively bleak. Was it for this she had left her job, her family and her friends in Boston?

At that moment the doorbell rang. Lettie Mae had not yet come out of the kitchen, and Virginia was nowhere in sight, so Cynthia answered the door. Beverly stood in the porch light's soft glow.

"Well, hello again," Cynthia said with a smile. "Come in."

Just as Beverly stepped inside, Lynn flew down the stairs. "I'm ready," she said.

"We're going to Zack's," Beverly explained. "Tonight's ladies' night. Want to come along? Love to have you."

A look of absolute dismay flashed across Lynn's face. She covered it up quickly, but not quickly enough for Cynthia to miss it. She was sorely tempted to take Beverly up on the invitation. If she and Lynn ever spent some real time together, J.T.'s daughter just might find she wasn't such a bad sort after all. But on second thought, Cynthia decided ladies' night at Zack's probably wasn't the place for that to happen. The popular nightspot would be filled with Beverly's and Lynn's friends, so there wouldn't be a chance for real conversation.

"No, thanks," she said, indicating the folder she carried. "I have some work to do. But you two have fun."

The cousins left in a flurry. Cynthia waited until they had driven away before going back to the guest house. Once there, she kicked off her shoes, sat cross-legged on the bed and settled down to read the contents of the folder.

She found the material both interesting and enlightening. There was a full financial report on the Double C Land and Cattle Company, plus detailed projections for the wine-making venture. They told her far more about J.T.'s beloved ranch than the man himself had ever been willing to reveal.

Cattle raising sounded romantic to people raised on the folklore of the Old West. Images of cattle barons overseeing vast kingdoms were deeply emblazoned on the American spirit. To listen to J.T. was to believe the Double C was a booming operation. Cynthia herself had assumed the ranch was a real money-maker. It wasn't. The family members did all right, thanks to stocks, bonds, trusts and interest payments from various sources. The Double C Land and Cattle Company was operating in the black—just—and getting by, but that was the extent of it.

Cynthia frowned as she looked over the figures. Then she shifted her attention to the wine-making projections. Granted, this was Tyler's baby, so he might possibly have painted an overly optimistic picture, but the venture seemed to have merit. She was hardly a novice at this sort of thing. For years her job had been financing other people's ideas.

There was a knock on the door. Cynthia closed the folder and placed it in the drawer of the bedside table. Thank God! The poker game apparently hadn't been as much fun as J.T. had thought it would be. "Come in," she called.

To her surprise, Tyler, not J.T., entered the room. "I asked them to deal me out of this hand. Said I had a phone call to make. Did you read what I gave you?"

"Yes. Come in and have a seat."

Two chairs and a low table stood in front of the window across the room. Tyler sat down in one of them and clasped his hands in front of his knees. "What did you think?"

"The ranch struggles, doesn't it?" Cynthia said bluntly.

He nodded. "At least we don't owe any money, and that's always a plus in ranching. Some years are better than others. But we're too big to be run by an owner and a couple of hired hands, yet not big enough to be agribusiness. The really big outfits have hurt operations the size of the Double C, and they've damned near eradicated the small family ranches."

"I only skimmed over the report, but even so, I found many places where expenses could be cut. Is it really necessary to employ so many people?"

Tyler uttered a little grunt. "No, but Daddy's not about to fire anyone. 'They've got families,' he says, and that's that."

"Isn't that rather foolish?" Cynthia asked in all seriousness.

"Cynthia, you've been here long enough to know there's not a soul on this ranch who's going to tell J. T. McKinney he's being foolish."

Cynthia had to grant him that. "Why did you give me that folder?"

"I wanted you to see firsthand that the wine-making thing is no whim. I'm dead serious about it. It's not going to be a hobby. And eventually it could sweeten the pot considerably and let Daddy go on raising his cows the way he always has.''

''Have you told your father that?''

Tyler rolled his eyes. ''Only about three dozen times. He refuses to believe ranching is a dying way of life. He's a cattleman, and in this part of the world that's almost a title, like Reverend or Doctor.''

''I still don't understand why you're telling me all this.''

''You must have considerable influence with him.''

Cynthia chuckled as she thought of the computer, the credit card, the baby and half a dozen other things. ''Much less than you might think.''

''When you questioned the wisdom of wine making, he sure backed off,'' Tyler insisted.

''I think that's because he had doubts himself. J.T. doesn't strike me as a man who is influenced by others.''

''You've learned a lot. Tell me something as an investment banker. Now that you've seen the figures, would you finance a winery here on the Double C?''

Cynthia thought hard before answering. ''Yes, I think so,'' she finally said. ''Given the success of the industry in the state, I think so.''

''Will you tell Daddy that?''

''I thought you didn't want him to know you gave me that folder.''

''You don't have to tell him you got the information from me. Tell him you've done some checking. Tell him you think the future of the wine industry is brighter than the future of the cattle industry. He won't like it, but he might start thinking along those lines."

Oh, Lord, Cynthia thought. *Something else for J.T. and me to spar over.* "Let me think about it, Tyler. Sometimes J.T. requires delicate handling."

"You *have* learned a lot." Tyler stood. "Thanks. I can't ask for more than that. Now I'd better get back to the game."

"How long do those things go on?" she asked.

"Depends on who's winning. If it's Daddy, they can go on for hours. Nobody leaves until he does or they run out of money. Well . . . good night."

"Good night, Tyler."

For a long time after he left, Cynthia remained on the bed, deep in thought. Did she want to help Tyler and risk yet another confrontation with J.T.? She felt she owed Tyler something since he was the first to accept her, but she and J.T. had so many other differences. Did she want to bring up something else for them to argue about?

Realistically, though, was she so sure they would argue? J.T. knew her background. If she told him wine making looked like a financially sound venture, wouldn't he listen to her?

She didn't know. That was the trouble—she never knew how J.T. would react to . . . well, to anything.

She looked at her watch. It was still early, and the poker game might go on for hours. She was edgy, indecisive and bored. The trouble with living in the country was one couldn't pop out to the drugstore for a paperback or catch a movie when there were idle hours to fill up. But on the brighter side, the ranch was a safe place to live. One could wander around at will without worry, and it was a beautiful night. A walk might clear her mind and help her make decisions. Swinging her legs off the bed, she put on her shoes and grabbed a sweater from the closet.

Cynthia found it hard to believe they were into November and she could still get by with only a sweater after sundown. J.T. had told her they often had shirtsleeve weather on Thanksgiving. That would take some getting used to. Her happiest memories of Thanksgiving were at her grandparents' house in the country. The children usually went sledding or ice skating to work off the gigantic meal. Did turkey and dressing with all the trimmings taste the same in shirtsleeve weather? A twinge of homesickness overtook her, something she had never expected to happen. She hadn't really been too content in Boston the past two years or so.

She wondered then if her discontent had made J.T. and a Texas ranch seem so appealing. She had been restless, seeking a change, and the Double C Ranch outside Crystal Creek, Texas was the biggest change from Boston she could think of.

Passing the bunkhouse, she heard the sound of masculine voices and the clink of chips. Head down and hands stuffed into the sweater's pockets, she walked on.

As interesting and enlightening as Tyler's information had been, it also was disturbing. The Double C needed to get its financial act together if it was to survive, but how did one convince a man who despised change? Now Cynthia understood why he insisted on that antiquated bookkeeping system of his. He didn't want anyone else to have access to the information. Tyler did, of course, but she'd bet her last dollar all the others were in the dark.

Cynthia sighed. She could be of so much help to J.T. if he would let her, but *modernize, streamline, economize, computerize* were dirty words to him. Once Cynthia was Mrs. McKinney, she could be of tremendous financial help to him as well. Her generous trust from her grandfather was largely untouched because she had been making good money for years. But if J.T. wouldn't let her put gas in the tank of his car, would he let her put her own money into the ranch? She seriously doubted it. He was the most maddening man on earth. She couldn't help but love him, but how she wished she understood him better.

She walked faster, trying to vent her frustrations with physical activity, and eventually came to some rocky terrain where the waters of the Claro River splashed over limestone ledges. The area was heavily wooded with cedar and twisted mesquite. She glanced over her shoulder and looked at the lights of the ranch house and bunkhouse in the distance, surprised she had walked so far. For a minute she simply stood listening to the water lap against rocks, smelling the aroma of earth and vegetation and staring up at the star-filled sky. Had it not been for the lights from the headquarters compound, she could imagine herself the only person for miles.

Suddenly she heard an unidentifiable sound, something like the scrape of metal. She turned her head in all directions, but she saw nothing. She stood stock-still and listened. At first all was silent; then she heard the muffled sound of voices, male voices. Some of the cowhands probably. By now she knew most of them by sight if not by name. Moving silently, she peered through a clump of trees. It was very dark, but she could see movement, and now she could make out what the voices were saying.

"Goddammit, gimme some light so I can see what I'm doing," one man said.

"We can't risk it," said another.

"Aw, ever'body's in the bunkhouse playing poker."

"Why ain't you with 'em? Don't that look suspicious?"

"Jerk idiot! How can I be there and here at the same time? I told 'em I'm broke. Gimme some light."

A flashlight came on, and Cynthia covered her mouth with her hand to stifle a gasp. A gate had been opened—that was probably the sound she'd heard—and a truck with a cattle trailer was backed up to it. A man stood outside the gate holding a flashlight. She couldn't see his face, but the man the light was trained on was tall and thin and wore a red plaid shirt and some kind of funny black hat. The hat wasn't anything like the Stetsons J.T. and his cowhands wore. This one had a flat crown, a narrow brim and a string tie hanging from each side. And right before her eyes, the man in the hat led two cows through the gate, and the man outside guided them into the trailer.

The rustlers! Cynthia stepped back and something crunched beneath her feet. The man inside the fence whirled around. "What was that?"

"I didn't hear anything," the other man said. "You're jumpy as hell."

For an eternity the man in the black hat stared, it seemed to Cynthia, right in her direction. She stood as still as death, but her heart was pounding so violently she thought it would jump out of her chest. She longed to turn and run to the bunkhouse, but then she would be seen, and how did she know the men didn't have guns?

Finally, the man turned back to his accomplice, who swung the trailer's tailgate closed. "This had better be it for a spell," the other man said. "We've pushed our luck about as far as we ought'a."

"It'll be it," the man in the hat said, "when I say it's it. Git gone."

The other man climbed into the truck's cab and slowly drove away without turning on his headlights. The black-hatted man closed the ranch gate and walked away, passing only a few yards from where Cynthia stood trembling among the clump of trees. She got a good look at his profile—hawk nose and prominent chin. If she ever saw him again, she'd recognize him, that was for sure.

She was forced to remain hidden in the trees until the man was completely out of sight, for what seemed like endless minutes. Then she began to run like the wind. When she burst through the bunkhouse door, she was so out of breath she couldn't make a sound. Every head in the place turned.

When J.T. saw who it was, his eyes widened. "Cynthia!"

Gasping for breath, she gestured wildly. He slapped his cards facedown on the table, got to his feet and took her by the arm, propelling her outside. "What in the devil's the matter? You can't go busting into a poker game."

"Oh..." She found her voice. "To hell with the poker game! The rustlers...I saw the rustlers."

J.T. gave a start. "Where?"

"At the gate...over in that direction."

"Are you talking about the east gate? What in hell were you doing that far out?"

"What difference does it make? I took a walk...and I saw two men...one inside the gate and one outside with a truck."

"Are you sure? I...hold on a minute. Shh."

A man was walking by. J.T. said, "Evening, Chase."

"Evening, J.T. Nice 'un, isn't it?"

"That it is."

The man walked on, and Cynthia distractedly turned to look at his retreating figure. She did a double-take, and her jaw dropped. Stepping closer to J.T. and lowering her voice, she exclaimed, "That's him!"

"What?"

"That man you just spoke to," she whispered. "He's one of the rustlers."

J.T. stared in the man's direction, then looked at Cynthia, and to her astonishment, he grinned. "Nope, sweetheart, no way. That's Chase Bennett. I've known him for years."

Cynthia sputtered in disbelief. "I saw him!"

"No, you saw someone who looks something like him. I promise you, Chase is no rustler. But that's good, Cynthia. Now we have a general description to go on, so..."

"General description? Listen to me, J.T. For once, just please listen to me! I'm going to close my eyes and describe the man I saw leading those cows into the truck." Her eyes snapped shut. "Tall and thin, red plaid shirt, funny black hat, hawk nose, prominent chin." Her eyes flew open. "Now, if the first time I'd ever seen him was a second ago when he passed us, could I possibly have described him so accurately?"

"It was dark."

"One of the men had a flashlight."

J.T. seemed to waver uncertainly, but only for a fleeting second. Then he shook his head. "It wasn't Chase. I'd make book on that."

Just then the bunkhouse door opened, and Ken Slattery peered out. "Anything wrong, boss?"

"No. Cynthia saw the rustlers."

"Hey, that's great."

"Trouble is, she says one of them was Chase."

Ken looked at Cynthia, then back at J.T. He, too, grinned. "Chase Bennett?"

"Yeah."

Ken shook his head. "No way," he said and went back into the bunkhouse.

"I don't believe this!" Cynthia cried. "I've handed you your rustler on a silver platter. Well, if you won't go to Wayne Jackson, I will."

She turned toward the guest house, but J.T. caught her by the arm and swung her around. He pointed his finger at her and jabbed it in the air. "Listen, Cynthia, you can't go getting things stirred up around here. You can't accuse one of my men of something so serious without proof."

"I'm an eyewitness!"

"Not good enough, especially in the dark."

She stared at that jabbing, pointed finger, and something inside her exploded! Her paternal grandfather used to shake his finger at her when he thought she'd been naughty. She'd hated it at eleven, and she hated it now. There really was such a thing as the straw that broke the camel's back. "This is it, J.T.," she said, so angry she couldn't think. "This is *it!*" Breaking free of his grasp, she ran to the guest house.

Again Ken stuck his head outside the bunkhouse door. "We're dealing a new hand, boss."

J.T. stared after Cynthia, unable to believe she was in such a snit. He really ought to go back and join the game. By morning she'd be over whatever was stuck in her craw, and they could discuss this like two reasonable human beings.

On the other hand, he'd never seen her so angry. Sure, they argued, too much it seemed to him, but when they did, she always seemed more frustrated and exasperated than really angry.

"How about it, boss?" Ken asked.

"Ah...no, deal me out of this hand. But I'll be right back." J.T. took off at a trot, reaching the guest house just as Cynthia slammed the door so hard the windows seemed to vibrate.

CHAPTER TWELVE

CYNTHIA OPENED the closet door, jerked out her suitcases and threw them on the bed. She turned to go back to the closet just as the front door opened and J.T. stepped into the room. "Listen, Cynthia, you're being..." He stopped when he saw the suitcases. "What in hell are you doing?"

She came out of the closet carrying an armload of clothes. Her chest heaved; she was close to tears. "What does it look like I'm doing? I'm packing."

It took a minute for that to sink in. When it did, he threw up his hands. "I don't believe this! You're turning a simple case of mistaken identity into a major crisis."

"I saw him!"

"You think you saw him. Now, come on, Cynthia, don't blow this out of proportion."

"Oh, J.T.," she said with a sad sigh as she laid the clothes on the bed. "It's not just this. It's...everything!" Pivoting, she returned to the closet.

"Everything?" he bellowed. "What do you mean by everything? Give me a for-instance."

She came out of the closet with more clothes. "Don't get me started."

"No, no, I want to know. What's everything?"

Flinging the clothes on the bed, she turned to him, a hand on a hip. "Okay, for openers, I'm sick of being accorded the warmth normally reserved for an occupying army. I've also had it up to my ears with being treated like the village idiot. I'm tired of trying to compete with a woman who apparently was a saint. Since the day I arrived here, I've felt as welcome as an outbreak of Asian flu. How would you like to crawl out of bed every morning knowing you were going to face a day of silly pranks, hostile stares and constant disapproval? I grew up in a world of mediation and compromise. I can't live with rock-hard obstinacy. And I damned sure don't want to spend the rest of my life walking on eggshells." She opened a suitcase and began folding her things.

"I think you're exaggerating... or imagining things."

"Think what you like. I'm neither exaggerating nor imagining. And you don't help a bit, J.T. You won't listen to anyone's ideas but your own. You believe what you want to believe, evidence be damned. I tell you what I saw with my own eyes, but you won't believe it. What could I possibly know?"

J.T. folded his arms across his chest and stood silently watching her make a hash of her packing. "You were mistaken, that's all," he said quietly. "It could happen to anyone. The police will tell you that two eyewitnesses to a crime seldom tell exactly the same story. It couldn't have been Chase. I've known him for years. I knew his daddy...."

Cynthia tossed her head impatiently. "And that, of course, makes him as pure as driven snow. I don't give a damn if the two of you shared an incubator in the hospital nursery. I know what I saw! As for your being a sterling judge of character, one of your close friends is a skirt-chasing philanderer!"

A hard, flinty look came to J.T.'s eyes. He strove to keep his voice low and measured. "Why don't you stop what you're doing? We'll both sleep on this. Things will look different in the morning. You're just upset."

"How perceptive. I don't want to sleep on it. I've had it up to here with this place." She made a slicing motion across her throat.

J.T. pursed his lips and stared at her thoughtfully. "It's really the baby, isn't it?"

"The baby's only part of it."

"No, I think the baby's most of it. You've been harping and harping on it—"

"I haven't harped. I merely told you I wanted a child, but as usual, it's what you want that counts."

"I told you how I feel about a second family at my age."

Cynthia uttered a bitter laugh. "Oh, yes, you've told me how you feel about everything. I know how everybody on this whole damned ranch feels about everything. I've never worked so hard at trying to fit in, trying to understand, trying, trying, trying, all for nothing. Well, I'm through. Now, please, all I want is for you to ask someone to drive me to Austin. Then I'll be out of everyone's hair, which will doubtless thrill them all to death."

"It's after eight. Who do you think will want to make an eighty-mile round trip this time of night?"

"Then perhaps someone will drive me to the nearest bus station." She whirled around and went into the bathroom to gather up more of her things. "One way or another, I'm leaving tonight."

"I'm asking you once more to sleep on it."

She came out of the bathroom, her anger ebbing, sadness replacing it. She shook her head. "No, sorry. J.T., there's so much about you to love, but it'll never work between us, never in a million years. We're just too different. Please . . . I want to go home."

J.T. tried to reach deep down within himself and pull out some contriteness, some compromise, something that would stop this before it went any further. But he couldn't. He didn't know how to give in and make concessions. And maybe Cynthia was right. Maybe they were too different. He wanted her to stay, but he knew he wanted her to stay on his terms. "Very well," he said, turning on his heel. "I'll see what I can do." As he reached for the doorknob, he looked over his shoulder. "In spite of what you think, I don't hold the patent on stubbornness. You've got your fair share of it, too."

Jerking open the door, he slammed it shut behind him and crossed the lawn to the bunkhouse. As he stepped inside the building, all heads turned in his direction. The look on his face stopped the action in its tracks. Tyler, especially, knew that look. It was the one that used to start him quaking in his boots when he was a youngster.

"I need a volunteer to drive a lady to Austin right now," he growled.

The men exchanged glances. Of course no one wanted to leave the game and drive eighty miles. Everyone hoped someone else would volunteer. Out of the corner of his eye, Tyler saw Ken make a move, but he preempted the foreman by slamming his cards down on the table. "Fold," he said and stood. "I'll do it. I've had nothing but lousy hands all evening. Good night, gentlemen. Wish I could say it's been fun."

J.T. stood aside to let his son pass. "The keys are in the Cadillac."

"Right," Tyler said and left the building. There was no need to ask what lady needed to be driven to Austin, and he didn't think for a minute she just wanted to spend a little time with her friend there.

"That'll be it for me, too, boys," J.T. informed the puzzled gathering. "Enjoy the game."

He didn't even glance in the direction of the guest house. He strode across the grounds and entered the house through the back door. The kitchen was dark and deserted, as was the dining room. One lamp shone in the living room, but no one was there. Lynn was

gone for the evening, and Hank would be in his house.
J.T. went to the bar at the far end of the living room,
took a bottle of whiskey from the cabinet and carried
it upstairs to his room. For the first time in more years
than he could remember, he intended to get quietly
and deliberately drunk.

"I HOPE the information I gave you isn't behind this,
Cynthia," Tyler said as the Cadillac cruised along the
highway to Austin.

"No, no, it was something else altogether."

"I can't tell you how sorry I am."

"I'm sorry, too," Cynthia said. "I really wanted it
to work."

"You know, maybe you should have waited until
tomorrow, seen it in a new light."

She shook her head sadly. "Things wouldn't be any
different tomorrow or the next day. J.T.'s J.T. and I'm
me, and we're just like oil and water."

They drove in silence for a few minutes before Cynthia said, "Before I forget, the folder you gave me is
in the drawer of the bedside table in the guest house.
You might want to get it before someone else does."

"Thanks." Tyler suspected that if Cynthia had been
alone, she would have been crying. He could tell that
from the way she kept swallowing hard and blinking.
Odd that he couldn't conjure up a picture of her
weeping. She always seemed so poised, so in control.
One simply couldn't imagine her having the frailties
and weaknesses of most women. He felt sorry for her.

Had she been any other woman his natural instinct would have been to pat her shoulder in sympathy, but remembering his own weakness where she was concerned, he kept both hands firmly on the wheel.

"Is your friend expecting you?" he finally asked.

"Yes, I phoned ahead. She's also checking flights to Boston for me." Cynthia turned her head toward the side window to stare out into the pitch-black night.

"Is she an old friend?"

"Yes, we met at college."

That was the sort of stiff, meaningless conversation they conducted all the way to Austin. Mostly there was silence. Finally, mercifully, Tyler pulled into the Honecker's driveway. Sally must have been watching for them. The minute Tyler switched off the engine, the porch light came on, and Sally stepped out, concern written on her face.

Tyler carried Cynthia's luggage to the porch, greeted Sally, then stood back, dreading the goodbye. Cynthia, anxious to get it over with, too, made it easy for him. Holding out her hand, she said, "You've been very kind, Tyler. Thank you so much. I'm sorry to have put you to the trouble."

He took her hand, holding it rather than shaking it. "Don't mention it. I was happy to do it."

"You keep after your father, now. Show him that folder. He's always said he'd go for the wine making if it would make him some money, and I think it will."

Tyler nodded. "Take care of yourself."

"I will. Goodbye."

"Goodbye, Cynthia."

Sally picked up one suitcase, Cynthia the other, and wordlessly the two women went into the house. "When I told Ted you were coming and why, he suddenly remembered someplace he had to be for a couple of hours," Sally said.

"Bless him. What did you find out from the airlines?"

"Two possibilities tomorrow. One at some ungodly early hour. I booked you an afternoon flight. Here, let's just set these here at the foot of the stairs," Sally said, indicating the luggage. "We'll take them up later. Come on, let's have a drink. You look like you could use one."

Cynthia took a chair near the fireplace while Sally mixed drinks. It occurred to her that this was the room where she had first seen J.T. Though it was useless now to wish she had simply admired him from afar that night and let it go at that, wish it she did. At least for a second or two. But then she remembered all those weekends in Boston. She had some good memories to go along with the bad.

"You look beat," Sally observed as she handed her a glass and sat on the sofa across from her.

"Emotion is tiring," Cynthia said, "and I've been through a bunch of them today—disbelief, absolute rage, sorrow, disappointment...name it." She took a sip of the drink, hoping the liquor would have a relaxing effect. Everything inside her was coiled as tightly as a snake.

"Want to talk about it?"

"Hell, yes," Cynthia said irritably. "And you're the
only one I *can* talk to it about. Lord, I dread facing
Mom and Dad. Fortunately, their code of honor won't
let them pry too much, but they'll be alive with curiosity and smug in knowing they were right all along."

"What happened?" Sally asked quietly.

Cynthia told her, and Sally frankly said the incident with the rustlers seemed to be more of an irritat-
ing annoyance than the death knell of a love affair.

"Oh, Sally, it was just one more damned thing
heaped on too many other things. J.T. is impossible.
He won't listen to anything but what he wants to hear.
Finally, in a great flash of insight, I realized what my
life would be like if I married him. Childless, that's for
sure. I would spend the rest of my days saying, 'Yes,
J.T. Absolutely, J.T. Of course you're right, J.T.' That
is, I would if I wanted to get along." She sighed sadly.
"I'd be brain-dead in a year. And it's such a shame,
because he has so many wonderful qualities, and we've
had some delightful times together. But he's just too
set in concrete about too many things, and I've found
myself giving in to him all the time. He is one over-
whelming personality. I've tried and tried to think how
I could have handled things differently, but I've come
up with nothing. He doesn't want a computer, fine, I
dropped it. I stayed out of the damned kitchen because the cook almost had a stroke every time I went
near it. I made up my mind I wouldn't make changes
until I was Mrs. McKinney. The baby... well, I never

gave up on that, but I planned to wear him down gradually, make him think he wants a child as much as I do. What concessions did he make? None, zero, zilch.''

The two friends sat talking for hours. Sally mostly listened, simply let Cynthia air her frustration and unhappiness. She realized she was getting only one side of the story, but she doubted this version strayed far from the truth. After all, she had known some J. T. McKinneys in her life—men blessed with the sure knowledge they were always right, men who tended to be thoughtless and inconsiderate, particularly in their dealings with women. Strangely, they often were also the kind of men who could charm the socks off a woman.

Sally had a hard time equating the Cynthia she had always known with the woman seated across from her. This Cynthia looked so miserable and heartbroken. The other had been intelligent, strong-willed and tenacious, and she'd almost always gotten her way, usually by employing reason. Sally had never seen her resort to womanly wiles, but womanly wiles were what worked with men like J.T. So the irresistible force had finally come up against the immovable object. Defeat was written all over her.

When Ted came home, he stopped long enough to greet Cynthia, but he quickly sensed that a masculine point of view was not wanted, and fled upstairs. "I'm sorry, Cyn," Sally said. "I really am. I was so looking forward to having you close. Now I'll probably never get you down here."

Cynthia stared vacantly across the room. "Oh, I'll be back. Maybe not right away, but I'll be back... someday."

But she wondered if she would. Texas, she feared, would always represent the major failure of her life.

THE FOLLOWING MORNING, Lynn and Hank waited patiently for Tyler and J.T. to show up for breakfast. Tyler finally did, much later than usual. "Where's Daddy?" Lynn asked.

Tyler took his customary seat and unfolded the newspaper. "The door to his room is still closed."

Lynn frowned. "At this hour? When was the last time Daddy wasn't up by six-thirty?"

Tyler didn't answer but pretended to be absorbed in the front page. The poker game had just been breaking up when he returned to the ranch last night, and some of the players had told him "the boss" had quit the game as soon as Tyler had left for Austin. Tyler had a pretty good idea what his dad had done—gone to his room to drown his sorrows. Wasn't that the traditional manly way of dealing with a romance gone sour?

Lettie Mae peeked into the dining room. "Isn't J.T. down yet?"

"You might as well start serving, Lettie Mae. Daddy might not be down for a while," Tyler said.

"Why not?" the cook demanded. "Is he sick?"

"Not physically," came the terse reply. Which probably wasn't true. The few times in his life Tyler had nursed a hangover, he'd been as sick as he'd ever wanted to be.

Lynn's head came around, as did Hank's. "What's that supposed to mean?" the old man asked.

Tyler looked up from the paper. "Cynthia left."

Three pairs of startled eyes focused on him. "Left? What do you mean left?" Lynn wanted to know.

"Left, as in adios, goodbye, bound for Boston."

Lynn looked at her great-grandfather, then back at her brother. "When?"

"Last night. I drove her to her friend's house in Austin."

Silence fell over the room for a minute as everyone digested that. "Wh-what happened?" Lynn finally asked.

"I have no idea," Tyler said. "Daddy simply asked me to drive her to Austin."

"How's he taking it?"

"I don't know."

"I knew it!" Hank chimed in. "I knew it 'cause I saw it. Well, good riddance to bad baggage. They must'a had a hell of a fight if she left and J.T. let her go. Lettie Mae, I'm hungry." The old man chuckled, adjusted his glasses and studied his paper.

The cook, who was as surprised by the sudden turn of events as Lynn, hurried back into the kitchen, returning in a few minutes with juice and coffee.

Lynn felt strange. Now that the thing she had thought she wanted so badly had come to pass, the oddest sensation washed over her. There was no relief, no elation. She wanted to believe her father had simply come to his senses, but somehow she didn't think that was the case. Something told her it was Cynthia who had decided to leave. What could have happened? Everything had seemed fine last night. The odd sensation intensified.

Lettie Mae had just finished serving the food when J.T. put in an appearance. All eyes turned to him expectantly. *Good God,* Tyler thought, *he looks like death warmed over.*

"Nothing for me this morning, Lettie Mae," J.T. said. "I'll have breakfast in town." He turned to leave the dining room, then stopped. "And take away that plate," he growled, pointing at the place where Cynthia usually sat. With that, he clomped out of the room, across the foyer and out of the house.

Lynn glanced nervously around the table. Cynthia's departure obviously wasn't something that would roll off her father's back. He looked like the weight of the world had settled on his shoulders, much the way he had looked for so long after her mother died. She recalled those awful days, when everyone had worked so hard to get close to her father and he had shut them all out.

Virginia came out of the kitchen with Lettie Mae right behind her. "Is it true?" the housekeeper asked. "Did she really just up and leave?"

"It's true," Tyler said.

"Well, if that isn't something."

"Why are all of you looking so stunned?" Tyler asked sarcastically. "Did you expect her to wait and say a fond farewell? I thought this was what you wanted, what you were going to work so hard to make happen. Now everything will get back to normal, whatever the hell normal is."

Lynn looked at Virginia, then at Lettie Mae. Now she could give a name to the odd sensation she felt. It was guilt.

CHAPTER THIRTEEN

"CYNTHIA, you've got to snap out of this," Alicia insisted. "You've been home for a week, and you've left this apartment exactly once. Even then it was only to have dinner with your father and me."

"That's not true. I went grocery shopping once."

Her mother sighed. "What on earth do you do all day?"

Wait for bedtime, Cynthia could truthfully have answered. She'd retrieved Tiffany from her friends, bought an armload of paperbacks, stocked the larder and cleaned the apartment from top to bottom. That had hardly consumed a week. Mostly she'd brooded, regretting her inability to make the relationship with J.T. work.

The silliest things reminded her of him. When she'd first returned to the apartment, she'd opened the refrigerator and seen it contained a can of coffee, a jar of apricot preserves ... and three bottles of J.T.'s favorite beer. The fit of sobbing that had produced had gone on forever. Another time, she had been thumbing through a magazine and had come across a spread on Indian food. The picture of a beef curry feast had spawned another crying jag. Every time the phone rang, she almost jumped out of her skin, even though she knew he wouldn't call. She had been the one to leave, and J. T. McKinney would never call and ask her to come back.

But suppose he did. Would she go back? Not without major concessions, and J.T. would never make them. It was over. Why couldn't she accept it and get on with her life? Why did she stay holed up in this apartment? She supposed it offered her sanctuary from curious—or worse, pitying—eyes. She couldn't face answering questions about Texas.

The evening she had spent at her parents' house had been especially trying. While they hadn't come right out and said, "I told you so," she had known they were thinking it. Her mother even seemed relieved. Cynthia knew what was in Alicia's mind. Now perhaps the daughter she had raised with such loving care would find a nice man from an old family who attended the Episcopal church and voted Republican— one of her own kind. Cynthia hadn't contacted friends because every one of them would think the same as her parents.

"I'm cold," Cynthia said, deliberately choosing not to answer her mother's question. She got to her feet and crossed the room to look at the thermostat for the umpteenth time. It was set exactly where it should have been. "I've been cold for a week," she complained.

"Inactivity," was Alicia's diagnosis. "When are you planning to go back to work?"

Cynthia shrugged. "I might call in Monday."

"Your father and I are planning to spend Thanksgiving at the country place this year. Naturally, we'd love it if you'd spend it with us."

"I'll see, Mom. Thanks."

"And I really would like to have you join Millie Barnes and me for lunch tomorrow."

"I don't think so. You and Millie are old friends, but I really don't know her all that well."

Alicia sighed again. "Well, if you insist on playing the hermit, I guess there's nothing I can do. Time will have to take care of everything."

"Truer words were never spoken," Cynthia said with a semblance of a smile, "but I really do thank you for being concerned."

"Of course I'm concerned. I'm your mother! Now, I really must be running. Do take care of yourself, dear. I've been told that when one is depressed, one falls victim to all sorts of illnesses."

"I'm not depressed. I'm disappointed."

"Indeed. Goodbye, dear."

Cynthia walked to the door and held it open for her mother. "Thanks for stopping by."

"I mean it, Cynthia. Take care of yourself."

"I will." She accepted Alicia's hug, then closed the door. Stretching her arms high above her head, she said, "Well, Tiffany, what shall it be tonight? Television, a book, laundry, order pizza, what?" The cat arched her back, then curled into a ball and purred contentedly. "Lucky you," Cynthia said with a sigh.

She walked to the balcony door and stared out. The day was overcast. Every day since returning to Boston, she had checked the Austin weather in the paper. A stupid thing to do when what she should have been doing was forgetting that part of the country existed.

Seven days ago she had boarded that plane at Mueller Airport secure in the knowledge she'd done everything humanly possible to make things work. But she'd had a week of lonely days to do nothing but think, and now she wasn't so sure. Perhaps she had come on too strong at first. She often did that—just walked in and took charge. The Double C wasn't her house, and the McKinney children weren't her family. They had all been together a long time; she was the outsider.

But quick on the heels of those thoughts came others, many concerning J.T.'s hardheadedness and insistence on doing things his way. If he wanted to keep on ranching the way he'd done for twenty years, she supposed she could live with that. But she couldn't live with knowing there would be no child. So she was right back at square one.

Pressing her forehead against the cool glass door, she closed her eyes and silently prayed that J.T. was every bit as miserable as she was.

J.T. WAS A BEAR. No one could go near him without getting snapped at. *Wonderful,* Tyler thought. *We all needed this.* Though they'd all had to deal with J.T.'s stormy moods at one time or another, Tyler realized they hadn't been forced to do so in some time . . . not since his father had met Cynthia. For that reason alone they should all have been grateful to her.

It was useless to hope Cynthia and J.T. would somehow get back together. Though the details of what had happened between them the night of the poker game remained unknown, Tyler was sure Cynthia was the one who had decided to leave. And J. T. McKinney would wrestle a bull with one arm tied behind his back before he'd run after a woman who'd left him.

Hank pretended not to notice J.T.'s black mood, though he was careful not to make any wisecracks about the socialite from Boston when his grandson was within hearing range. To the rest of them he staunchly maintained that Cynthia's leaving was good riddance.

Virginia and Lettie Mae simply gave their employer as wide a berth as possible. If he asked them to do something, they did it, but they certainly didn't seek him out. Lettie Mae, along with Hank, professed to be relieved Cynthia was gone, but Virginia was having second thoughts about her treatment of the woman. If they'd feared the household wouldn't be the same with her in it, it was worse with her gone. She, at least, had made J.T. happy, and a happy J.T. was a pleasure to be around. In some ways this was harder than when Pauline died. Then he had been grief-stricken and withdrawn. Now he was mean as a snake.

But it was Lynn who felt the worst. Seeing her father like this hurt her badly. Reluctantly, she now admitted to herself he was deeply in love with Cynthia. He must have been or her departure wouldn't have affected him so. Lynn was ashamed of the way she had treated the woman. She'd expended not an ounce of effort toward making friends with her or even acknowledging her presence. That alone probably wouldn't have sent her scurrying back to Boston, but it might have contributed to her wanting to leave. Lynn's conscience was beginning to demand she do something to make amends.

It wasn't easy, but she finally screwed up her courage and went in search of her father. She found him seated in his study. It seemed to her he had spent most of a week behind his desk, brooding. "Daddy, may I talk to you a minute?"

"Yes, hon. Come in and sit down. Got a problem?"

She slid into a chair facing him and folded her hands in her lap. "I'm afraid so. I've got a real problem."

"I'll bet it's nothing we can't solve. What is it?"

"It's you. I know you're unhappy."

J.T. blanched, having expected anything but that. "I've got some things on my mind, that's all."

"I wish you would level with me. I know it's Cynthia, and I think all of us are responsible."

J.T. was momentarily at a loss for words. No one in the household had so much as whispered Cynthia's name since she'd left. And if there was one thing he didn't feel comfortable with, it was discussing affairs of the heart with his daughter. "That's ridiculous," he finally managed to say. "You had nothing to do with it."

"Yes, we did. I don't know what the two of you argued about—I don't want to know—but I do know if she had felt welcome and comfortable here, she wouldn't have left because of a disagreement. All of us—Grandpa Hank, Virginia, Lettie Mae and I— maybe Cal, too, and Tyler to a lesser extent—did our best to make her want to leave. The only person in the whole family who was nice to her was Beverly."

J.T. sat back in his chair and rubbed a forefinger over his mouth. He recalled Cynthia's words: *I've felt as welcome as an outbreak of Asian flu.* He'd accused her of exaggerating. Perhaps she hadn't been. "Oh?"

Lynn nodded, embarrassed but determined to get it all out in the open. "Virginia was standing right here in this room when Cynthia began straightening up your desk. She knew it would send you into a rage, but she didn't open her mouth. When she told Grandpa Hank, Lettie Mae and me about it, we laughed like crazy."

J.T. couldn't have been more surprised. "Why?"

Lynn shrugged and stared down at her hands. "Just to keep things stirred up between the two of you. Virginia also put Mama's picture in the guest house. We hoped you'd think Cynthia took it there and that it would irritate you. I don't want to give you the impression that all this was Virginia's fault. The three of us, Virginia, Lettie Mae and I, looked for ways to make you mad at her . . . or vice versa.''

J.T. studied his daughter. A lot of people said shy, quiet Lynn had spunk. They were usually referring to her insistence on raising Thoroughbreds instead of quarter horses, which he had always attributed to stubbornness more than anything. Or perhaps to an attempt at making her presence felt. But, yes, he had to admit a lot of people were right. It took real spunk to face him with this confession.

"Again, I'll have to ask why. Why did you want us mad at each other?''

Lynn's chin trembled slightly. "She was just so different from Mama, so much younger and . . .'' She couldn't make herself say the word *prettier* so she paused. "Lettie Mae didn't want her in the kitchen. Virginia didn't want her to rearrange the furniture. Grandpa Hank said she was too highfalutin. Cal was steamed because she said something to you about his rodeoing. And Tyler . . . well, none of us could ever figure out what Tyler thought about her.''

"And you, hon?'' J.T. asked quietly. "What about you?''

Lynn briefly averted her eyes but quickly looked back. "Oh, I guess I wanted her to be more like Mama.''

"There's no one else like your mother, just as there's no one else like you.''

"I know. The truth is, I didn't expect you to ever be attracted to another woman, and when Cynthia turned out to be so young—" Lynn's cheeks colored "—I was afraid everyone would think you were foolish . . . like Bubba."

J.T. gave a start. Bubba had always been a sort of uncle figure to his children. But his children weren't children anymore, and like everybody else in Crystal Creek they would certainly know about the Bubba and Billie Jo thing.

"There is not one similarity between my relationship with Cynthia and . . . the other. Please tell me you're aware of that."

"Yes, now I am. I honestly thought Cynthia wasn't right for you, but Tyler told me what I really was doing was resisting change. I guess he was right. Anyway, I'm sorry for the way I behaved. It was stupid. And since you're so unhappy, I'm sorry she's gone."

She looked so contrite that a small smile touched J.T.'s lips, the first that had been there in a week. "Misguided, perhaps, but show me someone who's never been guilty of misguided behavior and I'll show you a liar. At least you had my best interests at heart."

"Not entirely," Lynn said. "I didn't want you so busy with a new wife you wouldn't have time for me."

"That would never happen. Never in a million years. Now, I wish you would relax and get that beaten-puppy look off your face. Nothing you or Lettie Mae or Virginia did had anything to do with Cynthia's leaving. There were just too many other things." A faraway look came to J.T.'s eyes. "Way too many other things."

Lynn didn't understand, but she felt so much better now that she'd confessed her sins and been forgiven. Standing, she rounded the desk and gave her father a hug. "I want you to be happy again." With that, she scurried out of the room.

J.T. swiveled in his chair and stared out the window. For a week he had made a conscious effort to erase Cynthia's memory, but nothing had worked. All he had to do was pass the guest house, and everything came back to him with painful clarity. After this discussion with Lynn, he supposed he'd have Cynthia on his mind all day. He thought about the night he'd found Pauline's picture in her room. She'd asked him to put it back where it belonged and not make an issue of it because she suspected someone wanted an issue made of it. He'd thought that odd, but now he realized she'd known what was going on and hadn't said a word to him about it.

Ah, hell! Angrily he turned, grabbed his hat and stood. He'd go nuts sitting around and brooding all afternoon. He was going into town. He hadn't seen anyone but his family and the ranch hands in a week. Surely he'd find someone or something that would get his mind off Cynthia.

He had just jammed the hat on his head when Virginia entered the study, looking sheepish and nervous. "J.T., can I speak with you a minute?"

"Of course." He braced himself for another confession and got it. He allowed Virginia to stumble through essentially the same story he'd just heard from Lynn. What bothered him most of all was that he had not suspected any of it. Carolyn had warned him, but he hadn't paid attention. Perhaps Cynthia had had good reason to blow up the night she left. After weeks and weeks of such treatment, wouldn't one little thing be the last straw?

He listened patiently to the housekeeper, then assured her that her petty little pranks were not what had caused Cynthia to leave—though he had reason now to suspect they'd contributed to her decision to do so.

"Well, I just feel better now that I've told you," Virginia said. "I really am sorry, J.T. You might want to think about calling her, and if you do. . . well, you can tell her she can move the sofa." Turning, she hurried out of the room.

J.T. shook his head in disbelief and walked on to the front door. As he reached for the knob, he thought of something. Changing direction, he went through the dining room into the kitchen and found Lettie Mae in her favorite spot, in front of the stove.

"Well, Lettie Mae, what tales of nefarious scheming do you have to tell me?"

The cook looked him up and down. "Huh?"

"Any skulduggery bothering your conscience?"

"No, sir. Me, I think everything's just dandy."

WORD HAD GOTTEN AROUND. J.T. knew that because he'd been to the bank, the post office, the farm and ranch store and now the hardware store, and not one single person had asked about Cynthia. Good. He wouldn't have to answer a lot of damned fool questions.

The cashier was ringing up his purchase when he felt a strong hand grasp his shoulder. He turned to see the smiling face of a young man about Lynn's age, perhaps a few years older. His face was slightly familiar, but for the life of him J.T. couldn't put a name with it.

"Howdy, Mr. McKinney. Remember me?"

"I remember the face but not the name, I'm sorry to say."

"Don't apologize. It's been about seven years since you last saw me. I'm Hal Sommervell, Sonny's boy."

Sonny Sommervell, J.T. thought with a grin. An old friend who had moved to Houston...was it really seven years ago? Craziest son of a bitch in Claro County back in their hell-raising days. He pumped the young man's hand enthusiastically. "Good to see you again. How's your dad?"

"Oh, he's fine."

"Good. And your mom?"

Hal's face clouded slightly. "We lost Mama about a year after we moved to Houston."

"What a shame. I'm so sorry."

"Yeah, it was awful sudden. Really knocked the props out from under us for a while, especially Daddy.

But he remarried three years ago, a real nice woman. Becky's been good for him.''

"Well, that's nice to know. Is Sonny still in the fence business?''

Hal nodded. "He's gonna retire next year, though. Says he wants to spend more time with the family. He and Becky have a two-year-old son, and that kid's given Daddy a whole new lease on life.''

J.T. felt as though someone had slapped him. Sonny Sommervell with a two-year-old kid! Sonny was his own age...no, a year older. "I...well, that's wonderful. I'm happy for him.''

Hal grinned broadly. "Yeah, it's a real kick to go over to Daddy's house and tick off, one by one, the things that kid gets away with that my sister and I never could. It's been nice seeing you again, Mr. McKinney. Daddy'll be glad to hear you're looking so fit.''

"Be sure to give him my regards. Goodbye, Hal.''

The cashier was waiting patiently. J.T. paid his tab, picked up his packages and returned to his car. Hal's news had him thoroughly rattled. Try as he might, he couldn't get Cynthia's words out of his head. *I think you'd make a great father. Think of the wisdom and maturity you have to offer a child.*

And never once had J.T. shaken the notion that it was Cynthia's desire for a child, not the rustler incident or anything else, that was behind her hasty exit from his life. She had said she deserved a child, and maybe she did. If she wanted one so much, she'd probably make a good mother.

Abruptly, he slapped the steering wheel. Dammit, he wasn't going to start thinking along those lines. Raising kids took the patience and wisdom of a saint, and he no longer had either.

Come on, J.T., his taunting inner voice said. *Who did most of the raising? Pauline, that's who. That's usually the case.*

No! He had no more business with a baby than he did with a million-dollar mortgage. Sonny Sommervell never did have the common sense God gave a flea.

Still, words kept swimming around in his head. *That kid's given Daddy a whole new lease on life.... That's not fair, J.T., and I think you know it. I deserve a child....*

He was lost in thought throughout dinner and hardly said a word, but by now everyone was accustomed to that and went on with the serious business of eating. At meal's end he headed straight for his study, hoping a quiet, solitary evening would help him marshal his thoughts. No such luck. He hadn't been behind his desk more than a few minutes when he smelled the cigarette smoke that always preceded his grandfather's appearance by a few seconds.

Sure enough, Hank soon limped into the room. His progress from the door to a chair was slow and painful to watch. J.T. was surprised to see him. Ordinarily, Hank would have been in his own house by now.

"Evening, Grandpa. What's on your mind?"

"Don't you think it's time you stopped mopin'?" Hank asked with his customary brusqueness.

"I'm not moping. I'm preoccupied."

"The hell you are. You're mopin' over that gal from Boston. You're well rid of her, boy. I've been around the track a few times, and I can spot the wiltin' flowers a mile away."

J.T. scowled. "Whatever else she is, Cynthia is no wilting flower."

"The hell she isn't. She wouldn't do you any good around here. Me, I like a little humility in a woman. That one's too feisty, got too much sass in her."

"You mean spunk, don't you? You've always said you admired Lynn's spunk."

"On Lynn, it's becomin'. On the other one, it isn't."

"That's silly, Grandpa, and you know it."

"Maybe. Once or twice in my life I've been accused of doin' something silly. If you think you need a woman, get yourself a real one."

"Tell me something, what's a real woman?"

"One like your grandma. She could feed the baby, gather the eggs, sweep the stoop and cook me a good breakfast before I was finished shavin'."

What a crock, J.T. thought. His grandmother, who died before he was born, had been in terribly frail health most of her life. His mother, Emily, had often recounted how she had taken care of her mother and done most of the work herself.

More than anyone J.T. had ever known, Hank remembered things as he wanted them to have been, not as they were. The truth was, his grandfather had had such a bad case of the oiler's itchy feet, he'd hardly ever been home, always out chasing one more big strike. If he made one—and he'd made a few—he'd just sunk his capital into another. The chase was the thing. J.T. recalled Hank's standard parting remark to his oil-patch buddies—"See you in the next boom." His grandfather had made most of them in his day. And Emily had resented that while not exactly deserting them, he had seldom been around when he was needed.

But if Hank wanted to remember his wife as the kind of woman who could do a day's work before sunup, what difference did it make? "I've got news, Grandpa. They discontinued that model several decades ago."

"That's the trouble with the world," Hank said obscurely.

"I thought it was the interstate highway system and the federal government," J.T. said, stifling a grin.

"Them, too. Fine damned mess the country's gotten itself into. Mamas goin' off to offices instead of stayin' home where they belong. People drivin' around like bats out'a hell, gettin' places faster'n God ever meant 'em to. Government stickin' its nose in everybody's business. Time was when a man was left alone to do what he wanted to. Did I ever tell you about the time Lefty Hall and I were workin' a rig near Ozona and this little pipsqueak from the Railroad Commission showed up..."

Of course he had told J.T. the story many times. The Railroad Commission, the regulator of the Texas oil industry, was another of Hank's pet peeves. He delighted in relating the tale of how he and Lefty Hall had run one of its agents off an oil lease with a BB gun. J.T. knew it word for word, but listened patiently, nodding and laughing at the appropriate times. Whenever J.T. became impatient with Hank, he remembered how little time the old man had left.

Hank was in a talkative mood. He asked J.T. for a little "sippin' whiskey to ease the pain." J.T. complied, even though Nate Purdy had been telling Hank to stop smoking and drinking for ten years. There again, J.T. thought, what the hell? His grandfather had already outlived his wife and daughter and all his old cronies. Let him choose his own poison.

The whiskey further oiled Hank's tongue. He was well into his third or fourth anecdote when he suddenly stopped and looked at his grandson. "I forgot to tell you somethin'. I had a dream this afternoon. Those missin' cattle. Someone you know took 'em."

J.T.'s head came up. Like the others in the family he didn't pooh-pooh Hank's dreams. The old man had been right too often. "Who?"

"Don't rightly know. It's jus' someone you're acquainted with."

At that moment J.T. looked over Hank's shoulder to see Ken trying to get his attention. "Excuse me, Grandpa," he said. "Come in, Ken. What's up?"

Ken walked into the room, a look of urgency on his face. "Evenin', Hank," he said, then propped his hip against the corner of the desk. "Boss, you know I told you the men and I were going to make a thorough patrol of the ranch until the rustlers were caught."

"Yes, I remember. We've had such lousy luck...."

"No more. I kept remembering your cousin saying it might be an inside job, so I figured I'd better keep this a hush-hush operation. I got three of my most trusted men, swore them to secrecy, and we've watched every gate on the ranch until the wee hours of the morning all week. Well, it finally paid off. Just a few minutes ago at the eastern gate. There they were, bold as brass. They didn't get any cows, and we got them." Ken's grin was one of absolute triumph.

"You caught them? Red-handed?"

"Sure did. Two of 'em. They damned near stole us blind right under our noses. Makes me madder'n hell when I think about it." Ken's head turned. "Okay, Marv, bring 'em in."

A Double C cowhand came through the door, dragging a man by one arm. Another of the ranch's cowboys pushed another man behind them. The first of the rustlers was an older man, someone J.T. had never seen before, meaning he was an outsider, probably not even from around Crystal Creek.

But he bolted to his feet, eyes blazing, when he saw the other man. It was Chase Bennett.

CHAPTER FOURTEEN

THERE WAS NOTHING ELSE to do. For the first time in his life J.T. was simply going to have to eat humble pie. As he stood before the door to Cynthia's apartment, he was as nervous as he'd ever been, chiefly because he had no idea what was waiting for him when the door opened. During the flight to Boston he had rehearsed half a dozen opening remarks. Unfortunately, he'd forgotten all of them.

Hesitantly he raised a hand and pressed the doorbell, then stood back and waited. A minute passed, and he pressed the button again. When another minute passed, he realized his ring wasn't going to be answered.

It had never occurred to him she might not be home. Had she already gone back to work? Glancing at his watch, he saw it was nearing four. If she was at the office, she should be home before long. Of course, if she wasn't, he might have a depressingly long wait in store.

But wait he would, at least for a reasonable length of time. Shoving his hand in his pocket, he withdrew his key ring. The key to Cynthia's apartment was still on it. He questioned the wisdom of just letting himself in, but finally he did it anyway. She couldn't be any madder at him than she already was. Turning the key, he pushed open the door and stepped inside.

A thousand memories assaulted him as he entered the familiar surroundings. So many Friday afternoons he had let himself into the apartment and waited for her to get home. The place was immaculate, as always. Tiffany studied him from one of her favorite perches—the top of a bookcase. She obviously remembered him, J.T. was delighted to note, for the cat immediately curled up and went back to sleep, satisfied that he belonged there.

J.T. peered into the kitchen-dining area, then moved into the hall and Cynthia's bedroom. An empty suitcase lay open on the bed. Was she going somewhere? Or maybe gone somewhere and decided she didn't need that suitcase? No, Tiffany was there, a sure sign Cynthia wasn't out of town.

Turning, he went to the kitchen and opened the refrigerator, then smiled. Three bottles of his favorite beer were still there. However, icy beer on a November day in New England wasn't very inviting. He felt chilled to the bone. Taking out the can of coffee, he brewed a pot. That done, he went into the living room and sat down to wait.

And to think about everything that had happened on that incredible day, the day the rustlers were caught. As stunned and furious as he had been that one of his own men had been stealing from him, his immediate thought had been of Cynthia. She had told him what she'd seen, but he wouldn't believe her. No wonder she was angry.

Coming as it did on the heels of so many other things—Lynn's and Virginia's confessions, the conversation with Hal Sommervell—the incident had forced J.T. to do some painful, deep soul-searching, and he hadn't particularly liked what he found. Originally he had been attracted to Cynthia because she was bright, inquisitive, energetic and independent. Yet from the day she first stepped on the Double C, he had systematically begun trying to repress those very qualities. Why?

It hadn't been easy for him to question his own character, but he'd persisted. Did he down deep in his heart want a traditional wife, a woman who stayed in the background and did wifely things, a woman who would never be controversial or different? Knowing Cynthia would never be that kind of woman, did he still want to marry her? If so, could he keep his damned mouth shut, at least most of the time, and allow her to be herself?

When he could finally answer yes to the last, most important two questions, he had called a family meeting. Announcing his intention of going to Boston to try to talk to Cynthia, he spelled out in no uncertain terms what he expected of them if she returned to the Double C. The house would be hers to do with as she pleased. The routine would be as she wished. Privately, he vowed he would introduce her to the financial side of the ranch's business. Let her see that for all its outward trappings, the ranch was no multi-million-dollar operation. He had kept many of his money worries from Pauline; he wouldn't from Cynthia. And maybe he'd adopt some of those newfangled notions of hers.

Tyler, Lynn and Virginia had no trouble with any of the new ground rules. Lettie Mae did, but wisely kept quiet. Hank, who never kept quiet if he had something on his mind, said, "So you're gonna go runnin' to her with your tail tucked between your legs," he'd scoffed. "Mark my words, boy, that 'un's gonna run you ragged. Course, I don't think she's gonna come back, so I don't plan on spendin' much time worryin' about it."

Sadly, J.T. wondered if his grandfather was right. But here he was, and he was going to at least attempt a reconciliation. If it didn't work...well, he supposed he'd have to worry about that when the time came.

THAT MORNING Cynthia had made two decisions. One was to go to the country house with her parents. She wasn't particularly looking forward to it, but anything beat spending Thanksgiving alone. The other was to get out of the apartment today, to go shopping, take in a movie, stop at the library, anything to keep her from moping around feeling sorry for herself.

So she had spent the lion's share of the day buying a lot of things she didn't really need, having lunch at an exclusive restaurant her parents had been raving about and stocking up on two weeks' worth of reading. She'd certainly need that in the country.

She was surprised to realize the city's hustle and bustle actually got on her nerves. Every store was crowded, everyone seemed to move at a dead run, the sales personnel seemed curt and rude. Once she would have felt right at home in the thick of it. Now she wanted to tell everyone to slow down. She thought of Crystal Creek, where people were never too busy to stop and talk. Was it possible to get accustomed to a much slower pace in such a short time?

In fact, she thought about Texas a lot. She missed more than the laid-back atmosphere. She missed the weather. She missed the J.T. who wasn't in a stormy mood. Sometimes she even missed old Hank's "Tales from the Derrick Floor." Even in the short time she'd known him, she'd heard some of them a couple of times.

Cynthia had experienced a lot of emotions during the past week, none of them very pleasant. One thing she hadn't experienced even once was a desire to return to work. What if she never did? But if she didn't have her job, what would she do? Damn J.T. McKinney for giving her a glimpse of what could have been a wonderful life, for getting her hopes up and then dashing them to the ground! This was what being stood up at the altar must feel like. All those grand dreams, hopes and plans, then poof! Up in smoke.

Her day out had done little to lift her spirits; it had only passed time. It was after four when she finally got home. Laden with packages, she had some difficulty with her key. Fumbling for the lock, she almost dropped dead when the door flew open and a man stood there. Then her heart began knocking against her ribs. Was she imagining it or was he really here?

"J.T.!"

"Need some help?" he asked.

"How...how did you get in?"

"I have a key, remember? Here, let me give you a hand." He relieved her of some of the packages and stood back to allow her to enter. Cynthia's knees felt weak. In fact, she was shaking all over. He was back, just like that. She didn't know whether to be glad or not.

J.T. glanced around and, seeing no better place, put the packages on the dining table, then took the others from her and placed them with the rest. When he turned around, he was ready to face the music.

God, she looked gorgeous. Her hair was windblown, and her cheeks were still flushed from the cold. He'd known he missed her, but until this minute he hadn't known just how much. He had to make this good.

Almost in a state of shock, Cynthia shrugged out of her coat and flung it across the arm of a chair. "Why didn't you call and let me know you were coming?" Her voice sounded strange, all quivery.

"I didn't want to give you a chance to tell me not to bother. I made coffee. Want a cup?"

One would think they'd just seen each other this morning, she thought in disbelief. *Coffee. Want a cup?* "I . . . ah, I guess so."

He walked off in the direction of the kitchen and returned with two steaming cups. "It's colder'n a well-digger's butt out there," he said.

She sat down on the sofa, and J.T. took a chair next to it. "Oh, it's not really cold yet."

"It is to me."

Cynthia took a sip, then said, "I know you didn't come here to discuss Boston's temperature."

"You're right." He set the cup on a nearby table. "We caught the rustlers," he said, facing her.

"Oh?"

"One of them was Chase Bennett."

A ponderous silence fell over the room. Cynthia didn't know what to say. She wouldn't have been human if she hadn't felt vindicated and a little smug. So, he had come to apologize, which couldn't have been easy for him. She didn't say anything; she didn't have to.

"I'm sorry, Cynthia. Sorrier than I know how to tell you. I should have believed you. I can't imagine why I didn't."

"Apology accepted."

"I . . . thought I knew Chase. I still can't believe it, but it seems the man I've known for so many years was financing a very expensive drug habit."

"What are they going to do to him?"

"I don't know. I recommended a rehabilitation center, but it's up to the judge." He reached out and touched her. She felt a jolt like an electric current race through her body. "I really am sorry," he said softly. "I should have taken your word for it. I wish to God I had."

"It's over. We don't need to say another word about it." A contrite J. T. McKinney wasn't easy to take. He made Cynthia feel off balance and uncomfortable.

"In fact, I'm sorry about a lot of things. I've had my eyes opened this past week. You were treated badly, and you didn't deserve to be. I've been told Virginia was in the study when you started straightening up my desk. She could have told you that was a no-no, and that would have been the end of it. Why didn't you tell me that?"

"When I was very young, that was called tattling."

"She also put Pauline's picture in your room. Did you know that?"

"I only knew someone had to have done it, because I damned well hadn't."

"You knew why, too, didn't you?"

Cynthia shrugged. "Sure...to make me look jealous. And it worked. The first thing you thought when you saw the picture was that I was jealous of your late wife, that I wanted to hide her photograph. That was never true, J.T. I hope you believe that. That you could sustain a beautiful, loving relationship for all those years touches me, it really does."

"I'm too quick to judge," J.T. admitted, "too slow to forgive, impossible to change, and I have a lousy temper."

His eyes were so warm, so sincere, so...brown. She had to keep her guard up. To remember she had been mesmerized by those eyes before, in this very room, only to meet him on home ground where he sometimes behaved like Conan the Barbarian.

She took another sip of coffee, then set her cup next to his. "Maybe, but it wasn't all your fault. I didn't help matters along. I've done a lot of thinking this past week, and I can see now there were times when a different course of action on my part might have smoothed the way. Lynn, for instance. The minute I saw how disappointed she was over the birthday barbecue, I should have offered to change our trip. Such a simple thing, but it might have been the one gesture that would have made us friends. And it's none of my business what Cal does for a living. I should have kept my mouth shut."

"Don't worry about Cal. You didn't say a thing I hadn't said many times over. I've got to get that kid out of the rodeo before he kills himself. As for Lynn, she's really sorry about everything. Her actions were all tied up with the way she felt about her mother, but she's had a change of heart. Everyone has." J.T. paused. That wasn't the whole truth and nothing but. Hank hadn't changed his mind, and J.T. didn't think Lettie Mae had, either. But he saw no reason to tell

Cynthia that. Tyler, Lynn and Virginia would more than make up for the other two.

He leaned forward, his voice earnest. "The point I'm trying to make, Cynthia, is that nothing's been the same since you left. You once asked me if we'd ever spend Thanksgiving or Christmas together. Let's do it this year. Please . . . I'm asking you to come back."

Careful, she cautioned herself. *He's so appealing, irresistible in fact, but has anything really changed?* Could he change? She didn't want to sit here and specify conditions, but neither did she want to return to the Double C and start the whole business all over again. "What makes you so sure things have changed?"

"We had a little household conference before I left."

"You ordered everyone to be nice to me, you mean."

"It wasn't like that."

"But what about us? The family's attitude toward me wasn't what sent me packing. You and I always seemed to be pulling in different directions."

J.T. ran his fingers through his hair. "I know . . . and if you'll promise you'll try to remember I'm all bark and almost no bite, I promise you I'll try to be more open-minded."

She rubbed her temple. "Oh, J.T., I don't know. I felt so useless at the ranch. There was nothing for me to do."

"My fault. I'm simply not accustomed to a woman who wants to be bothered with the nuts and bolts of a cow-calf operation, but if you do... Yes, I'll take you in as a full partner, show you the ropes, and...well, I'll at least look at what you say a computer can do for me."

He was making so many concessions. Cynthia had to give him credit for that. But were they genuine ones? It was easy enough to say I'll do this if you'll do that, but when the time came, could he really? He'd had things his way for so long. "I'll be honest with you—I can't live in another woman's house and do things the way she always did them. I like to cook. I want to redecorate that house. I know the kids, particularly Lynn, may resist, but I'll go slowly. I want my own husband, and I want us to have our own home, our own f—" She paused and looked down at her hands.

"Our own family? Is that what you were going to say?"

Her head came up. "Yes. J.T., I know how you feel but can we at least discuss it?"

J.T. heaved a sigh. Cynthia watched him grappling with what would be the biggest concession of all. "If you want a baby," he finally said, slowly, as if every word was an effort, "I'll do my damnedest to see you get one."

Cynthia's eyes lit up, but she remained skeptical. "Are you sure?"

"To be honest, I'm not completely convinced. But it might be good to hear kid sounds around the ranch again. It would certainly liven things up. Heck, we might not stop at one. We don't want him...or her to get spoiled."

Cynthia's head went back, and she chortled delightedly. Getting up, she threw herself in his lap, showering his face with kisses. "J.T., I know you're going to make a wonderful father."

"Does this mean you're coming back?" he teased.

"Of course. How else can I get my baby?" She curled herself in a ball and hugged him ferociously. He felt so good. From the beginning he had represented strength and solidity to her, and the past week without him had left her feeling weak and abandoned. "Oh, J.T., I've been so miserable without you. This has been the worst week of my life."

Stroking her hair, he kissed her temple, her ear, her cheek. "I've missed you horribly, sweetheart. We'll work everything out, you'll see. If things ever get touchy again, you just remind me of how I've felt this week. You and I are going to be very happy...very happy."

"I know," she cooed. "J.T.?"

"Hmm?"

"What really made you change your mind about the baby?"

He told her about Sonny Sommervell. "As I recall," he said in conclusion, "Sonny was a pretty stern father to those first two kids of his. But Hal says he's great with that two-year-old. And that led me to think about Wayne Jackson's last foster father. Maybe I would be a better old man the second time around, more understanding, less uptight. I'll give it my best shot. Anyway, he . . . or she will have you for a mama, so I won't do too much harm.''

"Bless Sonny and Becky," Cynthia said. "Let's be sure to invite them to the wedding.''

They clung to each other for several wordless minutes before J.T. said, "I forgot to tell you something of vital importance, something momentous.''

"What's that?"

"Virginia said you can move the sofa."

Laughter bubbled up from her throat. She kissed him soundly before uncurling from his lap and holding out her hand. "Come on."

He stood. "Where are we going?''

"To start working on that baby, of course.''

THEIR REUNION was a memorable one. J.T. was a masterful lover when aroused, and no one had ever inspired him as Cynthia did. And a week without her had made him hungry. He loved her into senselessness that night, until her mind and body were in no way connected. It was like it had been in the beginning, only better, because they had been through the rough seas and now cruised on smooth waters.

Cynthia languished in ecstasy, secure in the knowledge that this time it would work. This time she knew what to expect. This time everyone else knew what to expect from her. And since they had made concessions, she would, too. As she'd told J.T., she wouldn't come on like gangbusters. She would implement her changes gradually, so that one day all of them would forget the house hadn't always looked that way. It would be an interesting marriage, she thought, one requiring an enormous amount of give-and-take. Perhaps unconventional by J.T.'s old standards, but certainly never dull.

Snuggled in the warmth of his arms, she smiled in contentment. There actually was a pot at the end of the rainbow, and she had found it.

DOZENS OF THINGS had to be tended to before Cynthia and J.T. could leave for Texas. She had to arrange to have her furniture stored. There was no room for any of it at the ranch, not yet. Other personal items had to be shipped. She had to inform the bank she wouldn't be returning. Now she was relieved she hadn't bothered looking up friends. There would be no need for further goodbyes.

Naturally her parents were the first to learn that the wedding was on again. Alicia stopped just short of hand-wringing distress. "Oh, Cynthia, all this ambivalence... it's so unlike you. I still think..."

"I know what you think, Mom, but relax. This time I'm sure, and so is J.T."

"Did you ever find out what church he attends?"

As if that had anything to do with anything, Cynthia thought. "He's a Baptist."

A pained expression crossed her mother's face.
"Well, at least he isn't associated with some weird, far-out religion."

Cynthia laughed heartily. "If you knew J.T. as well
as I do, you'd know he's the last person on earth
who'd be involved in anything weird and far-out. He's
very conservative."

"Thank heavens for that."

Cynthia's biggest concern was how Tiffany would
fare on her first plane trip. She could leave her worldly
possessions behind without much qualm, but there
was no way she would leave her cat. "Bring her, by all
means," J.T. said. "Lynn will love her." Cynthia
wondered about Virginia, Lettie Mae and Hank, but
they would have to get used to Tiffany. The cat went.

At last, everything that needed doing was done, and
she and J.T. were winging their way back to Texas.
This time there was no apprehension or uncertainty.
This time she was in full control and full of plans.
Much later, as the Cadillac drove through the main
gate of Double C Ranch, she experienced a profound
sense of homecoming. It wasn't until they were
climbing the front porch steps that her control slipped.
There were a lot of memories lurking behind that front
door, and not all of them were good.

J.T. saw her falter. Taking her by the arm, he smiled
reassuringly. "Just walk in like you own the place," he
said. "Come to think of it, in a very short time, you
will."

Cynthia squared her shoulders. He was right. This was home now, her home. She waited until J.T. opened the door and stepped aside to allow her to precede him. Then she entered the house, every inch the mistress of the manor.

CHAPTER FIFTEEN

FOR CYNTHIA, Thanksgiving was a new experience that year. It wasn't like the ones she remembered from childhood, but she enjoyed every minute—and every bite—of it. The huge feast, served at one o'clock, as on Sundays, tasted as good in balmy weather as it did when the frost was on the pumpkin, she discovered. There were differences, of course. The turkey was smoked. The dressing was made from cornbread, not bread and sausage. There were green beans instead of brussels sprouts because J.T. loathed brussels sprouts. Candied yams replaced the mashed ones always served at her grandmother's house, and there was pecan pie instead of mincemeat. But it all was delicious. Lettie Mae, who truly was an artist with pots and pans, had outdone herself.

How different *everything* was this time. Oh, the cook still frowned every time Cynthia went near the stove, and Hank hadn't changed. He didn't so much greet her as size her up. "So you're back, huh?" he said, puffing on his cigarette and making certain most of the smoke drifted in her direction.

Cynthia, with great effort, did not allow her nose to so much as twitch. She suspected that nothing pleased him quite as much as annoying her. When she assured him she was indeed back for good, he said, "Well, if you're gonna be hangin' around, might as well call me Hank. By the way, I hate cats. Keep it away from me." Another puff on the cigarette and he limped off. *Charming old bastard,* Cynthia muttered to herself.

But everything else, everyone else had been welcoming. Virginia began addressing her as Miss C., which apparently signaled approval. The greatest change, however, was in Lynn. Shyly hesitant at first, she had gradually opened up. Tiffany had been the real icebreaker. As J.T. had predicted, Lynn took one look at the cat, scooped her up in her arms, and now she was the one the fickle animal seemed to want most. Cynthia had terminated their cold war for good by bringing Lynn a dress to wear to the wedding.

"I saw this in Boston," she'd said, "and it reminded me of you, so I bought it." The dress was a lovely royal-blue creation with a capelike collar that covered the shoulders and a skirt that fell in graceful folds to midcalf. Well made and expensive, it caused Lynn's eyes to widen, her mouth to drop.

"This dress reminded you of me?" she asked in disbelief.

"Yes, do you like it?"

"Like it? I've ... I've never seen such a dress."

"I guessed at the size."

Lynn peeked at the label. "Six is perfect. If it's too long, Virginia can take it up. I ... I don't know what to say, Cynthia. Thanks so much."

Such a simple thing, Cynthia thought. *Why didn't I do something like this before?*

The thaw between herself and Tyler had long since occurred, and he really did make her feel welcome. "I guess I have you to thank," he said the day after her arrival. "You must have talked to Daddy about the wine-making venture."

"We were awfully rushed, but, yes, I managed to get in a word or two. I couldn't tell if it did any good or not."

"It did. He gave me the go-ahead. I'll be leaving for California soon."

"That's wonderful, Tyler. Good luck. This should be interesting."

Now there was only Cal to win over, and that would have to wait for the wedding, when he had promised to be home. She had misgivings about J.T.'s younger son. If Cal still held her to blame for his father's insistence on his quitting the rodeo, she didn't have much hope they would be friends. J.T. was more determined than ever to get Cal off the circuit, and she'd had nothing to do with that.

However, she would worry about Cal later. For now, she had a hundred things to do and not much time to do them in.

DOUBLE C RANCH had never known such a protracted period of festivity. The Christmas decorations went up the week after Thanksgiving. Then, on December 12, Henry Clay "Hank" Travis celebrated his

ninety-ninth birthday. For at least a week beforehand
he had admonished anyone who would listen not to
make a fuss, meaning he would be terribly disappointed if they didn't. All of J.T.'s friends had been
invited to a big bash, even though Hank had alien-
ated half of them at one time or another during the
past thirteen years. J.T. counted on everyone's being
so in awe of a man who had lived one year shy of a
century that even Hank's abrasive personality couldn't
spoil the festivities.

He was right. The party couldn't have been a big-
ger success. Hank would have cut out his tongue before admitting he had a good time, but he did. And the
household had no more recovered from that than it
was time to get ready for the wedding.

The big day was one week before Christmas. Cynthia and J.T. were going to honeymoon briefly on the
Gulf Coast and be back at the ranch in time for the
holiday. Two days before the wedding, Alicia and Joseph arrived in Austin and were driven to the Double
C by Sally and Ted Honecker. The Honeckers chose
to stay at the Longhorn Motel, giving the Pages the
guest house. Cynthia, protecting the family's sensi-
bilities, moved into Cal's room, and when he showed
up, he bunked with Ken. Cynthia's main worry concerned her mother's first confrontation with Hank.

She didn't have long to wait. Hank chose to have
dinner with the family the first night her parents,
along with Sally and Ted, were with them. Limping
into the dining room, smoking and sporting a day's

worth of stubble on his chin, he looked for all the world like a refugee just off a freighter. Cynthia was certain he was being deliberately contrary. Her eyes flew to J.T.; his telegraphed an apology. Then he stood up. Ted and Joseph had stood the minute Hank entered the room.

"Hello, Grandpa," J.T. said.

"Good evening, Mr. Travis," Ted said. "I'm Ted Honecker. We met several years ago."

"We did? Don't remember."

Ted's smile faded. Cynthia closed her eyes and sighed, while Sally covered her mouth with a hand, hiding her smile.

Hank looked at Joseph. "And who're you?"

J.T. rounded the table to stand by his grandfather. "Grandpa," he said suavely, "this is Joseph Page, Cynthia's father. Joseph, my grandfather, Hank Travis."

Since Hank and Joseph were several feet apart, shaking hands was impossible. Joseph merely said, "How do you do, Mr. Travis."

"Howdy." Hank looked at Cynthia as though surprised to discover she had a father. Then he turned back to Joseph. "You should'a kept your little gal at home where she belonged."

The little gasp must have come from Alicia, Cynthia thought as she again closed her eyes.

Joseph, distinguished and sophisticated down to his shoelaces, offered Hank a little smile. "We tried, Mr. Travis. Yes, we certainly tried."

"And the lovely woman seated by Joseph is Cynthia's mother, Alicia," J.T. said.

Alicia murmured a response, and Hank said, "Evenin', ma'am. You've got a fancy name, too." He looked at J.T. "Am I supposed to stand on this goddamned hip all night, or are you gonna get me a chair?"

Cal, seated nearby, jumped to his feet. "Here you go, Grandpa Hank. Take mine. I'll fetch another."

Hank slowly and painfully sat down, then to everyone's relief, kept his mouth shut throughout the meal.

MUCH LATER, after the Honeckers had left for the motel, Cynthia walked her parents to the guest house. "You look tired, Cynthia," Alicia said.

"I am tired. There's been so much to do. I just hope I haven't forgotten anything."

"J.T. has a nice family. His grandfather certainly is...colorful, isn't he?"

"He's crochety, opinionated, stubborn and outspoken," Cynthia said. "He's also ninety-nine and has a hip that keeps him in constant pain."

"Dear me. I suppose one must make allowances for that." When they reached the guest house door, Joseph went inside, but Alicia paused and looked around, a tiny frown furrowing her brow. "Cynthia, are you very sure about this? The ranch is lovely, but it's so...so rural."

Cynthia smiled at her fondly. "One doesn't raise cows in the city, Mom."

"Of course, but . . . I just want you to be happy."

"I'm going to be. Count on it."

THE MORNING of the wedding dawned clear and bright. Virginia and Lettie Mae were up before dawn, barking orders to everyone who came near them. Then they set up an ongoing buffet in the dining room. The living room had been cleared of most of the furniture, and folding chairs had been set up with an aisle running down the middle. A makeshift altar had been created with rented candelabras and ferns. In the back of the room, the high school music teacher was setting up his keyboard. The cake arrived, then the flowers. Cynthia had certainly been efficient. Somehow everything seemed to have gotten done. Both the housekeeper and the cook were quite impressed.

Cars began streaming through the front gate at noon. The Episcopalian minister J.T. had found arrived and went in search of the bridegroom to run through the ceremony. As J.T.'s firstborn son, Tyler was given the honor of being best man. Cal was appointed host and tried hard to keep everyone supplied with food.

Carolyn and Beverly came early and found Cynthia, Lynn and Sally in Lynn's room upstairs. The bride was clad in slip and bra and looked one step away from physical collapse.

Beverly turned to say hello to Lynn, and her mouth dropped. "Where did you get that dress? Not in Crystal Creek, I'll bet."

Lynn beamed. "No, Cynthia bought it in Boston. Do you like it?"

"I love it!"

Lynn gloated silently. She was sure this was the first time she'd seen envy in Beverly's eyes.

Cynthia introduced Sally to the Townsend women and asked Carolyn how things were going downstairs.

"The place is filling up."

"I hope we have enough room for everyone."

"No one will mind standing," Carolyn assured her. "Don't fret."

Sally glanced at her watch. "We'd better get a move on, friend. On with the dress."

Cynthia stood and Sally slipped the dress over her head. "Oh, Cyn, it's so beautiful! Did you find it here?"

"Umm-hmm. Pamela ordered it for me." She had wisely decided to buy everything she possibly could in Crystal Creek. Though she didn't yet know it, she had forever endeared herself to many local merchants. Her dress, the invitations, the cake, the flowers, the rented equipment, all had come from local shops. She wouldn't be forgotten.

The dress was elegant, expensive and simplicity itself—white satin with long sleeves, sweetheart neckline and slender skirt that flared below the knee. "Oh, it's just gorgeous!" Beverly enthused.

At that moment Joseph appeared in the doorway, ready to escort his daughter downstairs. "We'll see you later," Carolyn said, and she and Beverly left the room. Cynthia glanced in the mirror and heaved a deep sigh. At last. If the wedding had been the next day, she wasn't sure the bride would have been able to make it.

J.T. WAS CERTAIN he had never seen such a vision. His heart was beating at rapid-fire pace by the time Cynthia came down the aisle on Joseph's arm. The bride and her father halted at the first row of chairs; J.T. stepped forward to claim her, and Joseph took a seat beside Alicia.

"Dearly beloved, we are gathered together...."

Carolyn's eyes moved across the aisle to Mary and Bubba Gibson. *I do so wish Mary would drop the stiff upper-lip and kick Bubba on his ass.*

Rose Purdy was watching Bubba, too. *He's going to get his, mark my words,* she thought.

"...which is an honorable institution..."

I can't believe she bought that dress in Crystal Creek, Beverly thought.

"...the ring, which symbolizes..."

Oh, she makes such a beautiful bride, Lynn thought, *and Daddy's the handsomest man alive.* She sniffed and fumbled for the tissue she'd known she would need. Seated next to her, Cal chuckled.

"...and repeat after me—I, Cynthia Anita, take thee, John Travis..."

"I, Cynthia Anita, take thee, John Travis..."

Tyler had to admit they were just about the best-looking couple he'd ever seen. The marriage might be the start of something really big at Double C Ranch. Who knew what wonders tomorrow would bring?

"I, John Travis, take thee, Cynthia Anita..."

Hank had refused to be seated at the front with the family, insisting instead on the very back row. Squinting, he surveyed the scene. Virginia and Lettie Mae were standing in the doorway, still in their working clothes. They had a busy afternoon ahead of them. Virginia was sniffling. *Silly old thing,* Hank thought. He returned his attention to the ceremony.

"...I now pronounce you husband and wife...."

Hank slowly and sadly shook his head. *It's done, and that boy's just tied himself to a handful of trouble.*

"Ladies and gentlemen, it gives me great pleasure to present to you, Mr. and Mrs. John Travis McKinney."

Lettie Mae sighed. *There goes my kitchen.*

If you enjoyed
DEEP IN THE HEART

don't miss

COWBOYS AND CABERNET
by Margot Dalton

the second installment of the
Crystal Creek series
coming to you in March

Ruth Holden, California wine expert, travels to Crystal Creek with the intention of convincing her father's old friend, J. T. McKinney, that Texas cowboys really shouldn't try to be wine makers. But it isn't long before she finds herself falling in love with Texas and with J. T.'s son, Tyler. However, a local girl bitterly resents Ruth for her intrusion into Tyler's life, and reveals a scandalous secret that could drive Ruth away forever.

Watch for it next month, wherever Harlequin books are sold.

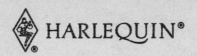

HARLEQUIN®

THE TAGGARTS OF TEXAS!

Harlequin's Ruth Jean Dale brings you
THE TAGGARTS OF TEXAS!

Those Taggart men—strong, sexy and hard to resist...

You've met Jesse James Taggart in FIREWORKS!
Harlequin Romance #3205 (July 1992)

And Trey Smith—he's THE RED-BLOODED YANKEE!
Harlequin Temptation #413 (October 1992)

And the unforgettable Daniel Boone Taggart in SHOWDOWN!
Harlequin Romance #3242 (January 1993)

Now meet Boone Smith and the Taggarts who started it all—
in LEGEND!
Harlequin Historical #168 (April 1993)

Read all the Taggart romances!
Meet all the Taggart men!

Available wherever Harlequin Books are sold.

FLASH:
ROMANCE
MAKES
HISTORY!

History the Harlequin way, that is. Our books invite you to experience a past you never read about in grammar school!

Travel back in time with us, and pirates will sweep you off your feet, cowboys will capture your heart, and noblemen will lead you to intrigue and romance, *always* romance—because that's what makes each Harlequin Historical title a thrilling escape for you, four times every month. Just think of the adventures you'll have!

So pick up a Harlequin Historical novel today, and relive history in your wildest dreams....

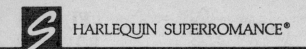

BE PART OF CRYSTAL CREEK
WITH THIS FABULOUS FREE GIFT!

The attractive Crystal Creek cowboy boot brooch—beautifully crafted and finished in a lovely silver tone—is the perfect accessory to any outfit!

As you share the passions and influence of the people of Crystal Creek ... and experience the excitement of hot Texas nights, smooth Texas charm and dangerously sexy cowboys—you need to collect only three proofs-of-purchase for the Crystal Creek cowboy boot brooch to become YOURS ... *ABSOLUTELY FREE!*

HOW TO CLAIM YOUR ATTRACTIVE CRYSTAL CREEK COWBOY BOOT BROOCH ... To receive your free gift, complete the Collector Card—located in the insert in this book—according to the directions on it. If you prefer not to use the Collector Card, or if it is missing, when you've collected three Proofs from three books, write your name and address on a blank piece of paper, place in an envelope with $1.95 (Postage and Handling) and mail to:

IN THE U.S.A.:
HARLEQUIN CRYSTAL CREEK PROMOTION
P.O. BOX 9071
BUFFALO, NY 14269-9071

IN CANADA:
HARLEQUIN CRYSTAL CREEK PROMOTION
P.O. BOX 604
FORT ERIE, ONTARIO L2A 5X3

Below you'll find a proof-of-purchase. You'll find one in the back pages of every Crystal Creek novel ... every month!

PREMIUM OFFER TERMS

Requests must be received no later than March 31, 1994. Only original proofs of purchase accepted. Limit: (1) one gift per name, family, group, organization. Cowboy boot brooch may differ slightly from photo. Please allow 6 to 8 weeks for receipt of gift. Offer good while quantities of gifts last. In the event an ordered gift is no longer available, you will receive a free, previously unpublished Harlequin book for every proof-of-purchase you have submitted with your request plus a refund of the postage and handling charge you have included. Offer good in the U.S.A. and Canada only.

Here's a proof of purchase—start collecting today!!

ONE
PROOF-OF-PURCHASE

088-KAW

Crystal Creek

CCPOPR